WEE
ROCKETS

Gerard Brennan

Cover design by JT Lindroos
Cover photo

Formatting by Polgarus Studio

Visit Gerard Brennan at:
www.blastedheath.com

ISBN: 978-1-492944-37-9

Version 2-1-3

For Allan Guthrie and Kyle MacRae

Also by Gerard Brennan

Requiems for the Departed (editor)

The Point

Fireproof

Possession, Obsession and a Diesel Compression Engine

Other Stories and Nothing But Time

Wee Danny

Breaking Point

Also by Blasted Heath

Dead Money by Ray Banks
Phase Four by Gary Carson
The Long Midnight of Barney Thomson by Douglas Lindsay
The Man in the Seventh Row by Brian Pendreigh
The Killing of Emma Gross by Damien Seaman
All The Young Warriors by Anthony Neil Smith

Keep informed of new releases by signing up to the Blasted Heath newsletter at http://www.blastedheath.com/. We'll even send you a free book by way of thanks!

Chapter 1

The streets of Beechmount stank of wet dog. The effect of drying rain in early summer. Light faded from the West Belfast housing area. Joe Philips yawned and slumped against the redbrick alley wall. Half past ten at night. He wanted to be in bed, cosy and watching a DVD until he drifted off to sleep. But he was the leader. The rest of the gang expected him to be there.

At least it was holiday time. No school to mitch in the morning. He popped his head around the corner and glanced down the avenue.

"I see one," he said.

They all looked up to him. Literally. In the last few weeks he'd taken what his ma called a growth spurt. He'd use his share of tonight's money to buy longer trousers. Too much white sock showed between his Nike Air trainers and his Adidas tracksuit bottoms.

"Anyone else about?" Wee Danny Gibson asked. He snubbed a half-smoked fag on the alley wall and tucked the butt behind his ear.

"No, just the aul doll. Easy enough number."

Wee Danny nodded and the rest of the gang twitched, murmured and pulled hoods up over lowered baseball caps. Ten of them in all, not one above fourteen years old.

"Right, let's go," Joe said.

They spilled out of the alley and surrounded the blue-rinse bitch like a cursing tornado. She screamed, but they moved too fast for the curtain-twitchers to react. Broken nose bleeding, she dropped her handbag and tried to fend off kicks and punches. Wee Danny scooped it up and whistled. They split in ten different directions. The old granny shrieked at them. They were gone before any fucker so much as opened his door.

###

"Why are we wasting time talking about this? I'll happily volunteer to go out there now and batter each one of the wee fuckers with a hurling stick!"

"Stephen McVeigh. Sit back down and shut up unless you have something constructive to offer."

Stephen glared at Father Cairns but slammed himself down on the seat with enough force to mark the laminate flooring with black rubber streaks. The squat, bald priest looked away. Nobody had the balls to back Stephen up. Everybody knew the only way to stop these hoods was to talk to them in the one language they understood. Violence.

"Ginger cunt," some spineless fucker behind him muttered. Stephen's hand automatically went to his red hair. A couple of people sniggered. *Bastards.*

The Beechmount Residents Association met every month at the leisure centre, and every month they skirted the real issues. The committee sat behind a long table at the top of the multi-purpose room and the concerned residents faced them in rows of stackable plastic chairs. Nobody wanted to deal with the bastards the Andersonstown News had dubbed the Wee Rockets. Since the IRA agreed to cease all paramilitary activity, punishment beatings were no longer common practice. And because Sinn Fein would not officially advocate the Police Service of Northern Ireland, and there was still a bad-feeling hangover from the RUC days, their investigations weren't supported by the residents. The vicious, robbing bastards could take what they wanted from innocent people with no fear of consequence. The Wild West.

"It's time for us to stage a protest." Father Cairns addressed the gathered residents. A general murmur of agreement filled the room.

Stephen snorted loud enough to be heard. He was ignored.

"Yes," Jimmy Mac, the association's chairperson, said. "We know that some of these wee scumbags must live around here. We need to put pressure on them or their families to come forward."

Stephen shook his head. "If we knew who they were we could just run them out of here. Why waste time with chanting in the street? The parents don't give a fuck about these kids and the kids don't give a fuck about who they hurt."

"Please watch your language, Stephen," Jimmy said.

A red-faced Father Cairns cleared his throat and nodded.

"Sorry, I curse when I'm upset. Last night's attack was a disgrace. Missus McKinney is in her seventies. "

"We're all upset. Just try to keep in mind the company you're in, Stephen," Jimmy said. "This isn't a football pitch."

"Look, I'm just saying that the softly-softly approach won't accomplish anything. In the days when the Provos ran this area these wee hoods would be rolling about the streets in wheelchairs."

"These are different days. We have to look ahead."

"You're just politicking, Jimmy. A protest is a waste of time."

Stephen folded his arms. He'd made his point. Someone else needed to run with it. Plenty of the people at the meeting thought like him. Now that he'd put a stop to the pussyfooting it'd be easier for the others.

Nobody took the opportunity. Jimmy slow-shrugged at Stephen as if to bait him into further discussion. Stephen shook his head. The muscles in his forearms bulged as he twisted his beanie. The black wool stretched in his grip, spoiling its shape. He was the only man in the room who really cared about his community. He'd have to do something about the little problems on his own.

###

"I have to leave the gang," Joe said.

He'd purposely waited until he and Wee Danny were alone. They were on their way back to the gang from a trip to the corner shop. Joe carried a plastic bag of loose cigarettes and penny chews. His height and thin moustache helped him pass for sixteen. He didn't mind buying the cigarettes for the rest of the gang. It was much easier than buying cider.

"What?" Wee Danny took the fag out of his mouth and squinted as a cloud of smoke blew back in his face. "What do you mean leave? Where are you going?"

Joe shook his head. "No, I mean quit stealing with you guys."

"What for? Sure it's good craic."

"Aye, I know. But I'm starting to stick out like a sore thumb. It won't be long until someone around here figures out who I am."

"My ma says I won't be long catching up with you. We're just at that age."

Joe nodded. He didn't want to tell Wee Danny his ma was full of shit. He was only a sparrow fart. You could tell by looking at Wee Danny's fists he would never be big. Joe's granny always used to say that pups and boys grew into their paws. Wee Danny couldn't even get a sovereign ring small enough to fit his fingers.

And anyway, his brother Paul was still a shortarse and at twenty-something his growing days were gone. The others joked that Wee Danny's ma still bought his clothes in Baby Gap. Not in front of him though. Small or not, he scrapped like a Staffordshire bull terrier.

"That doesn't help me right now though."

"The others won't like it, Joe."

"Do you think?"

"Yeah. Don't be saying nothing yet. Not until me and you come up with a story."

"Okay, mate. Are you not pissed off?"

"No. With you gone the gang's mine. Best news I've heard all year, you gangly prick."

Joe punched Wee Danny's shoulder. Wee Danny laughed and flicked his fag butt at him. It bounced off Joe's chest in a shower of sparks.

"You're a wee bastard," Joe said.

"Your ma says I'm massive where it counts."

Joe tried to think of something disgusting to say about Wee Danny's sister. He didn't get a chance.

"Here, Joe, what's going on up there?"

At the corner of Beechmount Avenue and Mica Drive a big guy with ginger hair stood amongst the rest of the Rockets. Voices rose.

"Shit. Doesn't look good," Joe said.

They jogged towards the commotion. As they got closer Joe picked out a voice shouting the odds.

"You don't own the street." Liam Greene's voice wavered but he raised his double chin to the big ginger guy. Stupid wee fatty always had to mouth off. He'd just make things worse, as usual.

Joe and Wee Danny joined the ranks. Joe wanted to say something but he couldn't think.

"What's wrong, mister?" Wee Danny asked.

"I'm trying to find out who robbed Missus McKinney last night. I thought I'd ask your mates since they're always hanging about here. They've offered me nothing but lip."

"You're Stephen McVeigh, aren't you?"

The big ginger's face softened into a surprised smile.

"How'd you know that?"

"You play football for Davitts. The same team as our Paul."

"Wee Paul? The forward?"

"Aye."

"Nippy wee bastard, your Paul. We'd be lost without him."

Wee Danny nodded as if he'd trained his older brother in the sublime art of goal scoring. Joe marvelled at his friend's confidence.

"Right, well you and your friends keep an ear out for me. If you hear about any hoods from St James's or the Whiterock coming down here to cause trouble, you let me know. I won't let this place go to the dogs."

"No problem, Stephen. Good luck in next week's match. I hear St John's are on a winning streak."

"Cheers, wee man. Talk to you later."

McVeigh cantered down Beechmount Avenue and turned into Beechmount Parade before the gang relaxed into tough guy mode.

"Fucking dickhead. Who does he think he is?" Joe said.

"Who gives a fuck?" Wee Danny asked. "So long as he doesn't know who we are."

"We thought you were going to suck his dick for him," Liam Greene said. The others laughed.

"You have to pick your fights, Fatso. You're just lucky me and Joe came along in time to pull you out of trouble. You looked like you were shitting it."

"Your ma," Liam said.

"Right, okay, that's enough," Joe said. "Listen, we're looking too suspicious hanging around in a group of ten. We should lie low for a bit. That big ginger guy must be too thick to put two and two together, but if one of the real community activists decides to do a headcount they won't be long figuring us out. I don't want them knocking on my ma's door."

There was no discussion. Joe passed out the cigarettes and sweets and the gang broke off in twos and threes.

"You want to come to my place?" Joe asked Wee Danny. "I think my ma's to go for the groceries after work. We might get an hour or so to watch the telly."

"Aye, let's go."

They got about thirty minutes lounging time before the front door rattled open and Joe's ma spilled in, hands full of shopping bags.

"And where were you last night?"

His ma didn't even wait to get her coat off before launching into the interrogation. It didn't matter that Wee Danny was sitting on their sofa watching the telly. She was going to have it out with him. Joe hopped out of the armchair in case he needed to dodge a slap. He was taller than his ma, but she was a bleached-blonde devil when she was pissed off.

"I was out with Danny and a few of the lads." Joe said.

"Do you want us to put your shopping away, Missus Philips?" Wee Danny asked.

"No, Danny. Sit there and be quiet." She turned to Joe. "Well? What were you and your mates doing?"

"Just hanging about, like."

"Hanging about where?"

"What's with all these questions?"

"Hanging about where, Joseph?"

"Down at the Dunville Park. We went to the chippie across the road from the gates and all threw in for a couple of sausage suppers and a bottle of Coke. Then we sat at a bench and ate."

"So you weren't on Beechmount Avenue?"

"No. The chippie on that street closed last week. Health and Safety shut it, I heard."

Joe's ma finally took her coat off. The black polo shirt she always wore to work was covered in flour. Her job at the bakery paid her off the books which meant she didn't have to declare it to the DSS. She got her housing benefits and jobseekers allowance on top of the fiver an hour she earned three days a week. Without it they'd be eating ASDA value beans every day.

"Missus McKinney's son was at the bakery today. He's in bits about what happened last night. Did you hear about it?"

"Aye," Joe said. "Heard someone talking about it in the shop."

"Were you buying cigarettes?"

Joe broke eye contact with his ma for a second before answering. "No." He could always make up a convincing alibi, but lying to his ma about smoking was impossible. He'd never understand why.

"You lying wee bastard. Give me them."

"Sorry, ma. It's just too hard to quit." Joe handed over three loose cigarettes. The white paper had crumpled near the filters. They didn't travel well out of the box.

"Jesus, are they still selling singles in that wee shop?" She looked at the brand logo. "Mayfair? Ah well, better than nothing."

Joe's ma fished a plastic lighter from the pocket of her blue jeans. She always smoked his confiscated fags. Just to rub it in. He watched her thin cheeks dimple as she inhaled. She puffed a solitary smoke-ring before blowing two jets from her nose, clouding the space between them. The smell tightened his chest.

"Get those groceries put away and I'll let you smoke the butt."

###

Stephen grunted and shoved. His triceps and pectorals screamed but he fought through the pain. The clank of the loaded, twenty kilo bar settling into its brackets couldn't compete with his wail of ecstasy and relief.

"Good man, Stephen," Wee Paul said.

Stephen opened his eyes. Black spots danced, distracting his focus from Wee Paul who looked down at him from the head of the weights bench.

"I might have one more set in me," Stephen said.

"That's enough, mate. We can't have you injured for next week's match."

Thank fuck you said that, Stephen thought. Another eight reps would kill him. He'd already raised the stakes a little too high when he got Wee Paul to throw another couple of fives onto the bar. The last push scared him. And with Wee Paul spotting him, if he'd dropped it he'd have been fucked. Thankfully, he was at his peak. He sat up on the bench and rubbed his stiffened wrists. Wee Paul handed him a plastic bottle of water. He left slippery finger tracks in the condensation as he choked it down.

"Why are you pushing yourself so hard, Stephen?"

"Need to get a bit of aggression out. I'm not long out of the Residents Association meeting."

"Talking about poor aul Missus McKinney?"

"Yeah, plenty of talking. That's the fucking problem. All talk, no trousers."

Wee Paul nodded. Short, rapid bobs that went on for too long. He looked like one of those bobblehead characters all the music shops in town were selling. His little brother, Danny, nodded the same way.

"How's your wee brother doing in school?"

Wee Paul tilted his balding head. "Our Danny? Why do you ask? How do you even know him?"

"I met him on my way up here. He recognised me when I was asking his mates a few questions. Just thought the crowd he was hanging about with looked a bit dodgy. Has he been getting into trouble lately? Anything like that?"

"What are you saying, Stephen?"

"Don't get me wrong, mate. I'm sure your brother had nothing to do with Missus McKinney's mugging. I mean, you'd know if you had a scumbag like that in your family. Wouldn't you?"

"Of course I would." Wee Paul barked the words.

"But do you think he'd tell you if he knew his mates were getting up to no good?"

"Did you ever tout on a mate, Stephen?"

"That's kind of my point there, Paul. I wonder would you ask your Danny if he's heard anything. Tell him it's family before mates. Tell him you're worried your own granny might be the next victim."

Wee Paul shook his head. "I'll think about it. Take off the fives and fifteens until I get a go on this bench."

They swapped places and Stephen spotted Wee Paul as he went through the motions. The wiry muscles in the smaller man's arms strained as he counted out ten reps. The look on his face informed Stephen the wee man's thoughts were elsewhere. He was worried about his brother. *Good stuff.* Stephen didn't trust that cocky wee shit or his hoodie-wearing friends. Especially the lanky one with the bum-fluff moustache.

After another set each, Stephen told wee Paul he'd to see a man about a car.

Retired mechanic, Brian "Mackers" MacDonald, was the man to see about buying runabouts in Beechmount. Uninsured cars that were too old or fucked up to pass an MOT but could get you from A to B. Mackers' cars were parked all over the place. Customers rapped his door and told him what they wanted. He disappeared back into his house, retrieved a green parka and a key from within, and walked his client to the matching car. Some used them as disposable transport. Others for getaway wheels. Stephen wanted a patrol car.

The once blue Ford Escort had seen better days. Stephen kicked a balding tyre and rust flakes rained from the wheel arch. Replacement body parts scavenged from scrap-yards hadn't been spray-painted. A red door, a green bonnet and a black front bumper created a patchwork quilt paintjob. The driver's door opened with a protesting creak. Inside, the car smelt musty. Cracks ran through the plastic instrument panel. A little tree hung from the rear view mirror, its magic long departed.

"I'll give you forty quid for it."

Mackers rummaged in his hairy ear with a thick, old man finger. He smiled an NHS smile and drummed his fingers on the bonnet of the car parked on Ballymurphy Street. Stephen wrinkled his nose at the waxy fingerprints the old boy left behind.

"Fifty," Mackers said.

"See you later." Stephen got out of the car and brushed past the crooked old entrepreneur.

"Okay, son, forty it is. Come on back and don't be so huffy."

Stephen didn't offer to shake on the deal. He handed Mackers two wrinkled twenties and settled into the driver's seat. The engine chugged for the first few yards but eventually settled into a semi-regular splutter.

No time like the present, he thought. He decided to take the knackered motor out on its first patrol.

The runabout bucked as he changed gear. Everything in the car seemed to rattle or clank. The radiator light blinked at random intervals. The ancient magic-tree swayed from side to side as he took corners on the narrow streets of the West Belfast housing estate. He approached the junction onto the Falls Road.

Wee Danny and the tall prick with the sparse moustache sat on the low windowsill of the closed down chippie on Beechmount Avenue. Their seat faced an ancient IRA mural. A chained fist hovered over a badly drawn map of Ireland. The street sign set into the brick wall hosting the mural had been blackened out with spray paint. Above the deletion the words *RPG Avenue* were now scrawled.

He stopped at the red light and got a good look at them. Wee Danny was smoking, which his brother Paul would be delighted to hear. The tall one nattered on about something. He punctuated whatever he said with too many hand gestures. The long, skinny arms made his movements awkward and exaggerated. But Wee Danny hung on his words. He'd mistaken Wee Danny as the ringleader earlier. The cocky wee shit's attitude had thrown him off. The tall kid was the real leader. So the tall kid had to be dealt with first. Always target the main man.

The traffic lights turned green and Stephen moved on. Wee Danny looked his way as the Ford's engine backfired. He said something to the tall one and they both turned to stare at him. He stared back and took his time pulling out onto the road. The tall one blew him a kiss and Wee Danny laughed. Stephen shook his head and manoeuvred the runabout onto the Falls Road. A couple of hundred yards up the road he turned left into a narrow lane that led back into Beechmount. He took his time completing another circuit.

The blare of a car horn set Joe's heart racing. He hated being so nervy. Criminal paranoia. It was bad for the body and the mind. The driver responsible waved at him. Stephen McVeigh. His piece-of-shit car rattled past.

"He's driven past us three times now, Joe," Wee Danny said. "And he's given us the hairy eyeball every time."

"What's he beeping at us for?" Joe asked.

"To let us know he's watching us, I suppose," Wee Danny said. "Do you think he's on to us?"

"I think he's asking questions about everybody. He's decided he's a vigilante or something."

"Are you worried?"

"No. Are you?"

Joe lied. "No. Fuck away off."

"Good." Wee Danny looked at his watch. "When are these bastards going to get here?"

"Text Liam and see what's keeping them."

"I've no credit."

"Ach, fuck this then. Will we get some cider instead? I feel like getting pissed."

"Your ma will kill you, Joe."

"Only if she catches me. Come on. Will we just go have a drink at the park?"

Before Wee Danny could answer, Liam Greene and three other Rockets turned the corner. They announced their arrival by yelling insults at Joe and Wee Danny.

"So what's the plan tonight, Joe?" Liam Greene asked when the insults finally died off. His big cheeks were red from the effort of walking and talking at the same time. Joe felt an urge to slap him. Tell him to cut back on the Crispy Pancake sandwiches.

"I fancy a wee carryout at the park."

"After we earn a bit of cash?" Liam asked.

"Nah. I can't be arsed running about tonight. I'm sure you'd appreciate a rest too. You must be knackered after last night."

"Fuck up."

Joe waited for the rest of them to quit their sniggering then said, "What about you lot? Fancy a drink?"

The three who'd arrived with Liam looked to him for an answer. *What the fuck is this?* Joe thought. He glanced at Wee Danny who looked just as confused.

"They want to do some robbing," Liam said. The others didn't look directly at Joe but they didn't disagree with the fat bastard either.

"Can they not talk for themselves?" Wee Danny asked.

"We did our talking in the taxi down," Liam said. "We're all in agreement."

Joe tugged at the back of his baseball cap; the adjustable strap seemed too tight. Cold sweat ran from his armpits to the waistband of his trousers. "Are you the leader here, Liam?"

Liam looked up into Joe's face. His eyes widened. The fat boy's cheeks jiggled when he cleared his throat. "No, Joe."

"But you're making agreements in taxis with my gang. Sounds like you want to be the leader."

"Look, Joe, I'm sorry."

"What are you sorry about, Fatty? Making plans behind my back?"

Joe took a step forward and Liam retreated. The other three moved away from him, deserted him. One of them stumbled off the kerb onto the road. Wee Danny lit a fag. On the road, a car skidded to a halt and stalled.

"Get off the road, you stupid cunt."

A pretty blonde with a rough country accent poked her head out the window of her car. A student from St Mary's Teacher's College on the Falls Road by the look of her. Her little Clio had stopped just inches from the shocked Rocket. The tension broke as Wee Danny pointed and laughed exaggerated hee-haws at the angry student. She rolled up her window and shook her head as she gunned the engine. They cheered when she got it going on her second attempt. The cheer rose as she spun off and jumped a red light at the junction.

"Stupid bitch," Wee Danny said.

Joe nodded and pointed at Wee Danny's fag. His little mate passed him the shrinking butt and he pulled hard on it. Liam didn't speak. Joe blew smoke towards him.

"So you *can* keep your mouth shut."

Liam shrugged.

Joe stomped the ground in front of him. Liam flinched at the sudden movement. His chubby cheeks burned red. *Thank fuck,* Joe thought, *he's not up for a scrap.*

"Chill out, Liam," Joe said. "We're all mates here, aren't we?"

Liam nodded then stared at his own feet. Joe's heart slowed its roll. He was in charge again. He didn't want to be, but he wouldn't be phased out of his position by Liam Greene. People didn't forget that kind of thing. Show weakness and you're fucked.

"Here's the rest of them now," Wee Danny said. He put a finger and a thumb in his mouth and whistled loud enough to hurt Joe's ear. One of the other four whistled back. They carried blue plastic bags weighed down by what had to be three-litre bottles of cider. *Barrack Busters.* Another decision taken from Joe's hands. But he let this one slide. When the whole gang was together, Joe took control of the situation.

"No one will annoy our heads at the park," he said. "If we drink on the street we'll have to keep moving about. I just want to sit still."

"Right, let's go then," Danny said. "I'm gasping for a drink now."

Liam didn't throw in an opinion. *Good,* Joe thought, *remember your place.*

Dunville Park, their favored haunt, wasn't far from Beechmount. Five or ten minutes at an idle pace. It was smaller than the Falls Park which lay further up the road from Beechmount, but that way was all uphill and the older kids usually took all the best spots. Dunville Park was less concealed, but for a small group it did the job. They rarely got moved on from the swings and benches at night time. It was accepted that kids had to drink somewhere. Better the park than a residential street corner.

Joe leaned against the frame of the swings. He held a plastic bottle of cider in one hand and picked at the peeling primary colour paint on the swing's frame with the other. Wee Danny twirled on one of the intact swings. The chains scrunched as they twisted together. Liam worked on wrapping another swing around the crossbar. He took sips of cider in between. The rest of the gang were scattered about the recreational area. Some sat around the huge terracotta fountain and others lay on the grass. Because it was summer they would be undisturbed until ten o'clock. Then a council jobsworth would lock up for the night. When the park keeper was gone, they'd scale the fence back in.

The late evening air blew warm and the smell of exhaust fumes from the Falls Road traffic cleared a little. Joe sucked up the moment. The cider buzz, friends in good humour, nothing to dread in the morning, bright nights in a little city. The sweet life.

"This is fucking great, isn't it?" Wee Danny said.

Joe laughed. "You must have read my mind, mate."

"Fruits," Liam said.

Wee Danny spat a tobacco-spotted green gob. It missed Liam's head by inches. Liam made a kissy-face at him.

"Fuck up, Liam," Joe said. "If you want to be a fucking moan, go away on home to your ma."

"Sorry, Joe."

The fat fucker had obviously gotten in over his head earlier. He wasn't keen to repeat the experience. But Wee Danny didn't want to let it lie.

"You didn't say sorry to me, Fatso."

"Why should I, Frodo?"

"Who the fuck's Frodo?" Wee Danny asked.

"Ach, you're a stupid bastard. He's that wee dwarf out of Lord of the Rings."

"Hobbit, Liam," Joe said.

"What?"

"Frodo's a hobbit. The dwarf's the one with the long beard."

"Whatever. He's still a shortarse."

Wee Danny hopped off the swing. Liam didn't back down.

"Well, we don't call you Wee Danny because you're a fucking giant, like. You're a tiny wee shrimp. Probably have a wee, small dick to match."

"Keep talking, Fatso," Wee Danny said. "You're making this very fucking easy for me."

"You couldn't beat the deuce of clubs without Joe behind you."

"Is that right, dickhead?"

"Why don't you show me different?"

Joe's stomach clenched. In just seconds, the perfect summer moment had turned sour. It looked like he was set to referee a scrap. Liam, stupid fucker that he was, was headed for a serious kicking. After that they'd never get back the mellow atmosphere he'd been enjoying. But what could he do? If he stepped in now it'd look like Wee Danny couldn't stand up for himself.

"Are you sure you want to do this, Liam?" Joe asked, knowing what the answer had to be. Fuck it, it was worth a try.

"Fucking right I do. This wee dick thinks he's hard as nails. I'd love to hammer him."

"What about you, Danny?"

"I'm going to wreck this cunt."

Joe sighed and twisted the cap back on to his bottle.

"Fine, then. Try and keep it kind of clean."

Chapter 2

Louise Philips blinked back the threat of a tear. She pulled the spoon from her cup of tea, tapped it on the edge of the pure white mug and sat it on a saucer in the middle of the table.

"What's wrong, Louise?"

Louise jerked her gaze from the teaspoon on the saucer. Karen Magee stood in her usual place in the immaculate kitchen. She leant against her glossy worktop within hand's reach of the stainless steel sink and the white larder. Louise had already turned down an M&S biscuit, but Karen would stand there until one of them decided to give in to temptation. They followed the same routine every time Louise visited her friend.

Karen lived across the street. She had a degree and a good job but she'd stayed in Beechmount to look after her mummy. The poor wee woman couldn't open a tin of beans for herself because of her arthritis. Louise didn't know where her friend got the time between running errands for her mummy and working in the city to keep her house so clean. Too clean. Can't get comfortable clean.

"How's your mummy?" Louise asked.

"Don't change the subject. You near wore out that spoon you were stirring your cuppa so long. Something's up."

Louise sighed. "I'm worried about Joe."

Karen tutted. The sound of it pulled at the knot in Louise's upper back.

"What's he done now?"

"Ach, don't be like that."

"Sorry, but he's putting years on you, Louise."

Louise looked down into her cup. The tears rolled. Karen made one of her clucky apology noises. She left her spot by the sink and bent to hug Louise. They stayed like that until Louise patted Karen's back. Karen glanced at the damp patch on the shoulder of her navy work suit jacket but didn't complain. Louise felt bad about soaking it. *Hope it's not dry clean only*, she thought.

Karen handed her a piece of kitchen roll and pulled out the chair opposite. Louise reached across the wee table and grasped Karen's hand.

"I always thought Joe would be nothing like his daddy. Dermot fucked off so long ago Joe doesn't even remember him. Never asks about him either. I don't think he knows what he looks like. I've a few photos of us all but I never offered to show them to Joe and he's never asked if I have any. But he just looks so much like him and I think I might be too hard on him because of that. But I don't know what the wee boy is up to because I can't be on his back all the time, and he's probably doing nothing wrong at all, but Dermot was such a bad bastard and I was so stupid and…"

"Louise. Slow down. What are you trying to say?"

"Did you hear about Missus McKinney last night?"

Karen blessed herself, a rapid up, down, left, right led by her middle finger. "Oh Jesus, that was awful. How many aul dolls is that now?"

"One's too many."

Karen gasped. "Wait a minute. You don't think your Joe has anything to do with them muggings, do you?"

Louise shook her head, then nodded, then shook her head again.

"You don't but you do?"

Louise nodded.

"What even put the thought in your head?"

"He's never at home."

"He's a teenager. How do you know he's not just out smoking or sneaking a wee drink of cider?"

"That's it. I don't. But I've no way of knowing for sure."

"Is that all the evidence you have?"

"Well, no, not really. New stuff keeps turning up in his bedroom. Clothes and DVDs. And he hasn't asked me for money in ages. I give him pocket money but he used to ask for a top up every week."

"Maybe he's selling a bit of blow."

"That's possible I suppose. I'd rather he was doing that than robbing pensioners in the street, but… God, I don't know."

Louise fought the urge to puke on her best friend's immaculate kitchen floor. Her stomach shunted itself into her throat and her mouth watered. She pulled in deep breaths and surfed the wave of nausea until it passed. Then she looked her friend in the eyes.

"Do you think I could have one of those biscuits now, Karen?"

Liam froze as Wee Danny rushed him. He watched the first punch sail through the air. White light flashed. His head snapped back. Before he fully understood he'd just been hit, Wee Danny's left fist split his lip. He stepped back. Wee Danny followed. The others cheered. Liam raised his hands. Wee Danny sidestepped and hit him with another punch.

"Stop it!" Liam's voice squeaked. Somebody laughed.

Wee Danny hit him again. Liam couldn't even see the punches coming. Tears blurred his vision. He stepped back again. The world tilted and he was on his back. The setting sun coloured the clouds blood red. Liam instinctively covered his head and rolled into a fetal position. He waited for the kicks to rain in.

"Okay, Danny," It was Joe's deep voice, "You've proved your point. Leave him alone."

Some of the spectators booed. His so-called friends. Booing because he didn't get hospitalised. Liam opened his guard and peeked through his arms. A Nike Air trainer filled the gap. Pain exploded in his nose.

"Danny! I said that's enough. Back off!"

"I'm going to kill the fat fucker."

"You don't kick a mate when he's down. Not even Liam."

Liam kept his face protected until the sounds of a struggle ended. Wee Danny had been restrained. He wiped tears and blood from his face with the sleeves of his white hoodie. It was ruined. His dad would kill him for losing a fight. Unless he told him he was jumped by three guys. And he fought off two of them. He'd get one of the Fegan twins to corroborate.

Already his left eye was swelling shut. Bruises made you look hard. At least the kicking had that small silver lining. Respect from strangers he'd pass on the street. He poked at his inflated eyelid and snapped his hand back again. He looked at his attacker. Joe gripped the wee bastard in a bear hug. Wee Danny muttered reassurances that the fight was over.

"You're a fucking psycho," Liam said. He struggled to keep his voice steady.

Wee Danny laughed and Joe loosened his grip on him. The smaller boy's hands went straight to his pockets. Seconds later a lit fag hung from his lips. It was over. Liam tried to hide his relief.

They drank. The fight excitement faded. The group relaxed. Then they drank some more.

Half an hour later, Liam picked flakes of dried blood from his nostrils. He'd drunk enough cider to numb the physical and emotional pain. The constant replay of how badly he'd been beaten faded to the back of his head. If he hadn't swallowed his pride the others would have lost even more respect for him. Storming off was for girls. Huffing on a carryout was a mortal sin. He gulped down another mouthful of cider. Then he stood up, waited for his balance to catch up with him, and walked over to where Wee Danny and Joe shared a bottle. They were rapping along to a G-Unit tune playing from Wee Danny's Motorola.

He coughed when the mini hip hop performance finally ended. Wee Danny looked up at him and tensed. He was ready to go again. Liam wasn't. He extended his hand and tilted his spinning head.

"Truce?"

Joe nudged Wee Danny after the cheeky shite hesitated for a few seconds. He shook hands with Liam; his grip unenthusiastic and loose. Practically a fingertip shake.

"If you don't bother me, I won't bother you," Wee Danny said. He made sure he said it loud enough for the other guys to hear. Conversation around them ceased as the rest of the gang tuned in.

"Deal. I was out of order. End of story."

"Yeah you were."

Liam offered Wee Danny a cigarette. The peace offering was accepted and the rest of the gang lost interest. He sat on the grass with Joe and Danny and laughed as they fumbled through a Little

Britain sketch until they were interrupted by Wee Danny's G-Unit ringtone. He staggered away before they started another sketch.

Two of the gang sat on the lip of the dry fountain. Liam approached them, his mask slipping. They were the Fegan twins. Eddie and Matt. Non-identical but always dressed to match. Liam had once asked how they always ended up wearing the same colour. They'd looked at him, confused, and explained that they just put on whatever their ma left out for them. Liam thought it was weird, but didn't tell them that. He could probably take either of them in a toe-to-toe, but if they ganged up on him he'd have no chance. They were notorious for their tag team skills.

They gave him that confused look again. He felt closer to them than anyone else in the gang so he told them the truth.

"My da says there's more than one way to skin a cat. I'll get my own back on that wee shite."

Eddie, the elder twin, nodded. Matt chuckled. He could rely on them if he needed to.

The sun sank out of the sky and the moon beamed. Liam checked his watch, closing one eye to focus. Nearly ten. The park keeper would kick them out soon.

"Lads!" Liam's voice boomed. He enjoyed the sound of it cutting through the night. "Last orders! It's nearly locking up time."

Plastic bags rustled as they were loaded with half empty cider bottles. The gang mumbled and grumbled but got to their feet, falling into a ragtag formation. They moved as one to the gate. The less time they spent arguing with the park keeper, the sooner the guy left and they got in again.

###

Paul Gibson thumbed the red button on his mobile and fired the little Nokia at his brown leather sofa. It bounced off the firm cushioning and clattered onto the beech-effect laminate flooring. The back panel slid off on impact and the battery popped out. He cursed, collected the parts and pieced it together. He turned the phone back on and tried to call his brother again.

Danny never answered calls from family on a Saturday night. Acting the hard man in front of his mates, Paul supposed. He'd strangle the wee bastard when he saw him.

Paul's conversation with Stephen McVeigh had twisted his head. The big ginger prick was a pain in the hole a lot of the time, but Paul never pegged him for a liar. His less than subtle hints must have been based on some sort of information. Even if it was just a rumour, Paul had to figure out a way to put a stop to it. Around West Belfast rumours had a tendency to get people hurt. If it was more than a rumour… well, he'd have to break his little brother's neck.

Still no answer. He phoned his ma's house.

"Hello?"

"Ma. Is our Danny there?"

"Aye right! That wee bastard won't be home for hours yet. He's too busy with his friends to want to spend time at home."

He heard a rumble in the background. His father complaining about late phone calls, no doubt.

"It's our Paul. Stop yapping you grumpy aul bastard. Sorry, love. What were we talking about? Oh aye, our Danny. He'll not be in until I'm in bed."

"What does he be doing at this time of night?"

"Kicking a ball about or breaking windows or something. You know what kids are like these days. Why do you want him?"

Paul could practically smell the vodka breath from his end.

"Ach, I just wanted to borrow a DVD off him," he said. "She's out with her mates and Owen is down for the night. TV's shite."

"You're right there, love. Is your Sinead out again? You want to tie that one down."

"Okay, Ma. Good night."

"Night, love."

Paul sat on the sofa and flicked on the TV. Then he turned it off and stood up. He checked his watch. Half past nine. Danny was probably at the park but without a babysitter Paul couldn't track him down. Sinead wouldn't stumble in until the early hours. He sat down again, turned the TV back on and yawned. He rested his eyelids while he waited.

He dozed.

Paul's eyes sprang open. The scratching sound of a key trying to find its hole woke him. A few seconds passed as he took in his surroundings and straightened up his thoughts. He hated sleeping on the couch. Sweat soaked through his shirt and his neck complained when he looked to his right. The TV flickered an MTV music video, the sound low and tinny. A dried drool line ran down his cheek and he craved a shot of Listerine to freshen his mouth up. He tried to remember why he'd fallen asleep on the couch.

Sinead.

Danny.

Sinead's key turned in the lock. She shushed herself as she wobble-stepped her way into the living room. Paul sat up on the couch and smiled at her. She'd left the house primped to perfection; straightened hair, warpaint just right and working the graceful strut of a catwalk model. She'd obviously had a great night. Windswept and goggle-eyed, she flumped onto the couch, like a punctured inflatable sex doll dressed in beer-stained Top Shop chic. She'd look even better in the morning.

"What the fuck are you doing up?" she asked, her tone affectionate. She looked at her watch, blinked and gave up. "It's late."

"It's after one, but I need to go out."

"What?"

"I need to get a hold of our Danny. He's not answering his phone so I'm going to check the park and see if he's on a carryout."

"What's the rush? You could go see him tomorrow."

Paul didn't want to tell Sinead everything. She talked too much to be trusted. He toned down his suspicions.

"I heard he was selling dope to kids at school. I want to find out if it's true."

"The wee bastard. He better not be. See if he is, Paul, you give him a hiding."

"I will, but I have to go find him now."

"Right." She nodded like a sprung jack-in-a-box. Then her head jerked to a stop. "Wait a minute. What about our Owen? You can't leave him on his own."

"You're here."

"Aye, but I'm pissed."

"So?"

"So if I go to sleep and he wakes up looking for me I mightn't hear him."

"He's five. He hardly ever wakes up at night."

"What if there's a fire?"

"For fuck's sake, Sinead. There won't be a fire. But if you're worried, make yourself a cup of coffee and sit up until I get back."

"But I'm knackered."

"And I'd rather be in bed too, but this is important."

"You're ruining my going-out night."

"You've been out. I haven't ruined anything."

"You always ruin everything."

"Look, do what you want. I'm out of here."

He scooped the door key from Sinead's tiny knock-off Louis Vuitton handbag and stormed out. Sinead cursed after him, drunk and affronted. He stopped on the doorstep when he realised he'd forgotten to put on a coat. Sinead's voice penetrated the PVC door with perfect clarity. It wasn't safe to go back inside. He jogged to keep himself warm.

His footsteps clip-clopped a steady beat. The terraced houses streamed by on either side. It was peaceful but unsettling to jog through Beechmount at such a quiet hour. The familiar orange glow from the streetlights held comfort but the eerie quiet of sleeping neighbours and house parties still under control whispered wicked potential. His eyes flitted to the shadowed alley at the end of Amcomri Street. The security fence swung open on new and silent hinges. He imagined the Wee Rockets skulking out of sight amongst the wheelie bins, but didn't have the stupidity to run blindly in and challenge them. There'd be no grannies out and about at this time. He ran past with an almost clear conscience.

Taxis sailed up and down the Falls Road. The kebab shop, the Chinese takeaway and the pizzeria pulled in the scant few who'd left the pubs around Broadway early. Harsh fluorescents behind the massive streaked windows highlighted the slack faces of the people too drunk or tired to see the rest of the night through. The footpath remained puke and piss free for the time being. Paul felt comfortable in his stride. The park was in sight. Then a single-tone horn heralded an exhausted engine. He stopped too quickly and his knee barked at him; an old football injury rearing its head.

Stephen McVeigh's square, ginger scone was the first thing Paul saw, then he zoomed out to take in the shitbox he was driving; an old Escort runabout. He shook his head when the passenger door opened. A pathetic toot from the asthmatic horn insisted. He jumped in, the smell of old engine oil wrinkling his nose.

"What are you driving, McVeigh?"

"Never mind. Are you out looking for Wee Danny?"

"Yeah, have you seen him?"

"Earlier on I followed him to Dunville Park. He's been there with a crowd of young hoods all night."

"You've been driving about in this thing all night? Are you mental? You'll get carbon monoxide poisoning."

"Shush."

Paul shot a stern glance at his teammate. He needn't have bothered. McVeigh's attention was on the green iron gates of Dunville Park. The big man forced his car on another few yards. He U-turned on the Falls Road and mounted the kerb. The car rocked on its chassis like a busted mechanical rodeo bull. The old Escort was not the most efficient tool for espionage. Paul said as much to McVeigh.

"I want them to see me."

"Why?"

"It'll freak them out. Put them under pressure."

"And if they aren't the Rockets?"

"They are."

Still McVeigh stared at the secured park entrance but through the passenger window. Paul fidgeted with the glovebox in front of him, aware that he obstructed McVeigh's view. The catch-release button wouldn't move. He rapped the plastic with his knuckles.

"Here, this is broke, Stephen."

"The car cost me forty quid. You get what you pay for."

"I could probably force it open if you're curious. Never know what you might find."

"Leave it be."

"What's wrong with you, humpy-hole?"

"Just stop picking at my car and keep your eyes open for that scumbag brother of yours."

"Why are you so sure my brother's a scumbag? He's from a good family."

McVeigh snorted. Paul curled a fist but left it in his lap. *Wanker,* he thought.

"Paul, look, here they come."

###

Liam almost choked. He couldn't help but laugh as he ran down the Falls Road. They headed towards the relative safety of Beechmount's narrow streets. He carried the severed wing-mirror under his arm like a rugby ball. Joe ran ahead of him, taking full advantage of his ostrich legs. He whipped an extending car aerial through the air like a Burberry-clad Zorro. Wee Danny ran alongside Liam holding the other wing mirror. The wee shit yelped something at him but the thud of his heart and the thundering footsteps of the other Rockets blocked out the sound. He could taste the pastie bap he'd eaten at dinner. A cider burp added to the dizzying experience.

"Shut up and keep running, Danny." The words probably didn't reach Wee Danny's ears but Liam reckoned the sentiment was plainly read off his face. They ran on.

Behind them, the big ginger wannabe vigilante yelled threats. Liam didn't dare glance over his shoulder to see how close McVeigh was, but his voice got smaller and smaller. The Rockets followed Joe onto Beechmount Avenue, up Beechmount Parade and toward the grounds of Corpus Christi College. The clambering school of hoods scaled the outer wall easily and collapsed in a heap on the grass edging the staff car park. Again they were in the open but had a good vantage point to scope out oncoming threats. McVeigh couldn't be seen. The prick had given up.

The buzz in the air raised hackles and smiles. Liam almost felt like sharing the bag of grass in his zipped tracksuit pocket. He pulled out a twenty deck of Lambert & Butler cigarettes instead. Everyone but Wee Danny dipped in. He already sucked on a lit fag like a carpet monkey on a fat nipple. His was the only face not smiling. Liam knew and relished the cause of Wee Danny's anxiety but played dumb for a laugh.

"What's up, Danny?"

Wee Danny waved his wing-mirror at Liam. "Our Paul was in the passenger seat. He looked right at me when I pulled this off the car. You want to have seen the look on his face. I'm fucked."

Liam looked at his own souvenir from their planned attack. His wing-mirror had popped right off the driver side of McVeigh's old Escort. Access to his reflection came in handy. He could tell he'd control of his smirk before looking at Wee Danny again. Joe's idea to scare the shit out of McVeigh for stalking them had been a good one before Liam knew Wee Paul Gibson was in the car. Now that Wee Danny was in the shit, it'd been elevated to a dream come true.

"Shit one. So what're you going to do?"

"I'll have to take a hiding. Joe, can I stay at yours tonight?"

Joe nodded.

"Do you mean to tell me Danny Gibson is afraid of someone?" Liam asked.

"You don't have to sound so pleased about it, dickhead."

"Sorry, Danny, I didn't mean it like that. I just thought you were fearless. He's just your brother, like. It's not as if he'll kneecap you."

"Are you trying to wind me up? I'll shove this fucking wing-mirror up your hole."

"Ach, mate. Take it easy."

Joe stood up. "Liam's right, Danny. He's acting a dick, but no more than usual. You're just taking him too seriously. It's Liam for fuck's sake! Just slag him back and have a laugh."

Wee Danny mumbled something into his chest and Liam grinned. Finally, he was under the wee shite's skin, and this time Joe had stood up for Liam. Liam couldn't wait until Wee Danny showed up at the next carryout with bruises from his brother's fists on display. He'd really get on the wee boy's nerves then.

"Is there much cider left?" Joe asked the crowd.

A few of them held up plastic bottles. Not much at all.

Fuck it, thought Liam. "I have something to lighten the mood." He drew the bag of grass from his pocket, gunslinger style, and threw it at Wee Danny. It bounced off his chest and he caught it with a reflex snatch. Liam winked at the shocked Rockets. "What are you waiting for, Frodo? Skin up!"

Everybody but Wee Danny cheered.

###

Louise sipped on the fresh cup of tea. Her eyes stung, begging for sleep. Her shoulders slumped under the weight of her suspicions. The hard kitchen chair gave her pins and needles in her buttocks. If she'd waited for Joe on the sofa she'd have fallen asleep in a second. The wooden chair in her cold kitchen offered no comfort to snuggle into. The wee bastard wasn't going to sneak in past her if she could help it.

She lit a cigarette to go with her tea. Her mind drifted back to the time her insomniac ritual first developed. Dermot's swarthy skin and tightly curled, black shock of hair flashed vividly in her mind. His sly, tight-lipped smile bobbed to the surface and enhanced her pain. He frequently appeared in her thoughts when she was alone and at her most tired and emotionally vulnerable.

But this felt different. A cruel déjà vu. History repeating beyond her control. She couldn't count the times Dermot had kept her up, waiting and wondering. Twelve years since he left and the bastard still had the power to drag fingernails down the blackboard of her heart. Even the day they first met twisted her emotions inside out. She thought about that day, still unsure if it was a fond memory or the prelude to a waking nightmare.

He'd barged into the bakery and threw a brown paper bag over the counter. Louise had jumped at the sudden intrusion. The tall man with broad shoulders and a bad haircut curled his moustached lip in a sneer.

"Peelers are coming, love. Hide that bag of blow for me. They've searched me on the street five times this month and there's too much in there to claim personal use."

The cops didn't come into Beechmount to scoop small time drug dealers off the street in 1993. This man had done more than sell a wee bit of blow to justify such reckless action by the RUC. They wanted to arrest Mister Tall, Dark and Kind of Good Looking for anything they could pin on him. What he'd confess to after a night of hospitality in Castlereagh Police Station would be the real reason they wanted him.

"Why should I? I don't know you from Adam."

"Dermot Kelly. Now fucking hide it and act cool. They're nearly here."

Louise picked the little brown bag up off the floor and buried it in a basket of treacle scones on a flour-dusted shelf behind the counter. She stuffed one of the bakery's white paper bags with large sausage rolls and handed it to Dermot.

"That's two quid, mister," she said as the cops entered the premises.

The first one through the door bore the disapproving glare of a Free Presbyterian at a mixed religion wedding. A smaller, younger peeler traced the first one's footsteps. He looked excited. His eyebrows twitched as his eyes tried to take in every corner of the shop. Neither of them removed their hats. They intended official business.

"Well hello there, Officers Montgomery and McAllister," Dermot Kelly said. "You two in here for a wee salad bap or something? Always pinned you as burger men. You have that healthy, well fed look about you."

"Mister Kelly," the older cop said. "We have reason to believe you have been dealing drugs in this area. Please step outside."

"Officer Montgomery, I think you have been misinformed."

"Constable Montgomery."

"Sorry, *Cunt*-stable."

Constable Montgomery wrinkled his nose in contempt. "Step outside now, Mister Kelly."

"No, I don't think I should."

"We'll pull you in for resisting." Constable McAllister's young voice bounced up and down in pitch with an enthusiasm only matched by the urgency of his darting eyes.

Dermot laughed. "I don't remember you telling me I'm under arrest. I have rights, you know."

McAllister stepped forward but Montgomery placed a firm hand on the younger man's chest.

"You're right, Mister Kelly. We haven't arrested you. But in the interest of saving everybody's time, perhaps you could cooperate with us. If you're not guilty you have nothing to hide. Prove it and we won't have to go through the channels to make this official."

"What happened to innocent until proven guilty?" Dermot asked.

"You've been watching too many Hill Street Blues repeats, Kelly," McAllister said. Montgomery chuckled but patted his colleague on the shoulder. *Calm down, son,* the older cop said without speaking.

"I don't wish to cooperate with you, *Cunt*-stables. Please get the fuck out of my face."

Louise gasped at Dermot's language. Montgomery looked at her for the first time. She almost flinched. The cop seemed to sense this and his face softened.

"Sorry to have involved you in this, miss," he said. "We'll get out of here shortly." He turned his attention back on Dermot. "And I'll be seeing you again, very soon, Mister Kelly."

Montgomery strode out of the bakery, proud and unruffled. McAllister still had a way to go with regards to a professional veneer. He mouthed obscenities at Dermot as his eyes rolled about in his head.

"Get the fuck out of here before you get yourself in trouble, wee boy."

Dermot's words infuriated the cop further but in his frustration he could produce nothing more than a squeak before he tried to slam the door shut. The old hinges on the warped frame caused too much friction for a satisfying result. McAllister's face burned red. He stormed off after his partner. Dermot turned to Louise. His dark eyes glinted with excitement and the promise of danger. His smile curled upwards on one side, the lips fastened together hiding his teeth. She didn't trust that smile, but his eyes intrigued.

"What time do you finish here, love?" he asked.

"Half five."

"I'll see you then. There's a good comedy on at the pictures. I think you'll like it."

She didn't have time to accept or decline. He strutted out of the bakery and was out of sight before Louise's mouth unfroze.

"Okay," she said to herself, to prove that the ability to speak had returned.

That first contact set the tone for their entire relationship. Throughout their time together Louise's fascination with Dermot and her inherent mistrust of him waged war. She never knew if she loved him. Only that no other man had ever inspired such extreme emotion.

And now, twelve years later, she sat at her kitchen table, nursing a lukewarm cup of tea and waiting for Dermot's son. Joe. A chip off the old block without ever really knowing him. She wished she could figure out how to deal with Joe. It'd kill her to see him end up like his father.

At last, his key turned in the door. He chatted to someone as he stumbled over the doorstep. Wee Danny Gibson by the sound of it. They flopped onto the couch and the TV burst into life. Joe didn't even think to check the kitchen to see if his mother was up. Just like old times.

Chapter 3

Missus Phillips stood in front of the TV with two fists buried in her bottle blonde hair. Her face contorted and reddened and her mouth formed words too quickly to lip-read. To Wee Danny she was all picture and no sound. As far as he could tell she wanted to express a lot of anger, probably directed at Joe, but it didn't compute in his frazzled brain. Frazzled. *What a great word. Frazzled, frazzle, frazz... a-ma-taz.* Pressure behind his eyes derailed his train of thought. He looked at Joe, sitting beside him on the most comfortable sofa in the world. He was talking too. Wee Danny wasn't interested in Joe's words. His moustache was more interesting. It danced like a caterpillar on E as Joe's mouth motored at ninety to the dozen.

"Ninety to the dozen," Wee Danny said.

Joe turned to him and winked. Joe's ma reached out a huge hand and grabbed a handful of Joe's chin. She turned his face to hers. Wee Danny looked at the strands of hair caught between her fingers. She was literally pulling her own hair out. How bizarre. *Bizarre, in a car that won't go far. Far, a long, long way to run. Me,*

I'm high, so fucking high. Stoned to fuck. All on my own. His brother Paul would pull his hair out if he wasn't going bald already.

Paul. Shit. Paul had seen him fucking with McVeigh's car. Shit.

A typhoon of nausea in his stomach stiffened his spine. Then his head hovered above a sink. A sink with mugs and regurgitated dinner in it. He'd decorated it with the typhoon. Orange pebbledash. His stomach lurched again. The rest of the badness left his stomach and made him feel lighter. Relieved. *Better out than in.* He rested his head on the stainless steel draining board. A pleasant chill worked through his skull. Like background static, Joe's laughter drifted. A mild annoyance but significant. Joe's ma must have found her mute button. She silently spoke to Danny. Coaxed him to straighten up with body language. Her hand felt smaller than it looked as she cupped his face. He gazed into her eyes. Bloodshot, yellowing sclerae framed icy, blue irises.

"Your eyes are beautiful, Missus Phillips."

"Are you okay, Danny?"

"I think so. Sorry about the mess in your sink."

"I'm more worried about the mess in my living room."

"I can't remember messing up your living room."

"That's okay, Danny. I do."

She stepped back and smiled. Then she punched him on the nose.

"Did your ma punch me on the nose last night?"

Joe concentrated all of his energy into opening his eyes. Wee Danny, bare-chested and propped up on his elbows at the foot of Joe's bed, looked as bad as Joe felt. Maybe worse. He stared at Joe through puffy, purple eyelids. His nose looked swollen too. A crusty blood trail ran over his lips and down his chin.

"She sure did," Joe said. "I think it's broken."

"I thought I dreamt it."

"Nope. You deserved it though. You whitied like a bastard. The living room is going to stink for weeks."

"Ah shit. I feel wick."

"I don't blame you. I'd be well embarrassed too. What time is it?"

"Half past twelve. Still early."

"Better get up though. My ma's probably having a fit downstairs. No point making her worse by staying in bed all day. Besides, I'm starving."

Wee Danny produced a joint he'd palmed the night before, "to take the edge off," and they shared it before venturing downstairs. Every stair on the way down creaked louder than ever before. His ma was up and about. He could smell cigarette smoke and hear the kettle boiling. Even through an early afternoon blow-haze his nerves kicked at his insides. He focussed on an outward appearance of calm. He couldn't freak out in front of Wee Danny.

At the foot of the stairs Joe realised his ma wasn't alone. A man's voice rumbled under the sound of the almost boiled kettle. Jealousy surged through Joe's core. Some man was in there with his ma. Some man she'd neglected to tell him about. Joe shoved open the kitchen door and stormed in. His fists hung ready, clenched at his hips. They relaxed as soon as his brain processed the man's identity.

Wee Paul Gibson.

Still not wonderful news, but better than what he'd been prepared for. He heard Wee Danny curse behind him.

"Danny," Wee Paul said. "You should have phoned Ma to tell her you'd be staying here. She was worried about you."

"Sorry, Bro." Wee Danny's voice sounded sincere, but Joe guessed he was sorrier about getting caught than causing his ma to fret.

"Well, get your stuff together and say cheerio to Joe. I'm taking you back to my place. Ma went to chapel and she won't be back yet. I'll text her to let her know she can come meet you at mine."

"Okay, Bro."

Wee Danny hesitated.

"Now!"

The wee man bolted up the stairs like lightning to fetch his coat and baseball cap. Joe stood his ground in the kitchen, willing himself not to twitch under the scrutiny of his ma and Wee Paul. He focussed his gaze on a damp spot on the wall just above their heads. He'd heard somewhere that the old IRA boys used to do the same when the Brits had them in for questioning.

"Good night last night?" Wee Paul asked.

Tell the fuckers nothing! "Nothing special, Paul. Just hung about, like."

"The usual, then?"

"Pretty much."

Wee Paul nodded then turned to Joe's ma. "They just hung about."

Joe's ma shook her head. "You're a dopey wee bastard, Joe. Paul *saw* you! You stand head and shoulders above the rest of your mates and you don't think you'll be spotted every time you do something stupid? You didn't get your brains from me anyway."

"I didn't do anything, ma!"

"Ach, fuck up. You make me sick."

Wee Danny stood behind Joe again. He coughed to alert his brother of his presence. He obviously wanted to leave before things got too crazy. Joe couldn't blame him.

"And you're just as stupid, Danny," she said. "You follow this big eejit around like the wee sidekick you are. Do you not see how he's a shit magnet? If you'd any sense you'd cut him out of your life. Mark my words, if you don't, you'll end up in jail or dead."

"Nice opinion of your son," Joe said.

She hissed and stepped forward. Wee Paul flinched. He mumbled about getting back to his girl and the kid.

"What do you expect me to think of you? You're just like your da!"

Joe physically recoiled. She'd never even mentioned his da in front of him before. Now all of a sudden the absent male role model was the root of all their problems. Like she was a total saint. Joe's heart jack-hammered in its cage.

Joe said, "Why'd you have to say that, you cunt?"

The Wee Gibsons blew out a lungful of air in unison. His ma's face seemed to swell. She shrieked and launched her mug at him. He lifted his arms to protect his head. The projectile bounced off his elbow. Half a cup of cold tea splashed his face and upper body.

"What did you call me? What the fuck did you just call me?" With each indignant syllable she got louder and closer.

Joe backed away, bumping Danny out of his path without taking his eyes off the woman scorned. But she was an inevitable disaster. She attacked him with the ferocity and speed of a threatened alley cat. She kicked his shin. Her claws caught his cheek. A low punch knocked the air out of his lungs. Her tiny hands pushed into his chest. He stumbled into the living room. In frustration he curled his fists. This only aggravated the situation.

"Don't you dare lift a fist to me, Joseph Philips!"

He dropped his guard. She kicked him in the balls. Warmth spread up into his stomach. His knees buckled. He bent at the waist. She cursed at him. He looked up, hoping to make eye contact. She kicked him in the face.

At last, Wee Paul dragged her away. She struggled for a few seconds then relaxed in Paul's grip.

"Take it easy, Louise," Paul said.

She burst into tears. Huge, dripping, tumbling drops fell off her face and soaked into her T-shirt. Her sobs cut through Joe's pain. Wee Danny helped him stand up.

"You all right, Joe?"

"Not really."

"You kind of deserved that, though."

Joe looked at his mother. She'd turned to hug Wee Paul, buried her face in the crook of his neck. Paul regarded Joe with a disgusted curl on his lip. Joe shrugged and then shook his head.

"Fucking right I did."

"Jesus, that was fucking mad," Danny said.

"He shouldn't have said that to his ma." Paul said.

"I know, but holy fuck."

They waited for their own ma in Paul's decked out living room. Bob the Builder played on the widescreen. Wee Owen ignored the show and concentrated on stuffing a biscuit into the DVD player. Danny thought maybe Owen was a bit slow. At the age of five he should have figured out that only DVDs fit in there. Sinead, the lazy bitch, disappeared upstairs as soon as they'd arrived, leaving Paul to watch the child as usual.

"So you saw me last night," Danny said.

"Aye."

"And?"

"I'm freaking out for you."

Danny wanted a cigarette but couldn't have one in front of his football hero brother. He took slow, deep breaths like the guidance counsellor at school taught him after he was first caught smoking in the school toilets. Quitting advice. It did nothing for him. Paul maintained eye contact and Danny was afraid to break it. In the silence between the two of them, Wee Owen's mouth-breathing became an unbearable noise pollution. Danny had to break it.

"You don't need to worry about me, Paul." He managed a small smile and a wink.

"Like fuck I don't. Stephen McVeigh thinks you've been up to some serious shit. And he's going to be watching you and your mates like a hawk until he has some sort of proof of it."

"What's he think we've been at?"

"He reckons you're in the gang that's been out mugging grannies all over West Belfast these last few months. Them scumbags they call the Wee Rockets."

Danny felt the heat of his reddened face in his ears. His brother's calm and non-threatening manner made it harder for him to feign righteous indignation. Outright denial wouldn't carry any weight.

"And what do you think?"

"I think you better be very careful. McVeigh isn't listening to me. He just wants me to fuck with your head and guilt you into confessing. I can't believe you'd be so evil as to take money from defenceless pensioners, but he can't be convinced."

"What do you think I should do then?"

"Let your mates know about McVeigh and his crazy idea. It probably wouldn't hurt if you asked a few question to try and weed out the real culprits. But be careful about it."

"So you don't think I'm a Wee Rocket, or whatever they're called?"

Paul stood up and looked down on Danny. He put a hand on his little brother's shoulder and squeezed. The pressure hurt but

Danny didn't flinch. Paul's expression changed from worried brother to scary motherfucker in a blink.

"No, I couldn't think that of my own flesh and blood." Paul's grip tightened, pushing his thumb further into the soft flesh beneath the collarbone. Danny couldn't hold his poker face. He hissed in pain like he'd just burnt his fingers on a hot plate. Paul leant in even closer. Danny could feel his warm breath on his face. "But if I found out you were running with those cunts, I'd cut your throat. It'd be an easy thing to do since I wouldn't consider you a brother anymore."

"Paul, please let go of me." Danny cringed at the sound of his own voice. Weak and small.

Paul loosened his crushing grip and slapped Danny's cheek. It wasn't a hard slap but it stung Danny's pride. His own brother, treating him like a bitch. Something he'd not forget in a hurry.

"I'm glad we got that sorted out," Paul said. "Do you want a tin of coke?"

Joe washed the scratches on his cheek. He wondered if he could get any lower. It depressed him to think that he might have bottomed out at fourteen years old. His ma hated him now; he was sure of it. He found no comfort in the mirror above the sink in the bathroom. His reflection stared back at him, ugly and ashamed. The moustache he was so proud of seemed tatty and stupid. A barcode. The swarthy skin the girls at the park whispered about — just loud enough for him to hear — seemed yellowy; like the skin of old men who spend all day waiting for buses outside the Royal Hospital.

He focussed on the three parallel lines running from cheekbone to chin on the left side of his face. He'd suffered worse in schoolyard scraps and street fights, but those shallow scratches hurt his heart. Even the physical pain of his assaulted balls had faded, but his insides tried to crawl out his throat. His mother's post-fight expression replayed on a loop in his mind.

He splashed water on his face to avoid looking at his tears.

Sleeping pills. His ma kept her sleeping pills in the bathroom cabinet. She was supposed to take one a night but had given them up after finding out he'd been inviting friends back for the night while she lay in her bed, dead to the world. Another black mark against him. Something else to feel shit about. Inside the cabinet, three full blister-packs of eight tablets invited him to party. To just… slip away.

In his bedroom, he sat on the unmade bed and fanned the little plastic packets like a short-changed poker player. Twenty-four little pills. He didn't know if it was a lethal dosage. Would it just make him sick? Would he sleep for a week and wake up to another kicking for scaring his ma? Was it overkill? Could he afford to leave one of the blister-packs to help his ma get through the week after finding him? What would he look like when she found him? Scary? Peaceful? Lying in a room full of dirty socks and empty Coke tins. Would she smell him first or his dirty socks?

He'd heard that people who hanged themselves shit their pants before they died. Nobody had ever told him what an overdose did to your boxers. He wondered who wiped dead people's arses. The thought of his ma cleaning him up for his funeral freaked him out until he convinced himself that there were probably specially trained nurses at the mortuary for that sort of thing.

He popped the first pill out of its little pod.

The porn! He couldn't leave his dirty magazines under the mattress, waiting to be discovered. The glossy pages would cause a blockage if he tried to flush them down the bog. If he burned them he'd set off the smoke alarm. He could throw them out the window, but someone would find them and only remember the day they found a bag full of free dirt. Not the day Joe Philips...

No, it wasn't a good time for it. He swallowed one of the pills to see what it was like, but put the others back where he'd found them. His ma would need more time to calm down before he ventured downstairs and begged for forgiveness. He climbed into his bed and lit a cigarette. Smoking calmed him a little. The simple act of inhaling and exhaling the warm, blue smoke, the nicotine fix, whatever; the coffin nail did its job. He waited for the sleeping pill to kick in and let his mind wander. As it often did, it found its way back to the Wee Rockets' first victim.

Missus McCauley. The French teacher.

Missus McCauley wasn't from France. She once confessed she'd never even been to a French speaking country. She was from Poleglass. When she was growing up, living that far up the Falls Road had been a mark of affluence. She'd inherited the family home and watched the area's infestation and damnation. Her street gradually lost its good reputation over time and this apparently caused her to wallow in bitterness. Most people subscribed to this theory. Joe thought the old fucker just enjoyed being a bitch. She'd been his form teacher in first year and always had something against him. One day she pushed the wrong buttons at the wrong time.

"Joseph Philips. Do you have a note for yesterday's absence?"

"No, Miss."

"Missus."

"No, Missus."

"Why not?"

"I forgot it, Miss."

"It's Missus, Joseph. Wake up! How could you forget your note? Surely your mother knows you require one to account for every absence?"

"She does, Miss… er, Missus."

"So if your mother knows this, can I assume she was unaware of your absence?"

"You can if you want."

"What did you say?"

"You can *assume* whatever you want, Missus."

Liam Greene sniggered in the seat beside him. Joe sensed the rest of the class home in on the confrontation, suddenly snatched from their early morning daydreams. It fuelled his resolve to stick it to the old bitch.

"I might remember to bring in the note tomorrow, if that's good enough for you, *Missus* McCauley."

Some of the other boys laughed. McCauley's lips disappeared; her mouth became a one-inch slit. She looked at Joe as if he'd hopped up on his desk and dropped his drawers.

"You're a smart-alecky wee boy, Joseph Philips. I doubt you'll ever amount to much. Maybe I should phone your mother and have her come in. There's a lot I'd like to say to her, face-to-face."

"She's at work. But I can ask her to phone you when she has a chance; if you ask me nicely."

"At work?" McCauley's tightened mouth loosened into a knowing smile. "But I've been handing you free dinner tickets every morning for a year. I didn't think employed parents were eligible for financial support from the Education Board."

Joe's talent for lying to people in authority was yet to blossom. His face went red and he stuttered a few syllables before finding his response. "She's on a training scheme. The Brew sent her." Too late. His hesitation gave him away.

"Oh really? I'm sure the Belfast Education and Library Board would be thrilled to hear that. I must contact them and see how it affects your entitlements. I should probably phone the Department of Social Services first. To get my facts right."

"You don't need to do that, Missus."

"Oh I think I do. It's my civic duty."

Joe's mouth opened and closed. She had him on the ropes. He couldn't think of one thing to say that would improve the situation.

"Of course," she said, "I could just mind my own business. All you need to do is apologise for disrupting this morning's class."

McCauley placed her hands on her hips and gloated. Joe had no choice. He would have to look into the beady eyes staring at him from over the rim of her ancient bifocals and humiliate himself. Lick the fucker's arse to keep her mouth shut. Blackmailing bitch.

He opened his mouth to begin his apology. Then Liam Greene piped up.

"Missus McCauley, can I go to the toilet?"

McCauley looked at Liam and then the clock on the wall behind her. "There's a minute left until the bell goes. Can you not wait?"

"Only if you want to swim out of here."

"Liam Greene!"

"Sorry, Missus, but my back teeth are floating."

McCauley made a face. "Oh, get out you filthy boy."

"Thank you, Missus. You won't regret it."

Liam bolted out of his seat and slammed the door behind him with dramatic enthusiasm. A few of the boys chuckled. Joe smiled. His fat friend had taken the limelight off his confrontation with McCauley. She turned her attention back to him, but the moment was lost. The other boys in the class were shuffling in their seats, waiting for the bell to ring. Joe's composure had returned and he raised his eyebrows at McCauley. *I dare you.* The bell rang.

The students were afforded five minutes before the next class. Joe went to the toilets for a smoke. As Joe suspected, Liam waited for him there.

"Can I have a smoke of that?" Liam asked.

Joe nodded. "So long as you've washed your hands."

Muttering, Liam soaked his hands under a sputtering cold water tap and wiped them damp on the legs of his black school trousers. Joe handed over the burning fag.

"Thanks for that, Liam."

Liam narrowed his eyes, expecting a punch line. "For what?"

"You helped me out. Just there now."

Liam tilted his head. "What do you mean?"

"Did you really need to go to the bog just then?"

"Yeah, I was bursting."

Joe shook his head. He'd overestimated the fat fucker.

"But here," Liam said, "I wish I could have stayed to see you sweat a bit more. What else did McCauley say to you?"

"Nothing. The bell rang."

Liam tutted. "It was just getting good too."

Joe snatched the fag off Liam, took a puff and flicked it in the urinal.

"There was still a few draws left in that, you!"

"Fuck up. Help me come up with some way to get back at that bitch McCauley."

"We should put on balaclavas and pretend we're the Ra."

"Aye, right. The midget battalion."

"Slash her tyres?"

"She comes to work on the bus."

"We could mug her on the way to the bus stop."

"Liam, for fuck's sake, would you…" Joe stopped for a second. "Actually…"

And Missus McCauley became the first victim. Joe talked Wee Danny into the plan when they sat together for maths. Liam recruited the Fegan twins. They bunked off their last class to go to Joe's, change out of their uniforms and into hoodies, scarves and baseball caps. They attacked McCauley yards from the school gate. It was over in an instant, turned up fifty pound in cash and left the bitch with a broken arm. She took early retirement.

McCauley had never been the most popular teacher in the school and the suspects were plentiful. Questions were asked by the principal for weeks after the attack, but the boys kept their mouths shut and it all blew over.

And of course, getting away with it once wasn't enough.

There was another mugging when someone threatened to phone the vigilantes because Liam got caught stealing a garden gnome.

Another when Wee Danny reported a dirty look from a neighbour.

Another when the Fegan twins needed new trainers.

Another to initiate a new member into the gang.

And another.

And others.

And now Joe lay on his bed, weighed down with guilt and the dizzying effect of the sleeping pill. He wondered if he would die in his unnatural sleep. He thought about his father meeting him at the gates of hell. He prayed for forgiveness. He freaked out when he couldn't remember the last line of the Hail Mary. He gave up consciousness and surrendered himself to nightmares.

Louise needed something stronger than a cup of tea. She'd stopped keeping alcohol in the house the day she came home to find Joe drinking her vodka straight from the bottle. After the fight she wished she'd stashed a quarter-bottle in the toilet cistern, like Dermot used to. She wanted to talk to Joe about how she felt, but couldn't understand her conflicting emotions well enough to tell *herself* how she felt. A drink could simplify things. Her friend, Karen, didn't drink on Sundays. Ever. There was no point phoning her. But Louise phoned her and got invited around for a cup of coffee. Louise impolitely declined. She'd mend that fence later on in the week.

For the first time in her life, she went to a pub on her own.

She took a deep breath before pushing open the front door of Busby's, the Manchester United supporters' bar at the top of Broadway. Nobody turned in their seats to evaluate her. Celtic were playing Rangers. The widescreen TV at the other end of the bar held everyone's attention, including the barman's. Louise cleared her throat three times before she could wet her whistle. The vodka and lime burned her throat the first time. The others treated her just fine. When the match finished two nil to Celtic, Louise joined the clientele in a chorus of *You'll Never Walk Alone* and relished every syllable.

When a young man with ginger hair offered to buy her another vodka and lime, she accepted his offer. She asked him where she'd seen him before and he told her his name and that he lived in Beechmount.

Stephen McVeigh.

Not much of a looker, but he sure could listen.

Chapter 4

Stephen wanted a cup of coffee. Louise's haphazard kitchen yielded none. He settled for tea and closed the cupboard doors gently. He poked about in the fridge for breakfast while the kettle boiled. She didn't have much in. His body needed something healthy to tackle the ridiculous amount of alcohol she'd coaxed him into drinking. His eyes skipped past the fatty sausages on the bottom shelf. The best he could come up with was a large pot of natural yoghurt closing in on its best before date. He rescued a spoon from the kitchen sink and stirred the lumpy mass until the watery puddle at the top disappeared. The first spoonful met his tongue with approval. He gulped down the rest of the yoghurt before the kettle clicked and popped some hardening bread into the toaster for Louise.

After the night they'd had together it was the least he could do for her. Besides, he didn't want to leave until her son had seen him.

You have to know your enemy.

Wee Paul gave up Joe's address without a second thought; probably to shift focus off his little brother. Stephen was happy to take the information, but he wouldn't take it easy on Wee Paul's brother. After Joe, Wee Danny would be the next target. Then the fat kid.

Bite off the head and the body will die.

Stephen was almost certain that Joe ran the gang, but Wee Danny and the fat kid had displayed leadership qualities when he'd encountered them.

Take no risks.

But Joe had to be the first. Beautiful Lady Luck had smiled on Stephen when he finally plucked up the nerve to visit Joe's house. He'd parked at the far end of the street in case his Escort's engine alerted Joe and gave him time to run away or hide. It was to be a questioning only, but Joe wouldn't know that.

Before he'd closed his blue car's red door, a peroxide blonde stormed out of Joe's place with a face on her like a smacked arse. She moved fast and with purpose. Stephen followed her. She obviously knew Joe – was probably his ma – and looked pretty pissed off. Hopefully she was pissed off at a wayward son and was hoping to find sympathy somewhere.

Not only did Stephen get to insinuate his way into his enemy's closest family member, but he got to watch the Celtic match, get pissed and have a great shag. Lady Luck. What a doll.

He carried two mugs of tea in one hand and a saucer piled with buttered toast in the other. He used his knee to nudge open the door to Louise's bedroom. She sat up and almost smiled.

"You're still here." Stephen detected surprise in her voice. Low self esteem. Too easy.

"Of course I am."

"Don't you have to work today?"

"Nah, I take an extra week off before the July fortnight. Most sites are winding down during the second week of July and it's a boring time for a joiner."

Louise nodded at the plate in his hand. "You're not a chef then?"

He laughed. "I thought you'd like some breakfast. Toast was all I could think of. I ate your yoghurt by the way."

"Thanks. Toast is perfect." She hesitated. Then, "Did you meet Joe down there?"

"No sign of him. I guess he's still in bed. Teenagers sleep a lot."

"Aye, you're probably right."

He passed her one of the mugs and the toast. He didn't sit down on the bed with her. She didn't ask him to.

"Do you want me to go and check his room?" Stephen asked.

"Jesus Christ! No I do not."

"Okay, take it easy. I was just asking."

"How would you feel in his shoes?"

"After everything you told me about him last night, I can't believe you still want to protect him."

Louise looked away. "He's still my son."

Stephen nodded and took a sip from his mug. It did little for him but remind him he wanted a cup of coffee.

"Okay, Louise. Sorry if I've upset you."

"You haven't. It's just… Oh God, I still…"

"It's all right. Look, you probably need some time to sort your head out." *And I need a coffee and a shower,* he thought. "You have my number. Text me later if you'd like me to come around with a Chinese and a DVD."

"Thanks, Stephen. You've been really great."

"And you blew my mind."

Louise blushed and Stephen knew he'd be back that night. He'd see Joe then.

###

The sound of the front door closing woke him. Joe rolled out of bed and pulled back his curtains. The familiar, square, ginger head, bobbing away from his house, filtered through his slitted eyes, fought for significance in his abused brain and sprang his paranoia from its chemical cage. Stephen McVeigh knew where he lived. The bastard had come to complain about what they'd done to his piece-of-shit car. He listened out for the sound of his ma bolting up the stairs to get to work on round two.

Silence.

Maybe she couldn't even bring herself to dish out another hiding. He'd disgusted her so much that she couldn't see the point. He didn't know if he found relief or despair in the idea.

The sleeping pill had kept Joe under for almost twelve hours. He woke up in the early hours of Monday morning with a muzzy head and a dry mouth. He could see no sense in getting up at that time, so he'd taken a second pill from the bathroom and smoked cigarettes until the drug worked its magic. It took at least an hour before he felt anything resembling calm and another hour to actually fall asleep. He'd filled that time trying to prepare a speech for his mother, begging her forgiveness.

If he'd come up with anything he'd lost it by the time he woke up again.

His stomach growled.

Whatever his ma had in store for him, he couldn't stay in his room and starve. He changed into fresh clothes and left his room. On the way past his mother's bedroom he heard the shifting of bedsprings. But he hadn't heard her get back into bed after McVeigh left. Every stair in the house creaked. How could she have gotten back up them without making a noise?

In the kitchen, something seemed off. Joe couldn't put his finger on it, but he didn't feel comfortable. He put it down to the drugs, both prescription and otherwise, and looked in the fridge.

An unopened packet of sausages sat on the bottom shelf. He flicked on the deep fat fryer. When the little red light clicked on, he punctured the sausages with a fork and threw all eight of them into the bubbling oil. The crackle-pop of cooking fat set his stomach off on another thunderstorm grumble.

While his breakfast cooked, he leaned against the kitchen worktop and sipped on a pint glass of tap water. He thought about the direction his life was headed in. It was time to whip up the handbrake and pull a one-eighty. Fuck what the rest of the gang thought of him. If his mother ever found out about the muggings she wouldn't stop at a boot in the balls and a kick in the face. She'd either disown him or phone someone who'd happily shoot out his knees in the name of some dissident group.

He decided to hook up with Wee Danny as soon as he could and let him know first. Then he'd get the rest of the gang together for a bit of a session; blow only, to keep the mood calm. He'd tell them he was handing the gang over to Wee Danny and moving on to something bigger. Telling them he wanted to go straight wasn't an option. They'd think he'd turned yellow. Then he'd think of something to make it right between him and his ma.

First things first. He ate six of the sausages and left two on a plate for his ma to heat up for her breakfast. Then he phoned Wee Danny and spent ten minutes coaxing him out of his bed. They met at the shop.

"You got fags?" Joe asked.

"Yeah."

"Good. Let's dander then. I don't feel like standing about."

Wee Danny nodded and they made their way along Beechmount Avenue, smoking and spitting between sentences.

"You look a bit fucked up," Wee Danny said.

"Aye, I know. Did your Paul hit you a dig?"

Wee Danny shook his head. "No, but he said he'd kill me if he found out for sure I was robbing grannies. And I believe him."

"Shit. What makes him think you might be?"

"That wanker, McVeigh."

"Fuck! He was at my house this morning. Bet it was your Paul who told him where I live."

"Don't worry." Danny said. "He hasn't any proof."

"Still. It's not like he's a cop. Vigilantes don't need to follow rules."

"He's not a vigilante either, Joe. He's just a wanker."

"A big wanker who could snap my neck like a pencil."

"Did you lose your balls in that fight with your ma?"

Joe thumped Wee Danny's shoulder. Wee Danny stumbled onto the road.

"Jesus, Joe! Sorry. But there was no call for that."

"You got off lightly. So, come on. What are we going to do?"

"I think we'll have to lay low for a while. Tell the others that someone's watching us and we need to take a break."

"How do you think they'll react?"

"Who gives a fuck? It's your gang, Joe. *You* call the shots."

"But I don't want it anymore. I was planning on telling you it was yours now."

"Hah! Fucked if I want it anymore, mate. Far too risky."

They'd wandered out onto the Falls Road. Joe had no idea where they were headed, but he seemed to be leading.

"I'm just thinking," Joe said. "What if we just handed the gang over to Liam? You know he'd snatch up the chance to be the boss man."

"And what? Keep quiet until Stephen catches him?"

"Might be the best way for us to keep our noses clean."

Wee Danny shook his head. "No, that's too fly. I can't stand Liam, but he's still a mate. And the other lads don't deserve that.

We should tell him everything, but let him know he can take on the gang if he wants to risk it. Stupid bastard will still want to do it, but he might be a bit more careful."

"Ach, I suppose you're right."

"Of course I am."

They'd gotten as far as the crossroads where the Grosvenor Road and the Springfield Road met the Falls Road. Four sets of traffic lights kept hospital and motorway traffic chaos to a minimum.

Joe spotted a half a brick on the footpath ahead, probably left over from a recent attack on a passing PSNI land rover. He darted forward and scooped it up before Wee Danny had a chance to get near it.

"You pick," Joe said.

Wee Danny pulled up his hood. He pointed at an oncoming bus speeding up the Falls Road to beat the lights. "Who can resist a classic?"

Joe pulled up his own hood and launched the brick at the bus windshield. The experienced Citybus driver slammed on the brakes instead of swerving on impact. The safety glass concaved and cracks spider-webbed densely. Wee Danny whooped and they ran up the Springfield Road and cut into a residential area. A chorus of blaring black taxi horns sounded disapproval.

Scattered residents, out and about on their way to elsewhere, glanced at them as they zipped past. Nobody shouted for them to stop. They shouldered their way through a pack of nippers kicking a half-deflated ball about. Threats of beatings at the hands of elder siblings followed, but Joe didn't look back. He enjoyed the run. It was one of the few things he did well. Running away.

He forgot about everything as his world shrank to one physical challenge; landing one foot in front of the other. His lungs burned. His feet thwacked pavement. He wove through cars parked on kerbs. He skipped over dogshit. Thoughts of failure and disappointing his mother gave way to the thrill of getting-away-with-it. He smiled.

"Stop," Wee Danny said, his skin pale and his voice wheezy. He pulled on Joe's sleeve, barely able to keep pace. "I'm gasping."

And it was over. An end to escape. Back to reality.

They slowed to a halt and Wee Danny pulled two cigarettes from his pocket. They took a seat on a high kerb and smoked. Joe's hand shook as he raised the fag to his lips. *What a buzz.*

Louise's thumb hovered over the button pad of her mobile. It wasn't a question of whether or not she wanted Stephen to come around with a DVD and a takeaway. She did. But she hesitated because of Joe.

Joe had been the only man in her life since Dermot's midnight flit. There'd been casual flings on girls' nights out, but they'd been few and far between, and *never* at her house. Stephen had been a drunken fumble, and she couldn't even remember if he'd been any good. But he'd seemed interested in her that morning. He'd made her feel good with a few words. And she felt she deserved that. No, she *needed* that.

Her thumb made contact with the send button but didn't apply any pressure.

She thought about what she might tell Joe.

"Joe, this is Stephen. He's a friend of your mummy's."

Her voice sounded too upbeat. She went to the pine-framed mirror above the mantelpiece. Her reflection eyed her suspiciously.

"Joe, I want you to meet my new boyfriend." She blushed. "And there he goes, right out the door. Guess you don't need to worry about that guy, son. Silly old me, calling him my boyfriend after one night."

Louise placed her hands on the mantelpiece and bowed her head. She took a deep breath, looked up and made eye contact with her reflection. A smile tugged at her mouth as she tried her best to look natural. She giggled, bowed her head again, breathed and looked up.

"Joe, I'm shagging Stephen. If that pisses you off, good! You shouldn't have called me the C word. Now shake hands with the man before I kick you in the balls again."

She pushed down hard on the send button. When the phone told her the message had been sent, her stomach somersaulted. Regret instantly surfaced.

"Too late now, wee girl. Stephen's coming over tonight. Better scrub up if you don't want to scare him away."

In the bedroom, she sat at her hand-me-down mahogany dressing table and examined herself in her round makeup mirror. It magnified her insecurities to five times their normal size. An inch of dark roots offset lank, peroxide blonde hair. She frowned at her crow's feet and eye luggage. The lines running from the corners of her mouth to her chin had deepened. Was her nose bigger? How could her nose be growing? Why did Stephen want to see her again, anyway? He had to be at least five years younger than her. She'd been upfront about Joe, and what a nightmare he was. Stephen played football and had the muscles to prove it. She had stretchmarks and a saggy belly. He earned an honest living as a joiner. She did the double at a shitty bakery.

Had he just spotted an easy ride? She shouldn't have texted him. He only said he'd come back to make leaving this morning less awkward.

Her mobile beeped and buzzed. Stephen's text message confirmed he'd see her at nine. Hours away, but she felt panicked by the deadline.

Drink! She thought. *I want a drink.*

She needed to get something in to offer Stephen anyway. He'd said he would bring food and a film. He hadn't mentioned alcohol. He'd think it odd if she had nothing to offer. Makeup later. Drink now. It'd soften her self criticisms.

On her way to the off licence on the Falls Road, Louise spotted some of Joe's friends. Liam Greene and the Fegan twins. The three of them smoked cigarettes at the bus shelter close to the Beechmount Avenue entrance. The cancer-sticks looked ridiculously long in their pubescent paws. They didn't even have the decency to hide their fags when she waved at them.

"Hiya, Missus Phillips," Liam said, when she was within talking distance.

"Hi, Liam." She nodded to the twins. "Boys."

The non-identical Fegan twins nodded back. As usual, they'd been dressed to match by their mummy, from their baseball caps to their Reebok runners. Geeks.

"Have any of you been talking to our Joe today?" she asked.

"No. We haven't seen him since Saturday." Liam curved his mouth in a smile his own mother would like to slap. "I thought he was grounded. Because of the state we were all in on Saturday night. Did he get away with it?" The twins sniggered. Cigarette smoke blasted from their nostrils.

You're a sly wee bastard, aren't you? Louise thought. She smiled back at him. "Joe and I have an understanding. If he doesn't fall through the door, he's not in trouble. He's a *lot* bigger than you other boys. He can handle his drink better."

Liam's grin faded. He looked away from Louise.

There was no such arrangement, but she couldn't resist spoiling Liam's fun. She'd talk to Joe about sensible drinking when things cooled down between them.

"Will you tell Joe I'm looking for him if you see him, Liam? I think his phone battery must be dead. I keep getting his answer machine."

"No problem, Missus Phillips." The cockiness had left his voice.

She got about two yards up the road when one of them wolf-whistled. She glanced over her shoulder.

"It was him," they said in unison, each one pointing to another.

"Whatever," she said, wishing she hadn't given them the satisfaction.

She bought three tins of Harp lager, a bottle of Kulov vodka and a big bottle of Coke. She poured herself a generous vodka and Coke as soon as she got back to the house. A few gulps had her topped up from the previous night's session and her mood improved. She turned on the radio in her bedroom and slapped on her face as she sang pop songs and drank. Drinking and singing while she got dolled up used to be her favourite part of going out with her mates. It'd been a while since she'd done it, but its familiarity and simplicity soothed her. The backtrack loop of guilt that had tortured her since hitting Joe the day before finally packed it in. She put aside her self doubts and looked forward to seeing Stephen again. She drowned her suspicion of his intentions in vodka.

Stephen showed up fifteen minutes early, and Louise answered the door confident and tipsy. She almost purred when he kissed her cheek.

"Come in, you big eejit. What did you bring?"

He reached into a blue plastic bag and pulled out four DVDs. He fanned them out for her.

"I wasn't sure what kind of stuff you liked so I brought a selection. A horror flick, a comedy, one about the Troubles and, in the unlikely event that you're a martial arts movie fan, a Jackie Chan one."

"I like horror. Let's watch that. But we should have a wee drink first. Beer or vodka?"

"Oh, God. Definitely a beer after last night."

"You big wimp." She laughed at his pretend insulted face.

"I'll start with a beer and see where it takes me, then."

"That's the spirit."

"I thought we could phone for the Chinese later. Didn't know if you'd be hungry for it now."

"Suits me. I'll be back in a minute. Sit down and relax."

She skipped into the kitchen. He'd impressed her with his thoughtfulness. Bringing four DVDs to make sure they could watch something they'd both enjoy. Simple things like that said so much about a person. She could get into a man like that. And she wouldn't be afraid to let him know. It just took a little confidence and a lot of attitude. She could pull off sexy and sure of herself.

Drinking three strong vodkas before he'd arrived helped.

If she drank another three, Stephen was likely to get lucky again. She almost giggled. *Behave yourself, you wee hussy.* She topped up her drink and lifted a tin for Stephen.

"Would you like a glass?" she asked as she handed him the beer.

"No thanks. This is grand."

Another point in his favour. He was happy to drink beer from the tin. No airs and graces.

She hesitated for a second then sat on the armchair instead of the sofa. She wanted to talk to him without craning her neck sideways. He raised his eyebrows and smiled at her. *So talk to me,* his expression said.

"Did you get up to much today?" Louise asked.

"Just did a wee bit at the gym. Then I went for a run. I should be doing a few things about the house, but I didn't have the head on me for it today. How about you?"

"Well, to be honest, I've just been waiting about to talk to Joe but he hasn't been in all day."

Stephen sat forward. "Really? Do you know who he's with?"

"Probably Wee Danny. I saw a couple of his other mates earlier on and they said they hadn't seen him."

"So he's not with the whole gang, then?"

"Gang? I'd hardly call them a gang. They don't even seem to like each other. Always calling each other names... Why the interest anyway?"

"Ach, no reason. Just wondering what he could be up to all day."

"You know what teenagers are like. Probably hanging about on corners, spitting and talking about girls."

Stephen grunted. "He should be here trying to patch things up with you."

Louise wracked her brains for a subject change. She didn't want to dampen the mood with talk about Joe. "Maybe we could stick the first half of the film on, eh? Then we'll take a break to phone the Chinese."

"Only if you come and sit beside me."

"Deal."

Being an old fashioned girl, she handed Stephen the remote controls. He got the film going and set the volume. Loud enough for the soundtrack to have the full effect, but low enough for them to whisper bitchy comments about the cast to each other. Stephen pretended not to be attracted to the young brunette heroine, claiming to have a thing for blondes, and she pretended to believe him. In turn, she lied about preferring passionate, red-haired Irish men to the tall dark and handsome types. They drank a little more and huddled close on the sofa. She jumped in all the right places and he squeezed her hand and chuckled. She couldn't remember having a nicer evening.

Then Joe came home.

They had just hit pause and were reading the takeaway menu when the unlocked front door opened slowly. Joe shuffled in, expecting trouble. His body language went from hangdog to guard dog as soon as he spotted Stephen sitting beside Louise and drinking a beer.

"You came home, then," Louise said.

"What's he doing here?" Joe barked his words, glaring at Stephen.

"His name's Stephen."

"I know who he is. What the fuck's he doing here?"

"You watch your mouth, wee boy." Louise stood up and Joe back-stepped.

Her own son, flinching away from her. How could things have gotten so out of hand?

"Maybe I should go," Stephen said.

"I don't want you to."

"It's okay, Louise. I can understand why Joe's upset." He turned to Joe. "I'm a friend of you ma's, but I don't want to rock the boat. If you want me to, I'll leave. It's up to you."

Joe looked at Stephen, then Louise. He pushed out his lower lip. A childish expression Louise hadn't seen on him in years. "Do what you want."

Joe stomped up the stairs and slammed his bedroom door shut.

"I'm sorry about that," she said.

"It's okay."

"You're so nice. Thank you."

"Ach, wise up. I'll be okay here for a bit if you want to go talk to him. You probably should."

Louise almost welled up. She nodded and followed her son up the stairs.

She found Joe lying on his bed with his duvet pulled up over his head. His Nike Airs poked out at the end of his bed. The smell of dirty socks and cigarette smoke filled the room. Louise opened a window then knelt by the side of Joe's bed.

"We have to talk, son."

No response.

"Come on, Joe. I don't want to fight. I want us to get on."

"Humpf!"

Louise gently pulled the duvet away from Joe's face. He looked at her with brown puppy-dog eyes.

"I'm sorry for losing the bap with you yesterday, son. But you're not completely blameless yourself. What you said… it really hurt me."

Joe nodded. "I know mum. It just slipped out. I don't really think you're a… you know… one of those."

"I appreciate that, love. I'll work on my temper." She should have said she would never hit him again, but she didn't want to say it out loud. It still felt too raw.

Joe sat up in the bed and Louise gave him an awkward hug. He squeezed back for a second then patted her back to let her know he'd finished. She kissed his cheek and stood up.

"So why is McVeigh here, then?"

"I met him last night. He seems nice, so we're watching a DVD and having a wee drink. You can join us if you like."

Joe shook his head.

"You sure? We were about to get a takeaway. You're probably starving."

He shook his head again.

There was no point pushing the topic. Judging by his glazed eyes and silence, he was off somewhere in his head. He'd left the conversation to have a think.

"Okay, son. But if you get bored later, come on down."

He nodded.

The doorbell ding-donged.

Joe snapped out of his daze and looked at Louise.

"Are you expecting someone?" Louise asked.

"No."

"Could be Karen, I suppose. Better go see."

As she stepped out onto the landing she heard Stephen answer the door. What sounded like a pleasant greeting got a sharp return. Stephen raised his voice.

"Why? Who the fuck are *you*?"

Louise stalled at the top of the stairs, afraid of what she might walk into. Joe stood on the landing with his head cocked, concentrating on the rising voices below.

"No, you tell me yours." Stephen said.

The mystery caller mumbled something.

"Like fuck you will. You may dander on now while your legs still work."

The anger in Stephen's voice broke her paralysis. She bolted down the stairs. Joe called her back, but she couldn't stand by.

She found Stephen blocking the door. The back of his neck burned bright red. "Stephen. What's going on?"

Stephen didn't turn around. "There's a wanker at the door saying he lives here. Won't believe me that he's got the wrong house and he's getting close to an awful hiding."

Louise couldn't see past Stephen's wide shoulders. But she heard the mystery man's voice. She took a dizzy spell at the sound of it.

"Louise, tell this ginger cunt to get out of my way."

The familiar voice set her heart into overdrive. "Oh my God. No."

Stephen turned and looked at her, angry and confused. "Do you know him?"

The visitor took advantage of Stephen's divided attention. Louise heard a hollow thump. Stephen yelped and went down. His hands went to his lower back. Kidney punch. She winced for him. The tall, dark, kind of good looking man stepped over Stephen's writhing body and smiled at Louise. Familiar smile, fatter face. She couldn't speak. Couldn't move.

She sensed Joe standing behind her. "What's going on?"

"Joe? Is that you? Jesus Christ, you've fairly grown."

"Who are you?"

Shit, shit, shit. Don't you dare tell him. Not now.

"I'm Dermot. Your dad. How the hell are you, Joe?"

Chapter 5

Pain thrummed in Stephen's lower back. *The sneaky fucker stabbed me,* he thought, panicking. He held his hands up to his eyes when he could bear to open them. No blood. *Thank God.* His hands went back to his kidney to massage the agony. He concentrated on breathing. In. Out. In. Out. He didn't want to risk standing. Not yet. Better to wait. Wait until he was ready to hit the fucker who'd floored him. He rested his head on the laminate flooring. Dust and the ghostly scent of chemical floor cleaner tickled his nose.

He could hear Louise.

"… come waltzing back here whenever you feel like it? What's wrong with your head? All these years and not so much as a birthday card for your own son. You're a useless…"

So he'd just been sucker-punched by Joe's da. Afraid to face him like a man. Sleeked bastard.

"Louise, please," Joe's da said. His voice had a spoilt child whine to it. "Just listen to me for two minutes. Then I'll leave. Okay?"

"You have *one* minute."

"Then I don't have time to go into why I left and where I was. Just know that I had no choice. It was for the best. But that's not what I'm here for. I'm not after forgiveness. You've moved on, and I expected that. But I'm back in Belfast, probably for good. I want to get to know my son."

"It's a bit late now," Louise said.

"I'm trying to put things right. Don't write me off straight away. Please. Just let me leave my number. Then you can think about it and let me know. I promise you, I've changed."

"You've changed? I just watched you force your way in here. You've been back in my life for a few seconds and already you've hurt one of my friends. You're poison, Dermot Kelly. I'd be a fool to let you near Joe."

Dermot Kelly, Stephen thought, *I'm going to break your neck for you.*

"I'm sorry I hurt your friend, but I needed to talk to you. What could I have done?"

"Tried later, you stupid bastard!"

Stephen almost smiled.

"Can I leave my number?"

Silence. Stephen looked up at Louise from the floor. Her blue eyes bulged wide and unforgiving as she glared at Dermot, hands on hips and chin raised. Two spots of red burned on her high cheekbones like geisha makeup. Joe twitched behind her, jaw hanging. Dermot held a scrap of paper out. Louise shook her head.

"Why don't you ask Joe? He can speak for himself, you know."

Joe blinked. He looked at the back of Louise's head then at his da again.

"What about it, Joe?" Dermot asked. "Will you give me a chance?"

"Um…" Joe's skin reddened. "Okay. Give me your number. But I… I'm not promising anything."

"That's fair enough, Joe." He handed his son the ragged strip of paper. "I'll go now and give you two some time to think."

"I've done my thinking, Dermot," Louise said. "Don't let the door hit your fat arse on the way out."

Dermot knelt down by Stephen. He caught a glimpse of Joe in twenty years time in the smirking bastard. "I'm sorry about hitting you, big man. I wish I could take it back." But Stephen could read the amusement in his dark eyes. And smell the onions on his breath.

"Fuck you." Stephen tried to inject venom into his voice. He sounded constipated.

Dermot nodded. "I deserved that." Then he left.

Louise went to Stephen's aid immediately.

"Are you okay?" She stroked his face and grasped one of his hands.

"I'll live." Talking hurt, but he tried to hide it. "Do you have any ice?"

"No, but there's a bag of frozen peas you can have. Joe, help me lift him onto the sofa."

They took an arm each and Stephen did his best to push himself up on rubbery legs. They lay him face down on the sofa. Joe went to the freezer for the peas.

"I'm so sorry, Stephen."

"You didn't do it."

"I know, but you were only trying to look out for me."

"I didn't do a great job though."

"You would have. I distracted you and that fly bastard hit you from behind. Typical. Afraid to go toe-to-toe with a real man."

It meant a lot more to him than he would have expected that Louise thought of him as a real man. It'd been quite a while since he'd made time for a girlfriend, and he'd actually been enjoying himself earlier. Maybe a little too much, in light of his intentions.

But he was sure he could keep sight of his plan. He'd gotten into Joe's home and now she'd trust him more than ever. On the downside, he had another wanker to take care of. Louise would probably thank him for getting at Dermot. With Joe, he'd have to be more subtle.

Joe had found the peas and handed them to Louise. He hopped from foot to foot as if he needed to go for a piss. Louise planted the bag of peas on Stephen's lower back. He hissed then sighed as he got used to the chill. The pain numbed a little.

"You should probably drink a lot of vodka," Louise said. "To help with the pain."

"I'll maybe wait until I can sit up again."

"Just let me know when you want me to help you move."

"Thanks."

Joe continued to do the need-a-piss shuffle. Louise turned to him.

"Son, say what you want to say and quit your dancing. I'm sure you've plenty of questions. Spit them out."

Joe stopped shifting his weight from side-to-side. He fiddled with the waistband of his hoodie instead. "Was that really my da?"

"Yes, love."

"Um… do you think I should phone him?"

"I think you need to decide that for yourself. Do you want to phone him?"

"I don't know."

"Well, sleep on it."

"Would you be mad if I did call him?"

Louise lit a cigarette, hesitated, then handed it to Joe. She lit another one for herself. Joe puffed like a chimney. Stephen bit his tongue, but watching kids smoke always bugged him. He couldn't believe a mother would encourage her own child to poison himself. Even an advertisement for contraception like Joe.

"I'd probably be a little mad, but I'd understand. If you do decide you want your father in your life, I'll still love you. But I won't sit in the same room as that shite."

Joe went quiet. He blew a series of smoke rings, his mouth working like a goldfish's.

"It's only half ten, son. Why don't you go see if Wee Danny is about? It'd do you good to talk to a mate."

He didn't wait around to be asked twice. As he walked out Louise called after him.

"What?"

"Be home before twelve. I don't want to go to bed not knowing where you are tonight."

He nodded and left. Louise turned to Stephen.

"We have the place to ourselves for a while. Think you can sit up?"

Stephen moved a fraction. A sharp twinge warned him to stay still. "Maybe wait another wee minute, eh?"

"I think I might have some straws. Do you want me to make you a drink? You can sip it where you lie."

"That's a great idea. Thanks for looking after me."

Louise bent down and caressed his cheek. He could smell perfume off her wrist. He didn't recognise the brand. She had warm hands.

"I wish I could do more for you, Stephen."

"Feel free to give me a gentle massage." He smiled at her and winked.

Louise tilted her head and an impish grin spread across her face. "Okay, big lad. And I tell you what. If you can get yourself turned around before eleven, I'll give this massage a very happy ending."

She laughed the dirtiest laugh Stephen had ever heard. A sound he could get used to.

Dermot Kelly tugged on his black leather driving gloves and flopped into the black C-Class Mercedes parked on the Falls Road. He gunned the engine and fiddled with the radio. *The Boys are Back in Town* by Thin Lizzy played on a classic rock station. He cranked the volume and flipped down the sun visor. His reflection smiled back at him in the little vanity mirror.

"He looks like you," he told his reflection. "Hardly any of her in him at all."

His reflection nodded in agreement, grin widening.

"I just hope he got my brains as well."

The reflection chuckled back at him and he flipped the visor up into place. He pulled the Mercedes out onto the Falls Road and cruised towards the city centre. The sparse weeknight traffic allowed him to travel at tourist speed. Old landmarks twanged his nostalgia. The Beehive, the Celtic Supporters Club, the Sinn Fein offices sporting the famous Bobby Sands mural and the Chinese takeaway unfortunately named the Shatt Inn. He'd never been able to order a curry chip from them.

He murmured to himself, "I can't believe you actually missed this place."

What he remembered as the old Falls Swimmers had been reconstructed into a new, bigger, plastic-walled leisure centre. Set against the old, grubby redbrick buildings it shared the road with, it stood out like a hooker at a nunnery. Backlit panels of green, blue and pink Perspex screamed for attention in the summer night.

He slowed almost to a stop and gave the place a good eyeball. Lucky for him he did. Not far up ahead, a spanking white PSNI land rover rolled to a halt at the traffic lights on Northumberland Street. It indicated right, to travel up the Falls Road. Towards Dermot and his stolen Mercedes.

He turned left onto North Howard Street.

What the fuck? he thought.

North Howard Street ran from the Falls Road directly onto the Shankill Road. Before he'd left Belfast, the road had been blocked by a huge, graffiti-covered security gate to keep the Catholics away from the Protestants and reduce sectarian unrest by making it less convenient. He'd planned to dump the car on the dead-end street and run, but was delighted to find the blue security gate was gone. The Peace Process at work. He could get used to this new Northern Ireland. He took the Shankill into the city centre and made it to Linenhall Street without another cop-scare.

Thursday night was traditionally the busy night on Belfast's unofficial Red Light District. Late night shopping drew in the farmer's wives from rural Antrim into the city. The farmers on taxi duty left the wives to work away and took their Toyota four-wheel-drives to Linenhall Street. Under the pretence of reading the paper at one of the city centre pubs, they picked up a young lady of the night for a fifteen minute fling. The hookers made a bomb on fuck-a-farmer night. But on a Monday night the street just didn't have that same buzz. Dermot passed only one other kerb-crawling vehicle; a Renault Espace family wagon with a 'baby on board' sign hanging in the back window. The driver hung out his rolled down window and spoke to a huge woman with a thick black perm and a short lycra skirt. The devoted family man, bargain hunting.

Dermot pulled in ahead of the seven-seater. He looked out of the tinted window at a blonde in her late twenties wearing a long leather coat. Her attire wasn't completely necessary in the cool summer night, but the effect stunned. A little something for the Buffy the Vampire Slayer fans. She slinked towards the Merc, the sway of her hips exaggerated to compensate for the heavy leather framing her thin body. Dermot licked his lips and pressed a button by the gear stick. The electric window opened with a hummingbird drone. He waited for her to hunker down to eyelevel.

"What can I get for two-fifty and a Mars bar?" he asked.

The Buffy clone shook her head. "You are a wanker, Dermot."

He loved that London accent. Nobody swore better than a Cockney bird.

"Slow night, then, Emily?"

"Bloody useless. Where'd you get the motor?"

"Didn't have the taxi fare on me, so I tossed some aul doll out of it on the Dublin Road. It's shit hot. I'll have to dump it soon."

"Pity. Take me for a spin before you do, will you? I want to get off me plates for a bit."

"Hop in."

Dermot navigated the luxury car up Linenhall Street and onto the Ormeau Road via Ormeau Avenue. He fancied a tour of Belfast to see what had changed. So he took University Street, past Queen's University and went on a loop of the city. Around the university area, students roamed in packs, causing traffic obstructions and getting thrown out of pubs for disorderly behaviour. They came in all shapes and sizes. Long gone were the days of long woollen coats, dashing scarves and little round glasses. Some clumped along in chunky S&M boots, dragging leather and black denim clad bodies along in a faux-depression fugue. Others skipped by in their mismatched converse, blue jeans frayed at the cuffs and hands hidden under long cardigan sleeves. Others still swaggered in GAA tracksuit tops to advertise their sporting prowess, county allegiance and Catholic upbringing. And there were more. Too many cliques to count. None of them carried books.

Emily snapped him out of his people watching.

"My arse is warm. Are these seats heated?"

Dermot slipped a hand inside her coat and squeezed bare thigh. "No, that's the effect I have on any woman I spend a little time with. Thought you'd be used to it by now."

"Yeah, love. You're fucking hilarious, you are."

"It's the way I tell 'em."

She snuffed at that. "So did you visit the ex?"

"Aye. Didn't go just as smooth as I'd have hoped."

"What happened, then?"

"Sort of went downhill when I floored her fuck-buddy."

He told her about the one minute plea and Joe's decision to take his number.

"You think he'll phone you, then?" she asked.

"Aye, it's a dead cert. Nobody could resist getting to know their long lost father."

"And do you think we'll get anything from it?"

Dermot recalled the look of Louise's house. Cheap laminate flooring and the standard clearance-reduction leather suite. Two-year-old TV and painted-over embossed wallpaper. He'd noticed the new PVC windows, but every house on the street had them, along with a matching door and a new two-foot wall around the tiny front yard. They'd obviously been paid for in some regeneration scheme. She had fuck all squared in a box.

"We'll not get much off her, no. But like I said, she has a fellah. I'll see what I can find out about him when Joe gets in touch with me. He might be worth a few bob."

"I knew it was a waste of time coming over to this fucking place. We're no better off than we were in London, Dermot."

"Other than the fact that we're not in danger of getting our heads handed to us by pissed off gangsters, you mean?"

"It would have blown over," Emily said.

"London crime syndicates do not allow things to blow over. They kill people. That's how they get rich, powerful and feared.

Their path to success is littered with dead Irish thieves and mutilated whores. But if you want to go back and take your chances, be my fucking guest!"

Emily rolled her eyes and turned away from Dermot. She looked out the window at the unimpressive Belfast architecture. Dermot wiped his lips with a gloved hand, momentarily enjoying the leathery smell. He counted to ten in his head before talking.

"Look, Emily, if we work together we can do well here. But we need to be on the same page. Forget London. It's been bled dry anyway. Too many people are sticking their fingers in that pie. There are opportunities here though. The IRA and UVF don't have the place carved up between them anymore. We can get in on the ground floor. But it's going to take some barrel-scraping and patience. Can you understand that?"

Another tut. He fought the urge to grab a handful of her wavy, blonde hair and bash her pretty face into the window. He needed her professional talents to keep them in bread and butter until he'd got to work on a few things.

"I don't think huffing is going to help either of us. For what it's worth, I'm sorry," he said. *Sorry I need you, you dirty, stinking whore,* he thought.

She turned to him, her pointy jaw set and her little head tilted. Her body language emanated skank attitude. "Whatever."

"We should dump this car. We've pushed our luck long enough."

Emily glanced out the window, onto the street and then looked about the car's luxurious interior. He could read the longing in her eyes. "Think you'll ever own one of these?"

"One for each of us. Silver for me, red for you. They'll make nice Sunday cars."

"You are full of shit."

"That's why you love me though."

She smiled at him. "Yeah, well, it's not your money, is it?"

"Not yet, baby. Not yet."

###

meat @ dville prk. 10 mins. need 2 tlk. gang stuff.

Liam felt queasy after reading the text from Wee Danny. He hesitated before replying.

ok

Nothing else came to mind. He hit send. His heart banged loud in his ears. Gang stuff? Liam considered phoning the Fegan twins and asking them to go with him in case he needed backup. He decided against it when he realised it might be construed as a sign of fear.

In the kitchen, he found some chocolate Pop Tarts at the back of the larder. He popped them in the toaster and fetched his trainers from the living room while they warmed up. Blood rushed to his head as he bent at the waist to tie his laces. The toaster kerchunked and he hurried back into the kitchen to fetch his breakfast before it cooled. He wrapped the sugar-packed treats in some kitchen roll and ate them on the move.

The sun beat down on the street, hot enough to melt tar. Kids ran about like stray pups in shorts, bumping into each other, screaming and falling over. One young girl swung around a lamppost on a length of blue rope. She sang the chorus of *Mickey Marley's Roundabout* in a woeful R&B vibrato. Liam, an ex-choirboy, cringed as he approached her. A car horn blasted as she swept out into its path. The little girl, around seven years old, gave the driver two fingers and resumed her suicidal spiral-swing. The driver trundled on, braking every couple of metres to avoid kamikaze kids nipping out from between gaps in the line of cars parked on the kerb. Liam crossed the road to avoid getting bowled over by the girl on the rope.

Wee Danny waited with Joe at the gates of Dunville Park. Liam instantly felt less nervous. Joe wouldn't let Wee Danny start another fight. As he crossed the road he saw why the boys chose to stand at the gates. The park teemed with sun-reddening kids and stressed parents. The squawks and whoops would melt your head.

"Not a lot of privacy here, eh?" Liam said.

Joe shrugged. "Where else can we go?"

Liam nodded to the empty bus shelter a stone's throw from the gates. He wanted to sit down.

"Aye, come on then," Joe said.

Liam took his seat and the other two stood in front of him. Wee Danny lit a cigarette.

"You're pulling them like a dentist pulling teeth, Danny," Liam said.

Wee Danny scrunched up his face. "You what?"

"One at a time!" Liam waggled his eyebrows, expecting a chuckle. Wee Danny squinted at him. "Ach, just give us one, will you?"

They enjoyed their first few puffs in silence.

"So, what's the craic, boys?" Liam asked.

They looked at each other and silently elected Joe as spokesman.

"Me and Danny want to leave the gang, Liam. It's all yours if you want it."

Liam nodded. "Funny. What's this really all about?"

"We're serious, Liam," Joe said.

"What? Why would you want to give it up? Sure we make good money and have a laugh."

"Because Stephen McVeigh is on to both of us. He's been to my house and he's been bending Danny's brother's ear. We'll get caught if we keep at it."

"So what? I get caught instead? Do you two think I'm fucking stupid?"

"Aye," Wee Danny said.

Liam turned to Joe and held up his hands, palms to the sky.

"Liam, me and Danny just figured that you'd want to make your own choice. We're offering you the gang, but you can leave too, if you want. At least we've told you about McVeigh."

Liam rubbed his chin. "I suppose we could see what the pickings are like further up the road. McVeigh might lose interest in us if we're not working Beechmount."

"Up to you, boss," Joe said.

Joe laced the word boss with sarcasm, but Liam still liked how it sounded. *Boss.* With full control of the gang, Liam could increase the number of nights on the hunt. He'd always been eager to do more, but Joe always had to play it safe. And he'd get more ambitious with the targets. No more robbing grannies for pennies. He'd have a go at the tourists, like he'd always wanted to. Relieve them of their holiday money and digital cameras. Make the effort worthwhile.

He reeled himself in and forced his brain to slow down. *Baby steps,* he thought. *Don't get ahead of yourself. Think this all through.*

"I'm going to have to think about this," Liam said.

"Do what you want," Wee Danny said. "We're out and that's that. If you want to pick up and carry on, fine. If not, the rest of them can sort it out amongst themselves."

"Right, but don't tell the others until I've decided. Don't want them getting big ideas if they think there's an opening."

"Like Danny said, we're out, Liam. It'll be up to you to get in touch with the others and let them know what's going on."

"So what are you two going to do instead? Sit and scratch your balls?"

"Don't worry about us," Joe said. "We've some ideas. But it's all hush-hush until that ginger freak stops sniffing about. For now, we're probably just going to lay low. Get pissed, get a couple of birds and enjoy the summer. That sort of thing."

"Aye? Well, good luck with that. Let me know how it works out for you."

Joe gave him a tight-lipped smile. Wee Danny lit another fag. Liam didn't reprimand him for not offering them around again. They stood in silence for a few seconds, none of them knowing what to say before parting company.

Then a thought struck Liam. "Joe, does this mean we're not going to hang about with each other any more?"

Joe shook his head. "No. We're still mates, like. We'll meet for a carryout on the weekends like normal. Then you and the boys can fill me and Danny in on your adventures."

"Aye, okay." Liam didn't feel a hundred percent convinced that things would work out that way. He felt like he should say goodbye or tell Joe it'd been nice knowing him, but didn't know how to say it without sounding soft or gay.

He flicked his fag butt onto the road and exhaled his final lungful through his nose. He looked up to Joe, shielding his eyes from the high sun with his hand, and then down at Wee Danny. It didn't look like they had much to say. Up to him to fill the gap as usual.

"Well, then. I suppose I'll smell you two fruits later. I'm away home to wake my ma up and see if I can get my lunch."

It'd have to do.

Chapter 6

Joe pulled Wee Danny's head off his shoulders and whipped him with his own spine. Blood pixels gushed from the ragged wound. Joe had set up the PS2 in the living room, taking advantage of the bigger, louder TV while his ma worked her Tuesday shift. He played Wee Danny at a two-player beat 'em up. Joe loved the button-mashing martial arts games. You could lose yourself in them, concentrating on timing and finesse, or you could go at it half-tilt and have a bit of craic with player two. Another round, and Joe laid into Wee Danny with a seven hit combination.

"You're shit at this today," Joe said.

"I can't concentrate."

"Why not?"

"I don't know. I just haven't felt right since we were talking to Liam earlier. That fat fucker gets on every nerve in my body. It's probably pissing me off that we've just handed him a meal ticket."

Joe thumbed a four-button sequence and knocked Wee Danny from one side of the screen to the other. "Sure we both agreed it was stupid for the two of us to risk running with them."

"I know, I know. But I still feel like we're losing out. And Fat Boy is laughing at us."

"So fucking what if he is? It's only Liam, Danny. He's always been a dickhead."

"Fuck's sake! Get up you useless bastard!" Wee Danny pounded on the joypad and spoke through clenched teeth. "Then why do you always protect him?"

"Because he's a mate! Now quit yapping and put up a fight here. I'm bored of kicking your arse."

"It's a stupid fucking game anyway."

Joe had heard enough about Liam Greene and the Rockets. They could get a record deal as the next big rap crew for all he cared. As long as his kneecaps were still intact, he was happy. He'd more important things on his mind, and Wee Danny should know that. They'd talked enough the night before.

"So, what do you think I should do about my dad?"

Danny hit pause on the game, dropped his joypad and reached into his pocket for his fags. "I had a think about this after you left my place last night. I reckon you should phone him."

Joe accepted a fag and lit up. "Really? Why?"

"Well, you're going to lose out on a whole lot of cash now that you've handed over the Rockets. And your dad's missed loads of birthdays and Christmases. The way I see it, he owes you big time. You'll not get a penny if you don't get in touch."

"What if he hasn't got any money?"

"Then you only phone him once. You're in a position to call all the shots. He's the one in the wrong."

"Fuck. You're right."

"Of course I'm right."

Joe thought for a few seconds. "What am I going to say to him though?"

"Well, big lad. What's the craic? Do you have much money?"

"Aye. That might need a bit of work."

Wee Danny shrugged. "Do we have to keep playing this?"

"What else is there to do?"

"I've got some E tabs. Want to try them?"

Joe sucked air in through his teeth. "Jesus, I don't know Danny. I've never taken that stuff before. Why'd you even get them? You should try and save some money, now that we're not earning."

"You need to get with the times, mate. Sure an E is cheaper than a twenty deck of fags these days. I bought a couple of Mitsubishis because they're selling grass for thirty quid an eighth this week. Fuck that."

"But Ecstasy's a nightclub drug. There's no point doing it here."

"I've got some of our Paul's old CDs with me. Come on, we can have our own wee rave."

Joe narrowed his eyes. "So long as you don't want me to slow dance."

"Fuck off, you fruit."

Joe stroked his moustache. He wasn't sure. A bit of blow was one thing, but Ecstasy still held its place as a Class A. The same league as cocaine and heroin. He shook his head to scatter his doubts. It was only a pill. "Ach, fuck it. Okay. But we may go up to my room. The stereo down here is shit."

"Dead on. We should neck the pills right now though. They take about half an hour to kick in according to the dealer. If you want, that'd be enough time to cook a pizza or something. I'm not sure if they give you the munchies or not, but there's no point starving if they do."

"Good thinking. We should drink shitloads of water too."

"Yeah, that's right." Wee Danny dug into his pocket and pulled out a little cellophane bag containing two aspirin-like pills. He handed one to Joe and dry-swallowed the other.

Joe shuddered. "I'm having a drink with mine."

In the kitchen, Wee Danny laid twenty fish fingers side-by-side on a baking tray while Joe inwardly talked himself into swallowing the pill, now floating in a mouthful of tap water. While Wee Danny tried to figure out the oven, Joe blessed himself and gulped. They had another few rounds on the PS2 while they waited on the food and the first signs of a buzz. Half an hour later, stomachs full, they carried water up the stairs in pint glasses and milk bottles.

Joe opened his bedroom window while Wee Danny fed three of Paul's discs to the sound system. Noise from the street invaded the room. Loud kids and louder parents. Beeping horns and revving engines. Sounds of the summer. Wee Danny cranked the volume knob. Aphex Twin knocked the dust off Joe's speakers. Old school mind-fuck. The bass line rattled Joe's fillings.

"Is it warm in here?" Joe asked.

Wee Danny shrugged. "We might be coming up."

"Cool."

Joe sat on his bed and tried to imitate the beat from the techno track in a combination of foot-stomping and knee-slapping. He couldn't keep up. But his jeans felt good. He ran his hands up and down the blue material from his knees to his hips and his scalp tightened in a pleasure shiver. He dug hypersensitive fingertips into his thighs and smiled. Then something important occurred to him. He needed to share it.

"See if I ever think about topping myself, Danny; will you slap me?"

Wee Danny blinked. "What?"

"You have to slap me if I ever want to kill myself."

"How will I know?"

Joe shrugged and flopped back on his bed. "I'll probably offer you a big bag of dirty mags."

"If you ever give me a pile of porn, I'll kiss you."

"Well, that's the end of that then. No fucking way I'm risking it now."

Wee Danny's laughter crackled in Joe's ears. Joe sat up. His legs shook but he liked the sensation. He watched Wee Danny's jaw work as if he'd a mouthful of Hubba Bubba bubblegum.

"Seriously, though," Joe said, "I don't want to die."

Wee Danny swayed from side-to-side in the middle of the bedroom like a metronome with a rubber needle. He took a deep breath, puffing out his chest then deflating it with a whooshing noise. "Me neither."

"I'm glad."

"I'm kind of excited."

"What about?"

"I don't know." Wee Danny laughed again.

"Your laugh sounds brilliant."

"So does yours."

"I'm not laughing."

"And I'm not singing."

"What?"

Wee Danny shrugged and slumped. Shrugged and slumped. Nodded his head and tapped his feet. "This tune is brilliant."

Joe stood up and danced. "I'm going to phone my da."

Wee Danny nodded in approval.

"And I'm going to ask him to meet me."

Wee Danny smiled.

"And I'll tell him I missed him, even though I never knew him."

"Joe, mate, that's beautiful."

Joe flinched as Wee Danny charged at him. But it was okay. His little friend wrapped little arms around him and squeezed. Joe looked down on his dandruff-speckled suede head.

"Your heart is out of sync with the music," Wee Danny said.

"Out of sync? What's that mean?"

"Do you never listen to the music teacher?"

"No. Should I?"

"You should listen to everyone... no... every*thing*."

Joe stroked the crown of Wee Danny's head then gently pushed him back. "Where's my phone?"

"I don't know. Try your pocket."

"Pockets can't talk."

"Stop melting my head." Wee Danny tried to sound tough but his goofy grin betrayed him.

"Will you turn off the stereo? I'll not be able to concentrate if I want to dance."

"Can we put it back on after?"

Joe nodded and Wee Danny danced his way to the sound system. He hit the power button and Joe almost felt the music stop, like it had cloaked him. Coddled him. And he could hear the kids and the cars from the street again. But those sounds offered their own comfort too. Joe whipped the phone from his hip pocket and the scrap of paper with his da's number on it from his back pocket. He dialled.

"Oh shit, Danny, it's ringing."

Dermot stalked the city centre car park, noting the wonderful variety in colour, class and engine capacity. Security wasn't much of an issue here. A dozen signs, nailed to the low wooden-fenced perimeter, shirked responsibility for damage to or loss of vehicles. A curmudgeon manned the MDF-walled ticket booth. Smashed CCTV cameras nestled in graffiti-coated concrete pillars. The pillars supported a motorway flyover which threw a shadowed chill over the parking bays. The cars sat abandoned and unsupervised in tidy rows. His for the taking; like sweeties from a child.

He'd spent the day trekking around Belfast City. He wanted to familiarise himself with the old whore sporting her EU funded facelift and discovered an abused city screaming for attention. *Look, we've taken away the barriers and the watchtowers. Everything is squeaky clean and bombscare free. Don't be afraid anymore. Spend your money here. The Guinness tastes just as good as it does in Dublin. I promise.* And Dermot knew he'd come home in the nick of time. New opportunities begged to be reaped.

His phone vibrated in his pocket. A mystery caller. He smiled, knowing full well only a handful of people had his number, and only one of those hadn't given him one in return.

"Dermot Kelly speaking. Can I help you?"

"Um, Da... Der..." Some unintelligible muttering followed before the caller finally identified himself. "It's Joe."

"Joe! Good man yourself. I'm glad you called. What's the craic?"

"Just... you know... the usual, like."

"Unfortunately, I don't know enough about you to know what the usual is. But we'll put that right, eh? Or are you phoning me to tell me to fuck away off?"

"Yeah... I mean, no... I mean..." Joe tutted. "Can we meet? For a burger or... something?"

"You sound a little jittery, Joe. Are you okay?"

"Yeah, sweet." His voice went up an octave. "Dead on, like. I'm just a bit nervous, I suppose."

"Oh, right." Dermot didn't want to miss his chance at getting on the boy's good side. So he didn't tell him it sounded like he could do with taking it a little easier on the E-numbers. Kids hyped up on food additives melted his head. "So, we shouldn't waste any more time. Are you free tonight?"

"Tonight? Yeah! I can meet you at the McDonalds by the Kennedy Centre. It's only two minutes away from here in a black taxi. I love McDonalds. Especially Big Macs. They..."

"Okay, Joe. Save some of that energy for later. I have to get a few things sorted out today, so I better nip on. But save your taxi fare. I'll pick you up, all right?"

Joe paused for an instant. "I don't know if my ma would be too keen on that."

"I'll not come to the door. Just listen out for a horn."

"What'll you be driving?"

"Don't know yet. That's one of the things I'll be sorting out today. I'll swing by some time around eight. Okay?"

"Yeah, great."

"Seeya later then, son."

Dermot pocketed his phone and turned his attention back to the neatly lined cars. Halfway down one of the rows sat an old Vauxhall Astra Mark II in red. The joyride of choice from his misspent youth. A time before electronic immobilisers and sensitive alarms. His intention that morning had been to scope out some new hunting grounds, but nostalgia's siren call beckoned. It'd make for a nice, low-risk buzz. He patted his light tracksuit top, feeling for the tools of his trade stashed in the lining. Seconds later, he jammed the flat-head screwdriver into the Astra's driver's door lock and twisted. The button popped and he slipped into the car. He cracked the ignition barrel and hotwired the engine. The old man in the ticket booth didn't so much as raise his head from his newspaper. Dermot flipped open the glovebox and found the little credit card-sized parking ticket. Rather than create a scene by busting through the yellow and black striped rising barrier, he paid the three pound tariff and cruised out onto Corporation Square.

The familiar driving position and handling took him back. He could almost hear the laughter of four passengers anticipating the next handbrake turn on the Monagh Bypass. Flashes of reverse doughnuts and games of chicken with Citybus drivers set his heart beating double-time and turned his stomach in the old combination of fear and excitement. Headlights flashing and car horns blaring. Engines revving and tyres screeching. Burning rubber and exhaust fumes in the air. Skinny youths rattling against each other like bottles in a milk crate. Then a frantic shag with a wide-eyed Millie in the backseat before burning out the disposable motor.

Great times.

He'd give anything to get that life back. A simpler time when anything he needed seemed to fall into his lap. No scrabbling for a few quid to keep afloat. No wondering where he might be sleeping after outstaying another welcome. No looking over his shoulder. No sleepless nights in squats. Although chaotic, his youth had always enjoyed a sense of security. Hoods like him belonged to West Belfast. They made up an integral part of the pecking order and as such, they would always find a maternal comfort on the streets. He'd taken that for granted until it was whipped out from under him by the peelers and the IRA. They'd left him with a choice. Run and hide or die.

He'd fled to Scotland on the ferry, hiding amongst an army of Glasgow Rangers fans on their way to an Old Firm match. Over a couple of years he worked his way down the island as a non-person, afraid to claim benefits and leave a paper trail, until he finally settled in London. Always two burglaries away from living on the street, he slept in hostels and flats between tenants. Emily eventually provided his first home for five years.

Her pimp had beaten her pretty bad and Dermot, a longstanding customer, had charged her a small fee to knock the shit out of him. She got a little more value for her money than either of them expected when the pimp's skull cracked open on a kerbstone leaving him severely brain damaged.

Dermot took the job as her live-in bodyguard and occasional fuck-buddy. Because Emily learned from her mistakes, Dermot never enjoyed pimp status. His payment for driving her to gigs and dishing out the hairy eyeball to overenthusiastic drunks was food and shelter at Emily's flat in Hackney. Emily didn't pay him a cut of her earnings, so Dermot continued to burgle houses and steal cars for currency. But without the added pressure of providing his own accommodation, life became a lot easier.

Of course, he managed to fuck things up again by getting on the wrong side of some London gangsters.

Emily had landed an easy number. A strip, a lap dance and a hand job, dressed as a prison guard at a coming home party for an aging Essex Boy. Tony Walsh, a big bear of a man, had just done a stretch of bird for armed robbery. Fifteen years of his life gone, and his mates celebrated the fact by throwing him a party and paying for a stripper. Not much of a consolation.

When the time came for Emily to jump out of a large cardboard cake Tony had cheered and laughed with the rest of them. He made all the right noises in all the right places, right up until she took him to the cellar of the little pub for his private treat. At that point, Emily later told Dermot, he'd gone to pieces and opted for a hug and a chat rather than the more erotic option. He wanted to talk about his son, who'd been buying crack cocaine from the Yardies. Ilford used to be a much nicer place before Tony left his two-year-old boy to pay his debt to society. But the Jamaican drug dealers had invaded the streets like vermin and little Jonnie Walsh had gotten familiar with the crack pipe.

This had been kept secret from Tony by his family and his gangster friends. They didn't want him to have to think about it in jail, and knew he'd prefer to deal with it himself when he got back on the street, rather than have one of the other Essex Boys lay down the law. Once Tony wiped out a couple of the main dealers in the area he could book Jonnie into rehab and life would resume.

But Tony was scared.

He confessed all to the pretty blonde in the prison screw uniform. The thought of going back inside for the sake of a few Yardie scumbags chilled him to his core. And if he was completely honest with himself, he blamed his son and not the dealers. Why should he have to take such a risk because of his son's weakness? Couldn't he just retire in peace? He still had money stashed from the robberies he hadn't been caught for. He could afford to just drift away from the lifestyle.

Emily could smell money. She told Tony that she might have the solution to his problems and gave him her number. He would phone her the next day to talk about a price.

Dermot listened to Emily's idea as he drove her home from the party.

"Are you nuts?" he asked.

"What's wrong with you?"

"I've never killed anyone in my life. What made you think I'd be up for this?"

"It's not like you'd be killing real people, Dermot. They're Yardies. Those wankers are always shooting each other in the back. It won't even make the papers."

Dermot shook his head. "It's not about getting caught, you stupid bitch. It's about knowing whether or not I'm capable of murder."

"Stupid bitch? Listen to me, you Paddy cunt. This is a golden opportunity staring us right in the face and you're not going to pussy out. I can't make a living on my back for the rest of my life, Dermot. We need to start working some better angles. This is a good start."

"Do you know what the going rate for a hit is these days?"

Emily shrugged.

"I'll be lucky to get seven grand a dealer. Seven grand! We'll hardly be set for life on that."

"And when was the last time you had seven grand, Dermot? Burglary and car theft hasn't exactly been lucrative, has it? With seven grand you could buy into something bigger."

"What, like drugs? So I can get shot too? Sounds like a great plan, Emily. Tell me, why did it take you so long to come up with the answer to our prayers?"

"You've got no balls."

"Ach, fuck off."

The heat of their discussion materialised as condensation on the car windows. Emily drew circles on her side with an index finger. "If I can get him to offer ten grand a hit, will you consider it?"

Dermot flicked on the demister. It rattled to life and droned. "How many hits are we talking about exactly?"

"He said a couple, so probably two or three."

"Well, which is it?"

"We'll say two for argument's sake. That's twenty grand for one night's work. Would you think about it?"

Dermot drummed his fingers on the steering wheel. "What if we could get the twenty grand without risking my neck?"

Emily narrowed her eyes. "How?"

"Well he's hardly going to ask us to bring him their heads on a plate, is he?"

"Obviously not, but I'm sure he'll have some way of finding out they're dead. These gangster boys all have eyes and ears on the street. He's not going to pay us on our word."

"We could buy off the dealers. Offer them a few grand to move on and get their underlings to feed back rumours that they're short a few Jamaicans."

"You're a right dumb berk sometimes, Dermot." With a violent swipe of her palm she rubbed out the circles she'd just drawn. "Do you know how much money a drug dealer can make in a nice area like Ilford? You can bet they have regular customers and the cops in their pockets. Why would they give that up for a few grand?"

"Maybe we could subcontract? Pay some youth to do them both for ten and keep the other ten."

"Or you could do the fucking job and we can have twenty."

"Fuck's sake!" Dermot rolled to a stop at the traffic lights on Morning Lane. They'd be home soon and he didn't want to continue the discussion all night. "All right, I'll think about it."

Emily put her hand on his crotch and squeezed gently. "There you go, love. You've got a pair after all." Then she flashed him a victory smile, knowing full well that the thinking was done and Dermot would do the business.

The next day, Big Tony called and agreed to Emily's price. Twenty grand for two dead Yardie drug dealers, to be paid after the job. Dermot and Emily met him at the pub from the night before. Big Tony gave them a time and a place to find the targets and warned Dermot not to fuck up.

Thursday night and outside the Liquid Bar, a nightclub on Ilford's High Road, a black BMW 5 Series idled by the kerb. Dermot knew that his targets, Death Man and Powerful, two twenty-something black men of Jamaican heritage, sat inside waiting for customers. Every Thursday night they set up shop in the same place until the Liquid Bar doormen started their shift at eleven.

Dermot watched them from an inconspicuous Peugeot 106. The little blue-faced clock on the dashboard read ten o'clock. He still had time to make his move, but it trickled away at an alarming rate. He pulled the Snub-Nose .38 from his coat pocket. The little five-shooter sat comfortable in his hand. Small but reassuringly heavy. Emily had suggested a machine gun but Dermot told her to wise up. They were dealing in real life and a bullet from a pistol killed as effectively as a bullet from a semi-automatic rifle. Machine guns were for movies. Professionals used easily concealable weapons. Emily hadn't been anywhere near as impressed with him as she should have been.

Death Man and Powerful opened their doors and stepped out of the BMW. Big Tony's physical descriptions had been on the money. Death Man, the taller of the two, sported a thick shock of ropey dreadlocks, held back by a Jamaican flag bandanna. He wore a baggy black T-shirt with a white Moschino logo and a pair of urban camouflage combats. Powerful's round belly and gorilla chest pushed against the fabric of a canary yellow hoodie with an AK47 assault rifle in silhouette printed on it. His jeans could have accommodated a baby elephant. The peak of a red baseball cap shaded his eyes. They lit a couple of conical joints and spoke to each other over the roof of the car.

Dermot swallowed a huge gulp of air. Time to move. He bounced out of his car and started across the street towards them. He'd intended to close the distance to point blank range but he lost his nerve and pulled the trigger.

The gunshot echoed in the street. The BMW's rear driver-side window shattered. Death Man, the closest to Dermot, spun on his heel. His finger-splayed hands went to his head. Powerful danced backwards and yelled something. The words were lost as Dermot squeezed off the other four rounds.

Bang. Bang. Bang. Bang. The gun bucked in his hand as he strode with his arm locked out in front of him.

Then silence.

Time froze. Dermot waited for the Yardies to topple over. They didn't.

"You shot my car, white boy." Powerful said.

"Why'd you want to shoot his car, man?" Death Man said.

"Ah, balls." Dermot said.

He'd missed them both. Not even a flesh wound. But he'd fucked up their car.

"Come here, boy," Powerful said.

Dermot backed away. "Sorry, fellahs. I didn't mean that. Mistaken identity, you know?"

Death Man yanked up the hem of his T-shirt and whipped a chrome handgun from his waistband. Compared to Dermot's it looked like a hand-cannon. A real Dirty Harry effort.

"Get your pasty ass over here before I shoot you in the face."

Dermot raised his hands and shuffled forward. He held the empty .38 by the trigger guard, pinched between his thumb and index finger, to show he didn't intend to use it. His stomach tried to climb out through his throat.

"I don't know you," Death Man said.

"Like I said, mistaken identity. I got you mixed up with some other guys."

"Because we're black?" Powerful asked. "You racist?"

"No, mate. I'm Irish."

Death Man flashed pearl white teeth. "Funny guy. But you're full of shit. Why did you try to kill us?"

Dermot sensed a way out. He jumped on it. "I can tell you who hired me. If you let me walk away."

Death Man glanced at Powerful, who shrugged. Dermot felt sweat from his armpits roll down his sides. He considered praying and realised he'd never been more scared.

"Okay then," Death Man said, "I'll bite. Tell us who wants to kill us."

"Actually, rather than tell you who, how about I lead you to him?"

"What, you don't trust us, white boy?"

Dermot said nothing, determined to choose life by not saying something stupid.

"We'll have to take your car, then," Death Man said. "Powerful's is fucked."

The big guy in the red cap growled. "What are you driving?"

Dermot pointed to the little blue 106 a hundred yards down the road. The Yardies seemed to be at a loss for words for a couple of seconds.

Death Man found his voice first. "If anybody sees me in that thing, I'll cut off your thumbs."

Powerful drove and Death Man sat in the backseat with Dermot. The hand-cannon glowed orange each time they passed a streetlight. As if Dermot needed more awareness of its presence. It distracted him from his co-piloting duties.

"Turn right here."

"There's no right, white boy."

"Shit, I mean left."

Powerful growled. "Wake up, boy. And give me more warning next time. I don't know this road."

"We're almost there anyway. Just pull into the leisure centre car park up ahead. He'll be in a black Saab."

Death Man nudged him in the ribs with an elbow. "You stay in the car until we've dealt with this Tony Walsh guy."

Dermot nodded. "He should be on his own. You'll have no problems."

Powerful parked the 106 close to the car park entrance. Big Tony's car occupied a space close to the metal shutters covering the centre's front door. The 106 shuddered to a halt and Powerful killed the lights. Death Man stepped out of the car and swaggered towards the Saab. He held his chrome .44 Magnum look-alike behind his back. Dermot shuddered as the dreadlocked Yardie thumbed back the heavy hammer. He braced himself for the gunfire, planning to flee the car as soon as the first bullet flew. Then the passenger door of the Saab flapped open. An aging skinhead jumped out. He brandished a sawn-off. Big Tony, the sneaky double-crossing fucker, never had any intention of paying Dermot. It was a set up. Probably to complicate a police investigation or prevent a gang war. And Dermot was the disposable nobody.

Powerful screamed. The sudden high-pitched blast left Dermot's ears ringing. It took a second to register the fat Yardie's panicked babbling.

"… the fuck's happening, white boy? What're we going to do?"

Dermot didn't answer. He looked beyond Powerful's big frightened face and out onto the Mexican stand off. The skinhead baby-stepped towards Death Man, talking though pinched lips. The Yardie stood his ground, the big revolver still gripped behind his back. The skinhead waved his sawn-off at him. Death Man shook his head. The Saab's driver door popped open. Big Tony, receding hair slicked back, unfolded to his full height and wheeled on the Jamaican. He rested his arms on the roof of his black luxury car, as if he needed help to support the huge automatic pistol he held in a double-handed grip.

Death Man finally produced his weapon. He pointed and fired at Big Tony. The Essex Boy disappeared behind the car. The Yardie turned to the skinhead. Too late. The sawn-off went boom. Death Man died. His body flew backwards, his torso torn apart by the heavy blast. Powerful screamed again.

"Desmond! No, man!"

Dermot reached through the gap between the front seats and shook Powerful. "Start the fucking car!"

"That fuck killed Desmond."

"And we're next. Go!"

The sawn-off toting skinhead glanced at the 106 and then tried to peer over the roof of the Saab, looking for Tony. Powerful fumbled with the keys. Dermot's heart almost stopped when the engine fired up. The 106's tyres screeched as Powerful sank the boot. They were going to make it. Then Powerful U-turned; towards the skinhead. Towards the other barrel of the shotgun.

"What the fuck are you doing? He'll kill us!"

Powerful didn't answer. Dermot ducked down. He heard the shotgun blast. Glass from the shattered windscreen rained down on him. Then the crash impact threw him forward to the melody of metal crimping. He bounced off the seats in front and landed in the foot-well. He clambered back up to a sitting position and surveyed the carnage.

The skinhead lay facedown on the Peugeot's bonnet, his legs crushed between the little car's bumper and the passenger door of the heavy Saab. If he was lucky enough to live he'd never walk again. Powerful would never breathe again. He'd taken the sawn-off's full brunt. Dermot couldn't look at the pulpy mess wearing a singed, pellet-riddled baseball cap. He opened his door and toppled out of the backseat. The calm night sky belied the scene of brutal chaos. A night breeze danced across the empty car park, kicking up empty crisp packets and blue plastic bags. Dermot wobbled on shaking legs as his adrenaline deserted him.

The Peugeot's one litre engine had stalled, but Dermot didn't want to leave it behind. There was too much physical evidence in there to tie him to the killings. Fingerprints, hair, skin cells. It could all be used these days, and Dermot's record hardly gleamed. England or not, it wouldn't be too hard to dig up his history from the Northern Ireland Office. He'd have to move Powerful and see if he could get it running.

The drug dealer hit the tarmac like a big sack of shit when Dermot pulled open the driver's door. The meaty flump raised the bile in Dermot's stomach but he was thankful he didn't have to touch him. Rather than climb over the dead man, he scooted around the back of the car and crawled in through the passenger side. The car started on the third try. Dermot could have cried with relief. He sat back in the blood-soaked seat, closed his eyes and pushed his hands through his curly hair.

Somebody moaned.

Dermot's eyes snapped open and he sat up in the seat. The skinhead still lay unmoving on the bonnet. That left either one of the dead Yardies or Big Tony as the source of sound. The Saab rocked on its suspension. Big Tony then. Dermot could hear the wounded man curse under his heavy breath. He popped the 106 into reverse. Big Tony's blood-slicked hand appeared. It struggled to find purchase on the Saab's roof. Dermot stomped on the accelerator. The 106 separated from the Saab and the skinhead flopped to the ground. Tony's head and shoulders emerged from his side of the stationary car. Dermot caught the muzzle flash from the automatic in his peripheral as he swept the car around one hundred and eighty degrees. Gunshots roared like thunder. Dermot sank low in the seat and drove on. He hit the road sideways and peeled off as fast as a punished 106 can ever be.

He'd watched for the Saab all the way back to Hackney in his rear-view mirror. But Tony must have let him go to clean up his own part in the mess. The dead skinhead would tie his gang to the Yardie hit and he'd probably needed hospital treatment. Dermot hadn't seen where the Essex Boy had taken the .44 calibre bullet, but catching one of those anywhere couldn't be good for you.

After picking up Emily, and firing a thousand I-told-you-so faces at her, he'd left the 106 in a bad neighbourhood with the keys in the ignition. They'd driven to Liverpool in a stolen delivery van and blagged their way onto a ferry. And Belfast welcomed him with open legs.

101

Chapter 7

Louise forced a smile for her son's benefit. Things had been awful between them for the last few days and it was time to be more positive. He'd just told her about his plans to meet Dermot that night.

"Well, what do you think?" Joe asked again.

She didn't want to take away from the excitement so obvious on his face. He'd just found his father, and Dermot seemed keen to get to know him. Knowing Dermot, it would probably end in tears, but it might not. And she had to allow Joe to enjoy that possibility. So she swallowed her pride and lied to her son.

"I'm delighted for you, Joe. I really am. What are you two going to do tonight, then?"

"Don't know yet. We're having a Mickey Dee's first. I suppose we'll just see where things go from there."

"Well, I hope it's a good night."

Joe nodded and smiled. He opened his mouth as if to speak then breathed out a soft sigh. He smiled again.

Louise wracked her brain for a change of subject. Something to extend the pleasant atmosphere between them.

"So what did you do today?"

"Not much. Wee Danny came over and we hung about here. He's away on home now."

"Did you eat anything?"

"Nothing much. Grilled some fish fingers."

"Do you want something to keep you going until later? Dermot… Your daddy won't be here for another few hours."

Joe's smile broadened. "Yeah, that'd be great."

"And maybe we could watch a DVD or something. We haven't done anything like that in ages."

"Do we have any we'd both like?"

"Stephen left a few films here last night." She watched Joe's face carefully. It didn't even twitch. "I'd my eyes closed for half of the scary one so I could watch it again if you like the look of it. Your choice. I'll get some food on and you get the DVD player going."

"Deal."

From the kitchen, Louise could hear Joe hum a happy tune as he shuffled through the DVDs. Guilt washed over her. Sometimes his height and attitude made it hard to remember his age. He was still a child and she needed to make more of an effort to give him the kind of attention a boy his age needed.

She toasted some soda farls and heated baked beans in the microwave. An old faithful, quick and easy. They sat on the sofa, plates on their laps and steaming mugs of tea with a packet of biscuits on a tray between them. Joe wolfed his beans down before the end of the film's opening credits then ripped open the digestive biscuits. He dunked them into his tea two at a time. The boy had hollow legs.

During a slow scene in the film Joe turned to Louise and cleared his throat. "Ma?"

"Yes?"

"Do you think you'll see Stephen McVeigh again?"

"Probably. He's seems like a nice guy. Do you mind?"

Joe puffed air through his nose. "No. You can do what you want."

"You don't like him, do you?"

"It's not even that. I just know that he doesn't like me."

"Why wouldn't he like you?"

Joe's jaw tightened and he shifted his focus back to the TV screen. "No reason. He just looks like a guy who doesn't like kids."

Louise knew he wasn't telling the full truth, but she let it go. "Son, you don't have to worry. I like Stephen and I'm going to see him again, but he'll never be as important to me as you are. If I find out for sure that he has something against you, I promise I'll drop him like a hot spud. Okay?"

"Really?"

"Of course really, you big geek!" She playfully punched him on the shoulder. "Now can we watch this film?"

Joe laughed. "Yeah. Thanks, mummy."

Louise smiled. She didn't point out that he'd called her mummy instead of ma for the first time in years.

###

Liam loved power. He always knew he wanted to lead the Rockets, but he never knew how good it would *feel* to be the boss.

After agreeing to take the reins he'd gotten in touch with the Fegan twins. Between the three of them they were able to round up the others for a meeting at the Falls Park. Encroaching dinnertime had thinned out the crowd and they sprawled out by the picnic benches furthest from the play area and adult ears. Liam shared the news with them in a steady and confident voice. No sweat.

After the murmurs of surprise, Liam continued. "So I reckon we should get to work to celebrate a shift in our... crew." He liked the sound of the word crew much better than gang. It had serious undertones. "As soon as possible."

"Who made you the leader?" Tommy Murray asked. The four-eyed wanker.

"Joe offered the gang to me this morning. Why? Do you think you should be the boss?"

"I just think there should have been a vote or something."

Liam stood up and pushed his chin forward. "How about this; if you want to take my job, you can stand up and fight me for it."

Tommy looked to the ground. "I was only saying, Liam. I don't want to be the leader. I was only saying."

Liam looked at the others. "Anyone else?"

Nobody took him up. Losing the fight to Wee Danny hadn't cost him too much respect then.

"Good," he said. "Now let's get back to my idea."

The Wee Rockets consented through silence.

Liam continued in his new business-voice. "Up to now we've been playing it too safe. Joe's a mate and I still respect him, but now that he's gone I think we can earn more cash by taking more risks. And I say we get started now. Right now."

"What are you thinking?" Eddie Fegan asked.

"That there are about a million more pensioners on the road at the minute than there'll be at ten tonight. We could do three and still have time to buy a carryout before the off licence closes tonight. So why wait?"

Mickey Rooney, the ginger nut from Cavendish Street, snorted. "Catch yourself on, Liam. The reason we've always waited until there's less people on the street was to lessen the chance of some hero tackling us. We'd have every taxi driver on the road chasing us with hammers and mini baseball bats if we went on a run now."

"Where're your balls, Mickey?" Liam asked. "It was worrying about that sort of shite that kept us back for so long. We have to move on and try new things. And I don't just mean altering the timetable. There's so much more we could be doing, but changing this one thing tonight is a step in the right direction. Next week we'll try something completely different."

The Fegan twins nodded their support and encouragement. Tommy Four-Eyes avoided eye contact but Mickey Rooney tilted his head thoughtfully. He seemed to be coming around to Liam's fresh approach. The other three Rockets didn't voice an opinion either way. Liam thought it a positive sign. It meant they were still interested.

"Do you see the man with the dog?" Liam pointed through the park railings onto the Falls Road. An aged humpback stumbled behind an energetic mongrel terrier. Every couple of steps he yanked on the dog's lead in a pathetic bid for authority. The brown and white mutt uttered a little yelp each time before bounding back to the lead's full extension.

The boys enjoyed the show until the mixed species couple disappeared into Milltown Cemetery.

"The graveyard?" Matt Fegan asked.

Liam nodded. "It'll be pretty quiet in there. Most people visit at the weekend."

"The guy's got a dog with him," Tommy said. "What if it attacks?"

Eddie Fegan made a hacking noise in the back of his throat. "It's fucking tiny! Lace the boot into it and watch it piss off."

Liam stood up. "No more talking. I'm going to the cemetery. If you want to come and help me, great. You'll get a cut of the money. If you don't, then don't bother me again. From now on we're cutting loose the dead weight."

He jogged towards the path, instantly regretting it as his heart sped up. But he'd committed himself to an energetic exit. He'd have to jog all the way across the four-lane road and up the slight incline towards the cemetery gates. Rather than glance over his shoulder to check on his backup, he pulled deep breaths in through his nose and puffed through his mouth. If he lost his breath he wouldn't be able to command his troop.

By the time he got to the gate, the twins were running on either side of him and he could hear the clump-clump of trainers on tar behind him. He stopped at the great stone arch over the cemetery entrance. Pretending to scope out the path ahead, he got his breathing under control before turning to the Rockets. Full attendance. Beezer, as his da would say.

"Right, we'll move in as two groups. Me, Eddie, Matt and Tommy will take the lead. You four hang back like you're not with us. Keep an eye out for witnesses. And if there's an awful lot of noise, sweep in and shut the old bastard up. Then we'll split. Every man for himself for half an hour. Meet up again at the new graveyard, um…" He paused to remember the name. "*City* Cemetery; the one at the Whiterock Roundabout. We'll find another jackpot before news gets out about this one."

Liam's group took the narrowing tarmac path that swept to the left and led them into the thick of the graves. They passed a black-humoured one way sign on their way to the older sites. The second group went off road, moving between headstones. Liam shuddered a little at the thought of them walking over the dead.

The old man had stopped in an untended section of the cemetery. Weeds stood higher than the black and grey tablets of stone. Clouds of midges hovered in pillars of sunlight. Liam placed a finger on his lips and rolled his feet from heel to toe, muffling his footsteps. Their target had his back to them, head bowed to look down on a grave. The tomb stone read, 'BELOVED WIFE'. As they got closer, he could make out the pensioner's mutterings.

"… and he still shits on the carpet. Awful pest of a thing. I should have bought a Labrador, they're easy to housetrain, but this one was free. I still haven't named him, but the other day my head was in the clouds and I called for Whiskey and this one turned to me. Would it be silly to name him after the last dog? Oh, hold on love." The old man bent a little at the knees and let out a thunderous fart. "Excuse me, Mary."

The Fegan twins snorted laughter. Liam shushed them out of instinct. The old man turned. He looked embarrassed and frightened, just like all the old men they robbed. That was the difference between the grandas and the grannies. The aul dolls always looked more pissed off than scared.

"Can I help you boys?"

The little mutt sensed something was up. It stood still for the first time, by its master's heel.

Tommy Four-Eyes spoke first. "Just give us your watch and your wallet and we won't hurt you."

The pensioner's eyes widened. "Fuck off."

"That's lovely language in front of your dead wife," Eddie Fegan said.

"Shut your mouth, wee boy! Have you no respect?"

The mongrel darted at Eddie. Matt stepped forward and planted a kick in its ribs. Dog and master howled in unison. Liam barged into the old man, and toppled him onto his wife's weed-topped grave. He went through the guy's pockets while Eddie and Matt teased the dog. They stamped the ground in front of it and the wee mutt snarled and yelped alternately. Liam glanced up to see what Tommy was doing. He stood a little back from the twins, rubbing his own arms and hopping on the spot.

"Four-Eyes, get over here and take his watch."

A reluctant and pale-faced Tommy knelt by the grave and grappled with the pensioner's arm. The old guy struggled against them, twisting and rocking like a fitting epileptic, making it impossible for Liam to get a good rummage in his coat pockets.

"Take it easy," Liam said.

The old man swung at him, missing his nose with a backhand swipe by inches.

"Ah, fuck this," Liam said. He thumped the old man's jaw. The struggling stopped. "Stupid bastard."

They left him, stripped of his wallet and watch, unconscious on his wife's final resting place. The little dog wandered away from the scene, trailing his red leather lead behind him. Liam thumbed through the wallet as they meandered to the gates.

"How much is in it?" Tommy asked, breathing hard, and then wrapped his lips around his little grey asthma inhaler. He sucked in a Darth Vader lungful.

"Five fucking quid." Liam jammed the wallet into his back pocket. "What was the dickhead thinking? All that fuss for a fiver!"

The others said nothing and that bugged Liam. They were disappointed in him. He'd just talked about turning over a new leaf and making serious money. And after his first run at the helm he'd made a fiver to be split eight ways. Fuck! He needed to salvage the situation.

"We're doing another one, lads."

"Aye, down at the City Cemetery." Tommy said. The colour was returning to his cheeks. "Which is why we should have split like the other four, instead of dandering along here like we haven't just left an unconscious wanker lying on a grave."

"No, I mean we're doing another one here. Right now. Nobody saw us. We have time before the geezer wakes up."

Tommy gave him a look. Arched eyebrows and curled lips. "You're pushing your luck."

"Nope, *we* are. Or are you going to run home to your ma?"

"I just think we should stick to the plan. *Your* plan. I mean, there's only four of us here now."

Matt and Eddie clucked like chickens. Perfect soldiers; always up for a challenge.

Tommy took a reddener from his neck to his hairline. "Fucking fine, then. Who?"

Liam pointed to the big stone arch. "The next person to walk through that gate alone. Man, woman or child. We'll hide behind the big skip there and at least we'll be close to the gate if things get sticky. A surprise attack from behind, quick and brutal. No struggling like the Mister Fiver-in-my-Wallet fiasco. And if they don't have something decent on them, I'm going to fucking lose it. I swear to fuck, I'll go fucking apeshit."

Joe looked at his watch again. Half past eight. No Dermot.

McVeigh's shitty horror movie had ended ages ago and he still sat on the couch with his ma. She scrolled through the Sky Digital TV guide with infuriating ineptness, pushing the yellow button when she wanted the green one and then trying to watch shows that wouldn't start for another twenty-four hours. He tutted as she hit the backup button again and started from scratch.

"I'm sure he's just been held up," his ma said. "He'll be here."

"Aye, right."

"Why don't you give him ten more minutes? If he doesn't show then go out and have a laugh with your mates." She squeezed his shoulder. "At least you can say you did your part. Then it'll be his responsibility to make it up to you." She paused. "Do you want a cup of tea?"

Joe nodded, mostly because she'd have to get up and leave the room to make his tea. If she kept going on and on about it he'd say something and cause another hassle. After the fun he'd had earlier with Wee Danny and the E, the crappiness of reality stung worse than usual. He'd still been a little chemically enhanced when his ma suggested they watch the film, but his come down had hit rock bottom halfway through. He'd heard about the depression after taking ecstasy at school; everybody at Corpus Christi got the anti-drugs propaganda in first year form class. But he hadn't expected his mood to plummet so soon after soaring high as a kite. It had to be the pill though. It's not as if he'd expected that much from Dermot. And what good was he anyway? Hadn't he done just fine without the big prick?

His ma set the steaming Manchester United mug on the arm of the sofa for him. She'd put in too much milk, but he didn't mention it. If she hadn't forgotten the sugar he'd be able to stomach it all right.

"We need sugar," she said. "I'll just run down to the shop. I'll be back before the tea cools." She grabbed her denim jacket from the balustrade and threw it on. Then she ran her hand along the nape of her neck and flicked her hair out of the collar. "I'll get you a Crunchie bar too, okay?"

Joe swallowed a sudden lump in his throat and nodded. "Thanks, ma. I… um… thanks."

She smiled on one side of her mouth and winked. It'd been a long time since she'd looked at him like that. She'd dug up the old expression at a good time. He managed a small smile in return.

Then they both jolted at the drum roll thudding on the front door.

Louise's look of surprise morphed into a scowl. "That must be Dermot."

"He said he'd toot the horn."

"He'll wish he had after I've finished with him."

The door rattled in its frame as it was attacked by the heavy-fisted knocking again.

"Take it easy!" Louise yelled through the door. She turned the night latch and took three stumbling steps back. "Karen?"

"Where the fuck is he?"

"Who?"

"Your Joe."

Joe felt an instant surge of guilt. His skin burned all over and his stomach drew his balls upwards. He'd never heard his ma's posh friend curse in all the time he'd known her. She didn't even sound like herself. More like a demon hijacking a woman's vocal cords. He tried to figure out what he'd done to her and came up blank.

His ma turned to him. "What have you done?"

Joe shrugged. He didn't know what to say.

Karen Magee's voice rasped again. "He's here?"

She almost knocked his ma over as she stormed into the living room. Joe stood up and raised his hands, palms out, to ward her off. She had panda eyes from crying. Joe wanted to tell her to calm down, that he hadn't done anything, but her messy makeup and gunslinger stance scared him into silence. He looked to his ma for support.

"What do you think he's done, Karen?" She spoke in a calm voice and approached her friend with bomb squad caution.

Karen spun on her heel. Her jerky movement almost emitted sparks. "My mummy's in the Royal. She got mugged at Milltown Cemetery. The animals broke her arm, her hip and fractured her skull. Looks like the doing of that fucking Wee Rocket gang." She shot the last two words out through a fine mist of spittle.

"You think my Joe hurt your mummy? Karen, when did this happen?"

"At about half six this evening. I couldn't go with her. I had to work late. But I thought she'd be all right. It's daddy's anniversary. She couldn't wait any longer to visit him. And those fucks robbed her." She turned to Joe. "She's in a coma!"

"Stop it, Karen." Joe's ma grabbed her friend's upper arm and turned her. She was not gentle. "Joe's been with me since I got home from work. We've been watching the telly since quarter past five. He couldn't have been there."

"Let go of me."

"Calm down."

"My mummy's at death's door! Don't you tell me to calm down."

"I'm so sorry to hear that. I love your mummy, I really do. But if you don't settle yourself and stop accusing my son of something he couldn't have done, I am going to give you such a kick up the arse. You should be at your mummy's side, not acting like a crazy bitch in my living room."

Karen burst into tears and collapsed against Joe's ma. Joe shook on the spot. His ma looked over Karen's shoulder at him. She made eye contact and frowned. Joe rubbed the crown of his head with both hands. He didn't know if he should leave them to it or wait for Karen to apologise to him. Karen's tortured sobs set his skin crawling. He needed a smoke or a drink or a pill or something. Anything.

His heart rate slowed as Karen's sobs finally faded to a kitten-like mewling. She mumbled watery apologies into the crook of his ma's shoulder.

"Shush, now. Sit down there. Joe, will you stick on the kettle please?"

He practically ran out into the kitchen. Only for the fact it would have prolonged his stay in the uncomfortable scene, he'd have kissed his ma for giving him an excuse to leave the room. As he reached for the kettle he heard his phone play Eminem's *The Real Slim Shady*. He'd left the mobile on the sofa. There was no way he was going to go back in there to answer it. He waited for it to ring off.

The music cut out as his ma answered the phone. "Dermot? Is that you? Where the fuck are you?"

There was a pause and some whispering from Karen.

His ma's voice again, "Car trouble? You're a… you know what? Never mind what I think. You can tell all of this to Joe. Have you enough credit on your phone to wait for him?" A pause. "Aye, big shocker. I'll tell him you phoned."

Joe didn't move from his spot by the kitchen sink. He expected a huge rant from his ma. She surprised him with silence. Karen spoke instead.

"Dermot? Dermot Kelly?" Her tone sounded a little more human.

His ma sighed. "Yeah. He arrived here last night. Caused a ruckus and left his number. Typical Dermot. Joe decided he wanted to get to know him. I couldn't stand in his way."

"And he's let Joe down already? Ouch."

Joe filled the kettle and switched it on. He considered slipping out the backdoor to avoid an awkward moment with Karen, but curiosity over Dermot's phone call pulled him to the living room. Karen fumbled her way through an apology and Joe blushed. He couldn't deal with it. Especially since he could have easily been guilty if the Rockets had come across Missus Magee before his recent departure. He shushed her as politely as he could.

"Forget about it, Karen. I'd have gone mad too. I understand."

"Thanks, Joe." She rummaged in her bag and pulled out a handful of tissues. She wiped her mascara-smeared eyes and blew her nose. The horn-like blast cut through the sombre atmosphere.

Joe's ma smiled at him, brimming with obvious pride. He felt like a piece of shit, but he managed a modest nod.

"I heard you on the phone to Dermot. Is he not coming?"

"He is, but he's running late. I didn't give him much of a chance to explain. Maybe you should phone him and ask him when he'll be here."

A two-tone car horn sounded in the street. He looked out the window and saw Dermot behind the wheel of a sporty Renault Laguna.

"I guess I won't need to phone him," Joe said. He grabbed his hooded top and took a deep breath at the front door before stepping out onto the street.

Liam swung the mop handle like a baseball bat. He turned his face away as the stick made contact with the window. The glass clattered into the Corpus Christi classroom. The others cheered. Liam turned and bowed to his rowdy audience, then returned to the circle of drinking Rockets and a diminishing bottle of cider. The mood buzzed on the school's car park. Liam twirled the mop handle like an Orangeman's baton before tossing it to Matt Fegan, the next batter. He motioned for the non-identical twin to stall for a minute. He had something to say.

"It turned out all right in the end, didn't it?"

They smiled at their fearless leader and raised their plastic chalices. The second job at Milltown Cemetery had gotten a little messy, but at least she'd a decent amount in her purse and a bit of gold around her neck. He'd hit her too hard and too many times, still pissed off about the old man with the dog, but made sure she was still breathing before they split. They picked a teenaged girl at the City Cemetery. That one turned up even more. Mobile phone, iPod, cash and jewellery. Fuck the oldies. They'd just upgraded. And he wouldn't let them stop there.

"Lads, today was the start of our very first spree. Tomorrow we hunt again. There is money out there for the taking. Let's get it."

Even Tommy Four-Eyes smiled at that. A little liquid confidence really made a difference. Liam thought he might suggest that Tommy have a few tins before the next job. See if it would make him a little more useful.

"Where do you think we should go in the morning?" Eddie Fegan asked.

"Where the real money is, mate. Tomorrow we're going into the city. I have an idea and Royal Avenue is the best place to test it out."

Chapter 8

Stephen chugged the first quarter of his beer. It went down so easy; frothy, bubbly, and chilled to perfection. His throat seemed to widen, inviting more. Few things in life came close to the first gulp from a perfect pint. Good sex held a steady second, but beer asked for a lot less in return. Thoughts of Louise surfaced to refute this old belief. Her dirty laugh and skilled hands hadn't cost him a thing yet. So far she'd been extremely low maintenance. He saluted her spirit with another sip from the cold, tall glass.

Freshly showered, in crisp clothes and feeling the physical effects of a good night's football training, he sat happy and comfortable on his barstool at the Manchester United pub. Wee Paul Gibson drank with him, complaining about his home life, as usual. But even the familiarity of the classic pub rant added an important element to the night. Life the way it should be.

"And I keep telling her," Paul said, "it's not natural for a five-year-old boy to be sleeping in his parents' bed. He needs his own space. I mean, he's at school now. Pretty soon his mates will be inviting him for sleepovers and all that craic. What's he going to do then? Take Sinead with him? It's not right."

"Aye, it's a sticky situation all right." Stephen felt like stirring it up a bit. He put on an innocent face. "So, I suppose the sleeping arrangement must put a bit of a strain on your… connubial activities."

"Our what?"

"You know. When a man loves a woman? What goes on behind closed doors? The old horizontal hokey pokey?"

"Oh, shagging?" Wee Paul shook his head. "Not a fucking mission. Some folks go through a bit of a dry spell after they have kids. I'm living in the Sahara fucking Desert. I've probably forgotten how to do it."

"Sure it's like riding a bike."

"Fuck off. I'm not desperate enough to ride a bike. Not yet, anyway."

"Well, if all else fails, you can always get a quick service down on Linenhall Street."

"Don't think I haven't thought about that, Stephen. Problem is I don't have a car. I'd borrow your Escort, but even whores have standards."

They laughed and took a short recess from the banter to pay their pints a little attention and order two fresh ones. The first round had gone down pretty fast, and Stephen had a feeling it'd be one of those nights. And why not? He'd no work in the morning.

"So what about you, Stephen? Getting any this weather?"

Stephen grinned. "You know, it just so happens I am. I met her here the other night. After the Celtic match."

"You landed a Hoops fan? Fucking sweet. I don't care if she's a boot, hold on to that one. I had to listen to Sinead moaning the whole way through that match. Last time I try and watch one at home." Wee Paul tilted his head. "So, *is* she a boot?"

"No. She's a bit of a Millie, but everything's in the right place and she's got more than a handful." He squeezed the air in front of Wee Paul's chest. "Nice arse on her too."

"Bossy?"

"Not at all. Kind of rare around here, so I think I will hang on to this one for a while."

Wee Paul raised his pint. "Fair fucks to you."

"There's just one flaw."

"What's that?"

"She's got a kid. And not a nice one."

"How old?"

"Same age as your Danny. Friend of his, in fact."

Wee Paul furrowed his expanding forehead. "Joe Philips?"

Stephen nodded.

"So you're seeing Louise Philips?"

"Aye."

"I was talking to her just the other day. Picked our Danny up from her house. She had a bit of a scuffle with Joe. Well, to be honest, she knocked his bollocks in."

"She told me about it. He's had it coming for a long time, as far as I can make out."

"If I were you, I'd be careful to never call her a cunt."

"Duly noted, mate."

"You're right though."

"About what?"

"She has a lovely arse."

Stephen's phone bleated. He lifted it off the bar and thumbed it to life. A text message from Louise.

"mad nite. mates mummy in hsptl. mugged @ cemetery. awful."

"Fuck's sake," Stephen said.

"What's wrong?"

"Another aul doll's been mugged. Louise's friend's ma."

119

"Jesus. It seems to be happening all the time now. Where are you going?"

"To see Louise. Maybe she'll have some information I can use."

"But you've half a pint here."

"This is important. Somebody has to do something about it."

"Don't forget we're playing on Thursday night. Try not to get beat up by a bunch of kids."

"Aye, right."

He shoved open the door and fresh air bit into his beer buzz. It pissed him off to lose out on a good session, but he had to take his leads where he could get them. If he was lucky he would catch Louise's mate and find out what they knew. At worst, he could wait around for Joe to come home and see if he could freak the scumbag out.

Louise answered the door with wide eyes and an open smile; surprised but happy to see him. Stephen pecked her on the cheek as he stepped past her, into the living room. A tired looking woman balanced a cup of tea on a saucer. It rattled in the saucer's indent as she bit into a biscuit. She scrunched up her face at him, as if trying for a smile and missing by a mile. Stephen nodded to her and sat in the armchair by the window.

"Do you want a cuppa?" Louise asked. She sat next to her mate.

"No, thanks."

"Karen, this is Stephen. Stephen, Karen. I wasn't expecting you to call over."

"Sorry to drop in like this. Just didn't know how to reply to the text you sent me. Thought I might think of something on the walk over." He shrugged slowly. "Still nothing."

"It's awful, isn't it?" Louise said.

Stephen nodded then turned to Karen. "Any witnesses?"

Karen looked up from her tea and sighed. She spoke mechanically and concisely, as if for a police interview. "Just before they attacked my mummy, they'd robbed another wee man. He struggled with them and got knocked out. When he came to he found mummy just inside the gate on his way out. He waved down a taxi and got her to the hospital. His descriptions could match any of the wee hoods around here. Except that they were younger than usual. The PSNI interviewed him, but you know what it's like. They don't have enough information to go on."

"Will your mummy be okay?"

Karen shook her head and sniffled. "She's in the ICU. We just have to wait and see."

Louise leaned into her friend and gave her a one-armed hug. "Your mummy's as strong as an ox. She'll be okay."

"Please, God," Karen said. "Look, Louise, I better get back to the hospital. I'm so sorry about my behaviour earlier. You've been very good to me. Will you tell Joe I'm sorry again when he gets back?"

"Don't you worry one bit. Joe knows you weren't yourself earlier, and you've been there for me often enough. Just let me know if you need anything. And call me in the morning to let me know how your mummy's getting on."

Karen nodded, passed her teacup and saucer to Louise and stood up. She turned to Stephen. "It was nice to meet you. Maybe next time I'll be in a better state to get to know you."

Stephen gave her a tight-lipped smile. "You too. Hope someone catches up with the wee bastards that did this."

"And breaks their knees," Louise said.

Karen, shoulders hunched and eyes to the floor, grunted a goodbye and left. Louise rolled her eyes and blew a long breath through pursed lips.

"What a mad night."

"Why did she need to apologise to Joe?"

"I'm dying for a drink. Come on through to the kitchen with me and I'll tell you. I can smell the pub off you. I suppose you wouldn't turn down a beer."

Stephen drank his beer from the can and tried not to act too surprised when Louise told him about Joe's alibi. His mind motored as she related the rest of the story right up to Dermot showing up almost an hour late to pick up Joe. He'd been so sure he'd nailed it. That it would be only a matter of time before Joe slipped up and got caught. That the community was only days away from getting rid of the Wee Rockets. Now he was back to square one.

"And you know," Louise continued, "I hate to admit it, but I'm so relieved. It's awful that this happened to Missus Magee, but at least something good has come of it. A couple of days ago I thought Joe was in that gang. Now I know he couldn't be. It's like the weight of the world has just dropped off my shoulders."

Stephen hugged her hard and wished he shared her enthusiasm.

Dermot watched Joe suck up the last of his chocolate milkshake, slurping and gurgling to his heart's content. *Behold, the fruit of your loins,* he thought and smiled to himself. On reflection, it seemed a slightly uncharitable thought; especially in light of the other clientele at McDonalds. The harsh fluorescent lighting did little for the pasty-skinned specimens stuffing French Fries and Big Macs into their pimple-dotted faces. Joe's clear, swarthy complexion and strong bone structure knocked him a few notches up on the evolutionary scale. The tatty moustache took away a little from the effect, as did the awkward angles his long limbs naturally fell into, but overall his physical appearance was a credit to Dermot's genes. They hadn't talked enough for Dermot to get an accurate idea of the boy's intelligence, but there seemed to be some activity going on behind his darting eyes. Certainly, he was no slack-jawed moron.

At last, the slurping stopped.

"Did you enjoy that, then?" Dermot asked.

Joe popped off the plastic lid and held the empty cup upside down. Not one drop hit the table. "No, it was stinking," he said and laughed.

"Yeah, I suppose it was a pretty unnecessary question."

Joe flattened then folded his cardboard burger carton and balled up the greasy paper bag his fries had come in. He put them into the milkshake cup and stuck the plastic lid back on. Dermot chuckled.

"You're a tidy guy, Joe."

"Hmmm? Oh, right. Not really tidy. I just don't like sitting at a table I can't put my elbows on. Makes me a bit fidgety."

Dermot glanced at the boy's jerking knee and tapping foot but said nothing. He didn't want to be pointing out all of his flaws during their first real conversation. "Was your ma okay about this? Us meeting, I mean."

Joe nodded. "She said she didn't want to stop me from getting to know you just because she hated your guts. I'm old enough to decide for myself whether you're worth knowing."

It stung Dermot a little more than he'd admit, even to himself, that Louise hated him. Anger he could understand, but hatred? Harsh. Still, he could play the emotional martyr. "You're ma's a great woman; putting your feelings ahead of hers. Not many around here would do that for their kids. You be good to her, okay?"

"Okay." Joe sounded a little reproachful. Like he was thinking, *who the fuck are you telling? I didn't leave her.*

Dermot didn't want to try too hard to impress this kid, but maybe he'd ease off on the moral stuff. "So do I have to get you back by a certain time?"

"My ma didn't say."

Dermot looked at his watch; a little after nine. "That's good. The night is still young. We could go to the pictures or maybe just go for a drive and chat some more."

"Or we could go for a pint."

"You would need some very convincing ID."

"Sure I'd be with you."

"As far as I remember, that doesn't count at this time of night. No, I don't think that's a good idea. What about a carryout?"

At the mention of a carryout, Joe's shoulders halted in their descent to Slump City. He grinned and winked. "Now you're talking. Where'll we drink it?"

"We can take the car to Clarendon Dock. I noticed they've cleaned it up and built some fancy new office buildings there. Plenty of benches by the water. Seems like a nice place to have a beer." It'd be safe enough to drive the Laguna about for the rest of the night. He'd stolen a set of registration plates from another parked up Laguna in an apartment complex car park in the city. A temporary fix, but they probably wouldn't be missed until the morning.

"Clarendon Dock? Never drank there before."

"Sure it'll make a change. You must be sick of Dunville Park by now."

"How did you…?"

"I was your age once before. Never went further down the Falls Road than Divis Flats until I turned seventeen. Thought it might be nice to show you the wider world a little sooner than I discovered it."

"I've been into the city before, like."

"I bet you have. But I'd also bet that you've never been there after dark. I'd say you've gone with your ma to get trainers or leather shoes for school then headed straight back up the road in a black taxi."

Joe blushed a little. "So?"

Dermot reminded himself to take it easy on the smart-arse comments. "It's nothing to be ashamed of. Don't take it like that. I just want to bring you somewhere different. Make our first beer together a memorable one. It's a pretty big thing, to me anyway. I'd have killed to sit and have a beer with my dad when I was your age."

"Oh, right. Okay."

"Good man. Let's hit the road."

Joe fiddled with the radio on the way down the Falls Road, experimenting with the bass and treble levels and the speaker balance. Dermot let him play, happy to take a break from conversing until he could loosen his lips a little with a cold one. The boom-boom bass kept the atmosphere in the car young and fun. They stopped off at the off licence in the Twin Spires complex and Dermot forked out for a tray of Carlsberg. Condensation ran down the side of the green tins while they sat on the counter and Dermot paid with a fistful of pound coins.

They parked the car on Corporation Square, outside the Greek Embassy, and ducked under the moving barrier at the side entrance to the prestigious business park. Dermot led them to a bench that looked out on the moored Seacat Ferry, and beyond that, the Odyssey Arena where the Belfast Giants played Ice Hockey matches, boy bands performed sell out gigs and you could eat, catch a movie, go clubbing and get pissed all under one roof. Reflected light from the building and its wide grounds ebbed on the murky body of seawater between the two large sites. A multi-coloured Ferris wheel spun a lazy circle in the centre of the summer funfair in one of the Odyssey car parks. Laughing, screaming and generic dance music carried on the wind to provide a pleasant low-volume soundtrack. Joe made appreciative noises and Dermot acted cool. Secretly he still felt overwhelmed by the massive growth in the area's private enterprise. Money, money, money.

He handed Joe a can of beer and cracked one open for himself. They drank silently for a few minutes before Dermot got things rolling. "You know, I don't think there's a better way to get to know someone than to drink a shitload of beer with them."

"Sounds good to me."

"Of course it does. You're getting free beer."

Joe stretched his legs out in front of him. "It's not just that. It's good to spend time with someone and not feel like you have to be the boss. I'm just along for the ride tonight."

The world-weary comment surprised Dermot. Especially after only a few sips of beer. "The boss? Are you a natural born leader then?"

Joe took a long draught from his can and belched. "I don't know. It's like… when I decide to do something, everyone else does it too. I don't even try to make them. It just kind of happens."

"That's a good thing though."

"Aye, right." He waggled his can, sloshing the beer inside, as he tried to express himself. "I end up double thinking everything, you know? Like I can't just worry about myself. I have to worry about my mates and all. I can't be arsed with it." He slurped down another heroic swallow of beer.

"Too much responsibility, eh? I can understand that. But I'm intrigued now. What kind of activities have you led your mates in? Have you been a bit anti-social in your young age?"

"That'd be telling."

Dermot laughed. "Fair enough." He pointed at Joe's can. "No rush. A few more of those and I'll not be able to shut you up."

Joe crushed his empty. "We'll see about that."

The beer went down easy and Dermot couldn't help but admire how well Joe held his drink. At fourteen he'd been a Two-Can-Dan, but then, the beer was probably a lot stronger in those days. The boy didn't get his resistance to alcohol from Louise anyway. A fact Dermot was happy to exploit during their time together. Many a night he would get her drunk on generous measures of vodka and slip out for a night on the tear without her ever knowing. She'd always assumed he'd been as drunk as her and passed out on the sofa too. He'd never bothered to correct her. He never knew how easy he'd had it with her until he left. But then, that's what they all say.

As the pile of crushed empties at their feet grew, Dermot felt safe enough to ask about Louise. "Did your ma tell you much about me?"

"No. Not a thing. But like, I never asked."

"You didn't miss me then?"

"I didn't know you. Couldn't remember you ever being there. How could I miss you?"

Dermot lit two cigarettes and passed one to Joe. The boy made a good point.

"You would have remembered me though," Joe said. "Did you miss me?"

Dermot's beer-numbed brain tried to think of a way to steer the conversation back to Louise. In the meantime, his mouth worked on Joe's question. "Of course I did. But I'd no choice but to leave. I'd hoped your ma would have explained it to you."

"Maybe she thought you would have phoned me some time, or something."

"Joe." Dermot wrapped an arm around his son's neck and pulled him in close. "You're right. I've no excuse for being such a shit." He kissed Joe's baseball cap and released him from the tender chokehold. "But I'm here now. And I want to make things good between us. Will you give me a chance?"

Joe straightened up his cap. "If you do something for me."

"What?"

"Tell me why you left."

The daylight had crept away, but the full moon above bounced enough light to colour the sky midnight blue. Even the stars managed to make their presence known, a rare treat for the city below. Dermot met Joe's unwavering stare. The boy barely fidgeted at all. "Okay, Joe." He didn't risk calling him son. "You deserve the truth."

Joe sat up straight on the bench and turned a little towards Dermot. He pulled two fags from his own deck and gave one to Dermot. He lit up off the butt of his last smoke. "Fire away."

"I'll keep this as short as I can. Want to finish talking before the beer runs out, you know?" He reached for another couple of cans. "I asked you earlier about anti-social behaviour. You were cagey, which is always a dead giveaway. It means you're as guilty of it as I was throughout my teens. We always know our own, eh? So yeah, I used to be a hood. Stole cars, broke into houses, dealt some drugs, snatched money wherever I could get it. You know the score, don't you?"

Joe nodded.

"Well, the older I got, the worse I got. Or the better I got, depending on your point of view. I'd built up a reputation as the maddest bastard on the Falls Road. Really there were madder and tougher than me, but I'd never have admitted that. I let my friends talk me up and never spoiled a good rumour with the truth. I figured the more respected and feared I became, the less I'd have to do to stay on top. Unfortunately, that kind of reputation can also earn the wrong kind of attention. It wasn't long before the Provos put word out that they wanted my kneecaps."

"And that's when you left?"

Dermot snorted. "Not at all. I figured the Provos were a little afraid of me too. Otherwise they'd have just done me instead of laying on the scare tactics. Nah, I went ahead and did what I always did, all the time feeling more and more untouchable. My trouble started when the RUC lifted me for dealing ecstasy from a stolen Vauxhall Nova in the middle of Beechmount. This was before the Peace Process kicked in and cops would have been safer in Beirut. They fairly caught me by surprise. Jumped out of an unmarked car between customers and bundled me into the boot. I thought it was the Ra until we arrived at Castlereagh Police Station. For the first time they had real evidence on me. Videotaped the dealing I'd done that night, got one of my customers to tout on me, took my prints off the car. I wasn't looking at a huge sentence, but they offered me an easy way out and I'd have been a mug not to take it."

Joe nodded. "I think I know what you're going to say."

"Yeah, some things never change, do they? They took me on as a tout. Turned out I wasn't the big shot I'd started believing I was. They wanted to get to a cousin of mine. Seanie Kelly, the IRA bomber. I'd been picked as a convenient stepping stone and made their job easier by being a sloppy hood. Anyone else would have gotten a tenner for each snippet of information. They got me for free."

"Shit, you had to set up your own cousin?" Joe leaned a little closer.

"Well I never liked the bastard. Spoke to him the odd time at weddings and funerals, but he knew what I was and I knew what he thought of that. In hindsight, he might have been part of the reason I'd never been kneecapped, but I didn't have any misplaced loyalty for him. So I helped Special Branch gather information and evidence and they scooped him. Charged him with a list of terrorist offences as long as the Lagan. He got life. A big deal at the time, but sure, he got out early under the Good Friday Agreement."

"So you got caught touting on your cousin and left, then. Makes sense."

"Well, not straight away. I'd provided them with enough info that they didn't need me as a witness, so I hadn't blown my cover. The peelers still had some use for me."

"How many Provos did you help put away?"

"Six. And I made things difficult for at least three others. A messy business."

Joe sat back on the bench. He seemed to be piecing things together in his drunk mind. "So when your identity got out you had to disappear." He spoke slowly, still figuring things out as he said them aloud. "And if you'd made contact with me you'd have risked getting discovered. Sort of the way the Americans on witness relocation have to promise never to contact the family they leave behind. You're like Ray Liotta in *Goodfellas*."

And Dermot was happy to let the boy kid himself with such a romantic notion. "So do you think you can give me that chance?"

"Aren't you worried you'll be recognised now?"

"Kind of. But it's been a long time, and the IRA agreed to cease all paramilitary activities last summer. I'll count on that as my 'Get out of Jail Free' card."

"Well, if you're not going to run off again, then I'm happy enough to keep on seeing you."

Dermot hugged Joe roughly. Then he broke up the awkward silence that followed with the sound of another can of beer cracking open.

"So that's enough about me," Dermot said. "What about you?"

"I don't know where to start."

"Well, how about we start with the important stuff?" Dermot scratched his head. "Like, are you happy?"

Joe took a few seconds to think about his answer. "Right now I am. It's been a weird week though."

"Right now is what's important. We all go through rough patches, but if you can keep your head down and bull through it, there's always a good time around the corner. And if it isn't, just fucking steal something. That always cheers me up."

Joe chuckled. "I'll remember that."

"There was a big ginger fellah at your house last night. I take it he's your ma's boyfriend. They been together long?"

"No." Joe's expression grew serious. "They only met on Sunday, apparently."

"And has your ma had a lot of boyfriends?"

"What? No! She's not a slapper."

"Of course not. I just wanted to know if you were used to that sort of thing. Your mum bringing men into your house, I mean."

"Well McVeigh's the first one she's ever brought home. And that was only last night."

And judging by how the boy spat out the ginger guy's name, he didn't have much love for him. "Do you know much about him?"

"Not a lot. Seen him about a bit. Lives in Beechmount, plays football and thinks he's hard. And he's *ginger*."

"He is, isn't he? So you're not a fan."

Joe shook his head.

"Well, maybe we could have a bit of fun with him. See what he's made of."

"I'm listening."

###

Looking over his shoulder at one-minute intervals to keep an eye on his manager, Paul surfed the internet for reviews of the Peugeot 307. He'd spent the morning doing his sums and thought he could probably afford to take on a Charles Hurst Usedirect finance deal for a 2002 model with all the trimmings. They'd be advertising for team leaders in the call centre next month, and after six years working as a phone jockey for Halifax, he had enough experience to do well in an interview. That would mean a little more money and he'd be able to put a bit aside every month to make the final lump sum payment. For once in his life he would count his chickens before they hatched.

And the night he bought it, he would invite Sinead out for a drive to christen the backseat on a quiet country road. If she turned him down, then he'd take a spin across the city to Linenhall Street, clear of guilt because he'd given the missus a chance to show some affection.

He'd joked about kerb-crawling with McVeigh the night before, but after the ginger one rushed off to play Columbo, Paul had ordered another pint and thought about his non-existent sex life. His introspection placed the blame in equal measures on Sinead and himself. She should have made more of an effort, but it didn't help that he'd been too soft with her. He never put her under pressure by complaining or begging. Neither of them talked about it anymore. It was as if sex no longer existed in their world. Even when Paul complained about Wee Owen's inability to spend an entire night in his own bed, he made it about the child's welfare and development and never about the impossibility of a decent shag.

And ever since McVeigh brought it up, his balls seemed to be humming. All morning in the office he'd been evaluating his female colleagues. Every glance of breast pushed against T-shirt, buttocks trapped in cotton trousers or bare calf liberated beneath a summer dress gave him a twitch in his boxers. Even the morning bus to work had given him a cheap thrill as it juddered in traffic. Something had to be done.

His mobile vibrated in his hip pocket, causing more activity down there. He rolled his eyes and only delayed fishing the naughty phone out for a few seconds.

McVeigh calling. Would that fucker not leave him alone? He knew he wasn't meant to take personal calls at work. If he'd wanted a chat he could have stayed and had a pint with him the night before, instead of inflicting pubescent notions on him then splitting. He pushed the red button and cut him off. Seconds later a text message came through.

"soz m8. 4got ur wrkin. call me l8r plz."

It was probably nothing, but curiosity got the better of him. Maybe the big eejit had actually stumbled across some useful information about the Rockets the night before and wanted to bounce an idea off him. The text seemed too amiable for him to have anything on Danny at least. He keyed in the toilet-break code that would take him off the phone system for five minutes, slipped off his headset/leash and took his mobile to the stairwell. McVeigh answered on the first ring.

"What?" Paul asked.

"Do you know where your Danny was at half six yesterday evening?"

"Probably watching The Simpsons. He never misses that show. Even the really old ones we've all seen a hundred times keep him glued to the armchair."

"But did you actually see him there?"

"No. I was at mine, shovelling the dinner into me before training. I never go to my ma's on a Tuesday. No time."

"But you think he was probably at home."

"I just said so, didn't I? What's this about?"

McVeigh took a huffy-puffy breath. "I think I was wrong about Joe Philips running them Wee Rockets. And if I was wrong about him, I'm pretty sure your Danny is innocent too."

Paul felt the relief of an ignored worry slipping away. "I told you so."

"Yeah. But now what?"

"Huh?"

"They were my main leads. I can't figure out what to do now. Who to follow. What am I meant to do?"

Paul thought for a second. "You could ask Joe what he knows. He *does* fall into the gang's age group. Could be he heard rumours about them at school that have a little substance."

"Nobody touts around here. Especially not at their age."

"True, but friends and family stick together too."

"How does that help?"

"Aren't you seeing his ma now? Make friends with him or replace his da or something."

McVeigh fell silent for a few seconds. "You might be on to something."

"Of course I am."

Paul checked his watch. Still a minute of his toilet-break left. He fired off a text message to Sinead.

"fancy goin 2 charles hurst tonite? feel like buyin a car."

He thought that a pretty dashing invitation. He hoped she'd show a bit of appreciation.

Chapter 9

The bald lunatic in baggy red trousers and a green vest juggled four flaming torches and tottered on a unicycle. An impressive display spoiled by his constant jabbering in an annoying Manchester accent. Liam had a strong urge to shout abuse but didn't want to draw any unnecessary attention. The juggler faked losing his balance and the crowd outside Castlecourt Shopping Centre gasped. Liam held his tongue. He stepped back from the ring of motley onlookers and tried to find a target.

On the periphery of the audience, a yuppie-type fidgeted and sweated in a charcoal-grey pinstriped suit. Liam didn't know why the stupid bastard would wear it on such a sunny day, but the white X chalked onto the back of his jacket stood out nicely against the dark fabric. Mickey Rooney had spent the last half hour hovering around cash machines in the heart of the city with a stick of chalk. Anyone withdrawing a thick bundle of notes got followed. Then, while they waited to cross the road, or stopped to check out something in a shop window, Mickey made two diagonal slashes on a coat, shirt or T-shirt without being spotted. X marked the spot.

There would be no risking their necks for a five-pound return. They had an easy way to find those worth robbing.

Yuppie-Type glanced at his gold watch and pursed his lips. Liam followed as the guy waded through pedestrian traffic, towards City Hall. Across the street he spotted Tommy Four-Eyes slip away from the rack of trainers on display outside a sports shop. Liam pointed at Yuppie Type and Four-Eyes nodded. He assumed the others were behind him. So long as they kept him in sight, things would work out fine.

The target turned on to Castle Street and Liam clenched a fist like a football spectator anticipating something special from a lucky break on the pitch. Less people moved along the narrower footpaths. Fewer witnesses. And more importantly, fewer potential heroes; especially since the black taxis had moved to their new depot and most of the bus stops were relocated to Fountain Street. The shops took a dive in quality on this street. Newsagents, greasy spoon cafes and market stalls that sold cheap batteries and four-for-a-pound lighters made up the bulk of the trade.

Halfway up the street, Yuppie-Type pulled a spanking new Motorola from his hip pocket, flipped it open and pressed it to his ear. Liam reacted. In a sprint, he closed the gap. He hoped the others would keep up. No time to check. Yuppie-Type, alerted by the clip-clop of Liam's trainers, glanced over a padded shoulder. Liam took a second to register the target's intimidating height. He'd looked average from a distance. Close up, he was a giant. But momentum stopped Liam from bottling out. He snatched the mobile out of Yuppie-Type's hand and ran.

Pedestrians scuttled aside as Liam bolted along the footpath. He kept an eye out for grabbing arms and tripping legs. The surprised expressions of those not ready to spring into action met his furtive glances. They had shopping to do. Not their problem. Liam broke right and hammered it up Fountain Place. Again he cursed his lack

of fitness. His lungs burned. Blood rushed to his face. His teeth
rattled in his mouth. He needed to put the pain out of his mind. A
busker's accordion blared and he forced himself to focus on it. A
Pakistani boy tried to sell him a Big Issue. Liam conserved his
breath by not telling him to fuck off. Low flying pigeons crossed
his path. He dropped his chin to his chest and bent at the waist to
avoid them.

Then he slowed to a halt.

He turned to face his pursuer. Yuppie-Type, barely fifty yards
away, dropped gears to jogging speed. Liam could see the sweat
glistening on his lined brow. A grim smile cracked his face. White
teeth gleamed against a sun-bed tan. His jog became a confident
stride. Liam bowed at the waist slightly and put his hands on his
knees. He looked beyond the oncoming target.

Seven Rockets formed a rough semicircle behind Yuppie-Type
and homed in. Liam ran at him. Yuppie-Type's eyes widened in
surprise but he raised his fists like a boxer. Liam dodged right,
avoiding a head-on collision. Yuppie-Type reached out and
grabbed a handful of Liam's T-shirt. Liam spun on his heel,
breaking the grip, leapt forward and shoved the target, putting all
his weight into it. Yuppie-Type stumbled backwards. And the
Rockets went to work.

As always, the Fegan twins attacked first. Eddie jumped on to
Yuppie-Type's back and bear-hugged his sweaty head. Matt kicked
the back of his knees. The man crumpled and Eddie landed on top
of him. Liam soccer-kicked him in his gleaming teeth as he tried to
push himself off the ground. Matt cheered. Eddie jumped on the
guy's back with both feet. Yuppie-Type flattened out facedown.
Eight pairs of trainer-shod feet kicked and stomped the shite out of
him.

Seconds later, Liam and the boys rolled the unconscious and
bloody man onto his back and rifled through his pockets. He found

a worn and wrinkled black leather wallet leaking crumpled receipts and fresh banknotes. He pocketed the wallet and went for the man's left arm. As he tried to figure out the clasp of the gold watch, Tommy Four-Eyes tugged on the sleeve of his T-shirt.

"What?" Liam asked.

Tommy nodded towards the bottom of the street. "We need to go."

Down the street, an elderly lady held a cop by the arm and jabbed her finger at the Rockets. The cop spoke into the walkie-talkie clipped to his Kevlar vest and sprinted towards them, almost dragging the little granny with him. The gang split into three groups and ran in different directions. Liam and Four-Eyes fled towards City Hall. Liam glanced back over his shoulder.

"Fuck," Liam said. "He's following us."

"Ah balls," Four-Eyes said. "We're in the. Shit now."

"There'll be enough of a crowd outside City Hall to get lost in. Just keep moving."

Four-Eyes struggled to speak through rasping breath. "Easy. For. You. To say."

"Are you having an asthma attack?"

"Think. So."

"Fuck!" If the cop scooped Four-Eyes it might allow Liam to escape, but there was the long-term to think about too. Could Tommy be trusted to keep his mouth shut?

"Can't. Breathe."

Liam looked at Four-Eyes. The asthmatic weed squinted back at him, pale-faced and panicky-eyed. Liam would have to help him. He linked arms with the lighter boy and pulled him along. Ahead, the pedestrian crossing on Wellington Place went from little green man to little red man. The four lanes of traffic got moving again. This made Liam's escape plan a little trickier.

"We can make this," Liam said.

Four-Eyes had worked his little grey inhaler out of his hip pocket. He tried to guide it to his mouth on the move, but as Liam jerked him into a sprint, he fumbled it and it bounced away from him. He croaked a barely audible protest and tried to resist against Liam's pull. Liam ignored him and charged on, sights set on the other side of the road.

Car horns blasted. Tyres screeched. Metal crimped. Glass shattered. Tommy Four-Eyes wriggled out of Liam's grasp. Liam reached the other side of the footpath. He didn't look back. But he knew he'd never forget the thud, the splat or the screams of the front row witness. A skinny Goth girl shrieked on the pavement where she had been waiting for the little green man; a spatter of blood beaded on her pale face. Tommy's blood. He was all done.

Liam barged past the Goth girl and ran on.

Joe scratched his head as he stared at the framed Bruce Lee poster hung over the fireplace in McVeigh's living room. Bruce stared back, fire in his eyes, sneer on his face, his bare chest slick with sweat.

"Do you like Bruce Lee?" Stephen asked.

Joe turned to him, glanced at his ma standing too close to the ginger prick, and shrugged. "Don't know. Never seen any of his stuff."

McVeigh blinked as if he'd been slapped. "Seriously?"

Joe shrugged again and looked away. "I don't like movies with subtitles. If I wanted to read I'd buy a book."

"You can watch the dubbed version on DVD."

"And listen to a bunch of Brit poofs shouting hi-yah? No thanks."

"Joe!" his ma said.

"Sorry, I mean *English homosexuals.*"

His ma tutted.

McVeigh smiled. "But Enter the Dragon was an American pro… Ach, you know what? Never mind. Different strokes for different folks, I suppose." The smile faded quickly. "Will we eat?"

McVeigh had invited them over to his place for their dinner. His ma had insisted that Joe go and make an effort to get on with her new fellah. Joe hadn't put up too much resistance. Scoping out McVeigh's house suited his needs. His da's plan could only benefit from it.

"What did you make?" Joe's ma asked.

"A phone call." McVeigh chuckled at his own joke. "Pizza arrived fifteen minutes ago. I stuck it in the oven to keep it warm."

"Oh, we love pizza. Don't we, Joe?"

"Aye, it's all right."

"Great," McVeigh said. "Sit down there and I'll bring it in. You don't mind eating in the living room, do you? I never bought a table for this place. Seemed silly to have one for just one person."

"Me and Joe are well used to eating in the living room. But keep the telly off or you'll not get a word out of this one."

Joe rolled his eyes and flopped down on the couch. McVeigh disappeared into the kitchen and got to work on banging cupboard doors and rattling his cutlery drawer. Joe looked at his ma, still standing in the middle of the Spartan living room. She jerked her thumb towards the ceiling.

"Sit up straight, you." She whispered through clenched teeth. "You're making the place look untidy."

Joe whispered back. "Ach, wise up, ma."

"I'm serious. He's invited us into his home."

"So *he* should be trying to impress *us*. Not the other way around." But he straightened himself up to keep her quiet. "Happy?"

"Thank you. He invited both of us because he just wants to make things a little less awkward between the two of you." She glanced at the door leading to the kitchen, then sat beside Joe. She dropped her volume to a mouse's whisper. "And I think he's worried about your father coming back. He keeps asking me questions about Dermot, as if he's fishing to see if I still have feelings for the bastard. It's kind of sweet that he's a bit nervous. Will you try to be nice to him? For me?"

Joe opened his mouth to answer but McVeigh swept into the room. He held the pizza box like a tray. Three plates and three glasses balanced on top and he had a bottle of Coke tucked under his arm.

"Grub's up," McVeigh said.

"All that clattering to find three plates?" Joe's ma smiled, the tip of her tongue pinched between her front teeth. "What are you like?"

McVeigh smiled at her. "I had to wash the glasses. They'd gotten a bit dusty."

Dusty? Joe thought. *Fucking hell!*

McVeigh handed out the plates and flipped open the pizza box. He took a newspaper from under the cushion on the armchair and laid it out on the middle of the wooden floor. The pizza went on top of this. Joe decided to drop a pizza slice on the floor to see what McVeigh would do. But as he reached for the double pepperoni, Eminem began a rant from his pocket. He stood up and fumbled for his phone, noting his ma's scowl.

"Who is it?" she asked.

Joe glanced at the screen. "Liam Greene."

She tutted. "I don't like that wee lad."

Joe shrugged. "I'll just be a minute." He turned to McVeigh. "Keep me a piece."

"No promises." McVeigh's smile didn't match his cold eyes.

Joe took the call on McVeigh's front doorstep. "What?"

"Joe. Jesus Christ. I fucked up."

Liam's tone stiffened Joe's spine. "What is it?"

"Four-Eyes. He let go of me. On the road. Fuck, fuck, fuck."

Liam let loose a creepy, unsettling moan. "Oh, God."

"Liam, what's going on?"

"Tommy Murray's dead, Joe. Dead as fuck. And it's my fucking fault."

Paul frowned at the Renault Clio. Sinead danced around the six-month-old demonstration model, smiling, cooing and generally sinking all hopes of getting a decent deal on the little red motor.

"Oh, Paul, it's gorgeous. Look at the colour of it. Lipstick red!"

Paul glanced at the car salesman and grimaced. The salesman winked knowingly and smiled. His clean-shaven face beamed confidence.

"Renault call this flame red, sir."

"Wow, sounds manly and dashing. I don't need to be ashamed to drive it. That's a plus."

The salesman didn't acknowledge Paul's sarcasm. Paul wanted to strangle him with his red silk tie. They'd gone in to look for a Peugeot 307. The guy said they'd none in, but they had a near perfect 2006 Clio for just an extra grand or three. Sinead's ears pricked up then and Paul knew he could kiss the idea of a black 307 goodbye.

He looked at the little Clio. Attractive enough with its new, sleek body design, but it looked a bit on the small side. Like a shrunken Megane. It might be easier for Sinead to park it, but would there be enough room for a week's groceries in the boot? And what kind of horsepower did these little things have?

"Is there much poke in it?" Paul asked.

"This model has sixty-eight horses under the bonnet, sir. That's not bad for a five-door diesel in this class. And its light body makes it seem closer to seventy-five anyway."

"The slowest 307 has ninety horses."

Sinead did the salesman's job for him, with considerably less aplomb. "Who cares about that crap? This one's cute."

"It's small."

"It's compact, Paul. I don't like big cars anyway. You know that."

And of course the salesman got his standard line in. "I should tell you there's another couple coming for a second look at this tonight. These demo models always go fast."

Sinead widened her eyes, jutted her chin and upturned her palms. *What the fuck are you waiting for?*

"Can you give us a minute?" Paul asked.

"Of course. I'll be inside doing some paperwork."

The salesman turned to slink off and Paul had to suppress a strong urge to bury a foot in his hole. He looked at Sinead and shook his head.

"What?" she asked.

"You're not exactly playing it cool here."

"You heard him. There's another couple coming."

"There's always another couple!"

"Keep your voice down." She tilted her head. "So are you going to buy this one?"

"It's a lot more than I wanted to spend."

"So add another year to the finance deal. Come on. We deserve to have something nice."

"307s are nice."

"Ach, they're clunky. This one's *cute*."

"It's a girl's car."

"Catch yourself on. There's no such thing as girl's cars. Just cars."

"Says you."

"Paul. I want this car. Don't I deserve nice things?"

He felt his face screw up. "I give you everything you want."

"Don't give me that look, Paul Gibson. I hate that huffy face. If you didn't think I was worth the effort you shouldn't have bothered. I only gave you a son." And she folded her arms, having dealt her ace in the hole.

"You wreck my head sometimes, wee girl."

Her scowling face softened. "Ah, you love me really. So are you going to get it?"

Half an hour, a credit check and four signatures later, they left the Boucher Road branch of Charles Hurst in a flame red Renault Clio. Paul drove, Sinead's only concession in the whole deal. He had to admit, it handled pretty well.

They called to Paul's ma's house first, to show it off. He tooted the horn but nobody came to the door. Irritated, he shut off the engine and used his own key to let himself and Sinead in. The house seemed too quiet. He couldn't remember the last time he'd arrived to find the television off. And at twenty past six he'd have expected Danny to be sitting on the arm of the sofa waiting for the opening credits of The Simpsons to roll.

"Stick the kettle on, Sinead. I'll go and see if anyone's upstairs."

He found Danny lying on his bed. A familiar musky scent hung in the air, fighting for dominance over pubescent body odour and dirty sock smell. Danny sat on his unmade bed with an ashtray between his feet. He didn't even attempt to hide the joint roaches when he registered his older brother's presence. Paul knew something was wrong.

"What's up, kid?" He tried to keep his voice upbeat. "You turned Bob Marley on me? You know that shite is bad for you."

"Sure I could be hit by a bus tomorrow. Ask Tommy Murray about that."

"What? Where's ma and da? Did something happen?"

"They've gone to Tommy's parents' place. Wanted to see if they could do anything for them."

"Why?"

Danny slow-blinked at his brother. "You haven't heard, then?"

"Would I be asking why if I'd heard? What's going on, Danny?"

"Tommy got killed in town today. Run over by a Citybus."

"Fuck off! Your mate with the thick glasses? Jesus."

Paul sat down beside his brother and squeezed him awkwardly around the shoulders with one arm. His little brother shuddered. He felt like a knotted muscle, ready to spasm.

"Are you okay, kid?"

"No. I'm freaking out. Couldn't even go with ma and da. I didn't think I could handle talking to Tommy's family. Nobody my age has ever died before. It's not right."

Paul had no idea how to comfort Danny. Truth be told, he felt freaked out too. Tommy Four-Eyes, fourteen and dead? He'd barely started living.

"You got any more blow on you, Danny? I could do with a toke."

###

Dermot dragged himself out of the bath. With a towel wrapped around his hips, he went to the makeshift bedroom and found Emily in a black bra and thong. She had one foot propped up on the box-spring bed base they'd been sleeping on since breaking into their squat. She bent at the waist and rubbed some moisturising lotion onto her raised leg. From behind, Dermot enjoyed the jiggle of her beautifully round ass as she worked both hands up and down her toned calf. He grabbed a handful and squeezed.

"Hands off the merchandise," Emily said. She looked over her shoulder at him, one eyebrow cocked.

Dermot twitched in his towel. He held both hands in the air, as if ordered by a cop, then pushed his crotch against her. "Look, no hands."

She pushed back and hot blood rushed to his groin. He groaned as she wiggled. "You like that, big boy?"

"You know I do." He bent over her and cupped her breasts in his hands.

"Hmmm, me too. Pity I'm late for work." She circled her hips, grinding into him.

"What?" He felt his towel come loose. It would have fallen to the floor but they'd pinned it between them. "Can't you leave it another hour? It's just gone seven."

She moaned softly. "But we need the money, honey. You said so yourself."

He peeled back the cups of her bra, freeing her stiffening nipples. "Take the night off. I'll make some real cash soon." He brushed his fingertips over her pink buds.

"Really?" Her thumbs hooked into the waistband of her thong. She slid it halfway down her hips. "Because I could do with an early night."

He'd have agreed to marry her under these circumstances. "Oh fuck. Yes, really. Take the week off. We'll be rolling in it soon."

"Are you going to see your old fence tomorrow?" The thong inched down a little further.

"Yes, yes, yes." He broke contact for a millisecond to whip the towel from between them. He threw it against the wall and shoved his hips forward again.

Another inch. "Promise?"

"Promise! Now come on."

The thong slid down her thighs and came to rest around her ankles. As she stepped out of them, Dermot fell to his knees and pushed her legs apart. He ran his hands up and down her inner legs. The thin film of lotion she'd rubbed into her skin lubricated his massage. He rose slowly, kissing and licking the back of her thighs. He stopped just short of her swollen clitoris. The muscles in her thighs tensed as she anticipated his moist tongue. Not yet. He worked his way back down her thighs and she groaned. Part pleasure, part agony. He kissed and nibbled the backs of her knees. Then he worked his way back up, pausing for an instant just before the summit. She shuddered in anticipation and he gave her what she wanted. When she was ready, she went to her knees and bent over the bed base. He slid into her from behind and the race towards climax was on. Moaning and thrusting backwards, Emily won, but only just. Dermot bent forward and kissed the back of her neck. She sighed.

"I should be paying you, Dermot."

"I need a smoke."

"Spark one up for me, darling."

He reached for his clothes pile and went into the pocket of his jeans. His phone fell out as he took out the box of fags. The screen displayed the missed call message. He hadn't even heard the ringer go off.

"I got a call from Joe," he said.

"I thought I heard something. I assumed it was you ringing my bell."

He grinned and gently slapped her backside, before retrieving his towel from the floor. Emily flopped back on the bed base and spread her arms in a Jesus pose, comfortable in her orgasm-pink nudity. Dermot checked his voicemail. Joe had left him a message.

"Da, listen, I called you for a chat. Something mad happened today. One of my mates… a guy I went to school and chummed about the streets with… he's dead. I… I don't know when you planned to meet me again, but it'd be good to get wasted with you. Your stories might help me forget about this. I don't want to think about Tommy. It's too… I don't know, sad? Scary, maybe? Whatever. Will you call me when you have time?"

Dermot thumbed the red button and lay down beside Emily. She rolled onto her side and threw a leg over him. He could feel her breasts squished against his upper arm.

"What are you smiling at, Dermot?"

"That was Joe."

"And?"

"One of his mates died."

"Okay. And that makes you happy because…?"

"Because Joe called me to talk about it. He trusts me already. Isn't that sweet?"

"Sure. Whatever you say. So what do you want to do tonight?"

"I think I should phone Joe."

"What about me? I'm taking the night off."

"Well, I got what I wanted from you." He shrugged, relishing the feel of her breasts moving with his arm. "I don't care what you do."

"You wanker!" She rolled away and sat at the end of the bed base with her back to him.

"What's the matter? Storming out no fun without clothes?"

"Fuck off."

"Emily, for God's sake. I was just messing about. I was thinking you could come with me to meet Joe."

Her tense shoulders dropped a little. "Really?"

Dermot enjoyed the contours of her back, highlighted by the bare forty-watt bulb hanging from the ceiling. "Yeah, really. Maybe you could wear your little denim skirt with the 'fuck me' boots. That'd cheer any fourteen-year-old up."

Chapter 10

Joe could smell Emily on his skin. She'd hugged him when his da introduced her and he'd tingled all over with chest-thudding excitement. She looked like a model for FHM or Maxim. Classier than a porn star, but only just. Cleavage, thighs, blonde hair and brown skin. He couldn't believe his da had a girlfriend like her. Nor could he believe that she was sitting on the sofa in his own living room. She slumped back, knees slightly parted, and Joe fought to keep his eyes from popping out of his head. His ma would kill him if she caught him trying to look up a guest's skirt. Besides, he could feel that threatening warmth in his boxers and would have been mortified to pitch a tent in her company.

Joe imagined his ma was less impressed with Emily. She'd offered that tight-lipped politeness usually reserved for teachers complaining about him on Parent Teacher Night. He guessed she didn't approve of the knee-length leather boots. Whatever she thought of the girl, his ma didn't give his da the satisfaction of acting annoyed.

"Do you want a cup of tea, Emily?" she asked.

"No thanks, Louise. I'm all right."

His ma nodded, not bothering to double-check. She didn't offer one to his da.

"I'm all right too, love," his da said.

Louise looked at him blankly. "Where do you want to take Joe tonight?"

"Just thought he'd like to go for a spin. Keep his mind off things."

"Are you in the mood to go out, Joe?"

Joe nodded, afraid he'd squeak if he tried to talk.

"Well don't be filling him full of beer this time, Dermot. I could hear him bouncing off the walls on his way to bed last night. And the smell in his room was awful this morning."

"Ma!" Joe didn't want Emily thinking he was a smelly wee kid.

"Ach be quiet, you. You're lucky I let you off with it. Plenty of mothers wouldn't. Don't push your luck."

"It's all right, Louise," his da said. "We'll be good."

She pursed her lips and huffed air through her nose. "Just bring him back before twelve. And in one piece. It was nice to meet you, Emily."

"You too, Louise."

His ma stood first. She ushered them to the door in silence. Emily grabbed his da's hand and led him away from the doorstep, high heels clacking on the small concrete yard then putt-putting on the tar footpath. Joe watched the swish of her hips for a few seconds then turned to his ma as she was closing the door. He smiled at her, she winked at him and he knew she wouldn't be pissed off in the morning. The door closed gently and Joe jogged a couple of steps to catch up with Emily and his da; they were halfway to Beechmount Avenue.

"What are we doing tonight then, da?"

"Well, I told your ma we wouldn't go drinking, so let's do something even better."

"What's that?"

His da stopped in his tracks and stooped to look Joe in the face. "I'm going to teach you how to drive."

Emily giggled. "Aw, look at his face. Precious. He don't know what to say."

"You're going to let me drive the Laguna?"

"No, I dumped that after I left you home last night. I'll pick something else up tonight."

The penny dropped. "You didn't own the Laguna. You stole it."

"Yes, I did. Does that surprise you? I told you about my past last night."

"Aye, but I thought that was your *past*. I never met a joyrider your age before."

Emily cackled and patted Joe's chest playfully. Joe's heart juddered.

"I prefer to think of myself as a thief, Joe. Joyriding can be fun, but it achieves little and draws too much attention. No, I steal cars to sell them on, or to get from A to B. I'm not really a joyrider, as such."

"So where are we going to go?"

"Well, it's not a good idea to steal a car from someone's doorstep. You never know when they might look out the window and come at you with a baseball bat. Best thing to do is find a car park. It severely decreases the chance of getting caught, especially since most CCTV cameras aren't worth a shit. You get a better selection too. I thought we'd go to the Royal tonight. Pickings were always plentiful there if I remember right, and it's close."

At the car park, his da chuckled when he saw the yellow and black-striped rising barrier at the visitors' car park outside the maternity ward. "Do they charge for parking everywhere in this money-grabbing city nowadays?"

Joe shrugged.

"Maybe we should go somewhere else, Dermot," Emily said.

"You're probably right, babe. But could you really be arsed walking to another car park? I think the Park Centre might be the closest, but that's a good fifteen minutes uphill."

"So what's your plan, darling?"

"We'll ram the barrier."

"Fucking hell!" Joe said. He giggled with nerves.

"Are you serious, Dermot?"

"Yeah, sure why not? We'll give the kid a show. We'll need something fast and solid though. No Novas or Escorts."

Emily ran a tongue along her front teeth. She looked pretty and demonic in one sensuous moment. "Maybe Joe should pick."

"Great idea! Son?"

"Are you serious?" Joe asked.

His da nodded.

Joe saw the one he wanted, even before they'd ducked under the barrier. Big, mean and leaking gangster attitude, the Honda CR-V stood out from the rows of saloons and hatchbacks. The black four-wheel-drive drew Joe to it with gravitational force.

He pointed. "That one."

His da whistled a long breath. "Nice taste. Definitely big and fast. Looks like the 2001 model. Only one crossbar in the grille, see? That one's got the simple but noisy car alarm and immobiliser. Not as easy to crack as the Civic or the Accord. Bit of a challenge."

"Oh, right. Well I can pick a different one if you don't want to risk it."

"I never said that, Joe. I said it'd be a challenge. Which means, an opportunity to show off. All I need is my trusty flathead screwdriver, wire clippers and a good-sized stone. Watch and learn."

His da drew his tools from different pockets in his combat-style trousers. Joe missed most of the magic. The window crimped and fell into the passenger seat. The alarm blared twice and the hazard lights flashed. Joe felt his heart jump into his throat. His da bent in under the steering column and the alarm ceased. A few seconds later, he climbed into the passenger seat and leant over the steering wheel. Then the big engine rumbled to life. Joe looked at Emily and she gave him the thumbs up. He gestured with a sweep of his arm that she should climb into the Honda first.

"Oh, right little gent, eh?"

Joe felt his cheeks redden and thanked God for the fading light. He followed her around to the passenger side so he could watch her step up into her seat. The denim skirt skimmed the bottom of her ass as she lifted her leg. Joe prayed for a strong summer breeze. No joy. Still, he'd an image to fall asleep to for the next week tucked away in his memory. He clambered into the backseat and sat in the middle.

"Buckle up, Joe," his da said. "This might get a little bumpy."

His da reversed the Honda out of its space and braked hard.

"Shite, I forgot about the steering lock. Must be getting sloppy in my old age."

He slipped the flathead screwdriver into the seam between the steering wheel and the steering column. Something clunked and Joe's da removed the screwdriver. He rotated the wheel with the palm of his open hand, lined the Honda up with the exit barrier and sank the toe. Joe felt like he'd been shoved in the chest. Emily's laughter morphed into a scream as they hurtled towards impact. Joe double-checked the seatbelt was secured in its buckle. And then they hit it. The CR-V barely rocked on its suspension. The steel bar tore out of its joint. Joe whooped as they bunny-hopped over the speed ramps on the way to Broadway Roundabout. Then they were cruising up the Donegal Road and from there up the Falls Road and onto the Andersonstown Road. They pulled into the car park of the Kennedy Shopping Centre. Most of the spaces lay empty as only Xtra Vision and the Curley's off licence opened past ten at night. His da stopped in the corner of the car park furthest from the shopping centre's main doors.

"Your turn now, wee man."

Joe didn't hesitate for a second. He was standing by the driver's door before his da slipped out of his seatbelt.

"Christ," Emily said. "You're keen."

He didn't need to adjust the driving position, his long legs fit perfectly, but he fiddled with the mirror a little to stretch out the anticipation. Then he turned to talk to his da in the backseat.

"So what do I do?"

"Well, this is an automatic, so it'll be wee buns to get going. Just keep your left foot on the floor, slot the wee gearstick into drive and push down on the long pedal on your right."

"And how do I stop?"

"Worry about that when you get going, son. There'll be time to figure it out. Look how much space there is."

Emily patted his thigh and his heart threatened to explode. "And so what if you don't figure it out, Joe? It's not your car."

Dermot chuckled. "Good point, sweetheart. Now let's get this fucking beast rolling."

Joe took a deep breath and stomped down on the accelerator. The four-wheel-drive SUV lurched, but didn't stall. Joe's teeth clacked together as he bounced in his seat. He eased off the gas and the forward motion smoothed out a little. They trundled on at about ten miles-per-hour. He felt insanely powerful.

"Don't forget to steer, darling."

Emily's calm voice reeled him in. He jerked the wheel to the left, narrowly missing an abandoned shopping trolley.

"Ach, you would have got ten points for that," his da said.

Joe looked over his shoulder to smirk at him.

"You should maybe face front until you get a little more experience behind the wheel, son."

He turned back and adjusted his course to avoid a parked Nissan Micra. Then he upped the speed a little. He took the car up and down the car park ten times and his confidence grew with each length.

"Can I take it out on the road, da?"

"Sure, why not? You're doing great. Take her on out the gates and swing left. We'll go on out the Airport Road and see if we can find an open field. See how she goes off road."

"Fucking sweet."

Joe made short work of his first public road outing, quickly learning the joys of velocity on the almost empty road. Only a handful of cars passed them in the opposite direction and at one point Emily calmly told him to inch to the left a little when a van approached them, riding a little too close to the dividing line. After passing a couple of locked gates, Joe suggested they ram their way into a field. His da laughed at the ballsy suggestion then told him to go for it.

"But pick one with a wooden gate, okay?"

As soon as Joe spotted a wooden gate, he veered off the road and crunched into it at an angle. Emily screamed. The steering wheel bucked in Joe's hands and slipped out of his grip. The passenger side headlight went out and the gate shuddered and cracked but didn't come off its posts. The powerful two litre engine grumbled on.

"So much for airbags," his da said. "Not one of them activated."

"So what'll I do now, da?"

"Reverse and charge again. If at first you don't succeed... you know the rest."

"I haven't learned how to reverse yet."

"Now's as good a time as any. Move the gearstick back to the R slot. That's you. Now apply a wee bit of pressure to the accelerator."

They bounced in their seats. The Honda had hit the grassy ditch opposite the gate.

"Jesus, you've a heavy foot, son. No worries though. Just stick her in neutral and rev up the engine a few times. Yeah, that's it, lovely. Listen to that big monster roar. Now, pop her back in drive, and floor it."

The weakened gate splintered and Joe rolled over the remains. The Honda's body rocked and jolted on the uneven terrain. He noticed Emily sink her fingers into her armrest and chuckled.

"Jesus, Dermot. This field's full of cows!"

"They're not dangerous."

"Says you."

"Ach, Emily. Look at the bloody things. They're practically hugging the ditches."

"Yuck! That one's shitting all over the place."

"Yeah, they do that. Joe, take us into the middle of the field. I'll talk you through a reverse doughnut. I'm pretty sure these things revert to front-wheel-drive automatically when you reverse. Pretty swanky, eh?"

"Can you show me how to do a handbraker too?"

"This isn't the best car for that, son. Too high and heavy. But we'll start with the doughnuts. Then we'll see."

The Honda tore up the field as the cattle cowered around the field's perimeter. A single beam of light from the intact headlight swept over the green grass. Joe took to the destructive driving like a duck to water. His da instructed and cheered him on from the back. Emily alternated between cackling and screaming. Every so often she'd egg him on by patting his forearm, and once by squeezing his thigh. The E tab he'd dropped with Wee Danny hadn't even felt this good. He only stopped because the orange reserve light blinked on. They were almost out of fuel.

"Sorry, Joe," his da said. "We'll need what's left to get back to civilisation."

Joe read the time off the dashboard. "But it's only after eleven. Do we have to leave now?"

"No, not yet. But we can't go on burning diesel. Just let her idle and we'll have a wee chat. Do you know this model has a foldout picnic table in the back?"

"I am not getting out of this car, Dermot," Emily said. "Not with all those bloody cows running about."

"That's okay, love. You stay here and work the radio. Me and Joe can sit out on our own. Have a little father and son time."

While his da figured out how to work the picnic table, Joe realised that he hadn't thought about Tommy Four-Eyes since he'd left the house. Guilt flushed his face. Tommy was dead and he'd been having the time of his life in a Honda CR-V, with the prettiest woman he'd ever met in real life beside him and his da singing his praises in the back. But not only that, Joe was painfully conscious of the relief he'd felt after Liam phoned him with the news. Relief that he'd decided to pack it in before the Wee Rockets suffered such a misfortune and, ultimately, relief that Liam carried the burden of guilt for the accident and not him. Grief for the loss of a friend seemed to play a smaller part than it deserved in his mixed bag of emotions.

His da snapped him out of his introspection.

"Hah. Got the bastard. Now for a wee nightcap." He pulled a half bottle of whiskey from one of the big pockets stitched to the leg of his combats then waggled it in Joe's face. "Want a shot?"

"Ma told us not to drink."

"No, your ma told me not to fill you with beer again. I'm only offering you one shot of whiskey while we chat. Totally different kettle of fish."

"Oh, right. Okay then."

Joe took the offered bottle and gulped down a shot from the neck. His eyes watered as the whiskey-burn edged down his throat and into his chest. "Gah! That's fucking stinking!"

"It's an acquired taste, son. Have another sip in a few minutes. It'll go down a lot easier."

"I might not take you up on that."

"We'll see."

They sat on the sill of the Honda's boot, and Joe rested his elbows on the foldout table. His da gulped down a huge mouthful and blew a short blast of air through his lips. Joe wrinkled his nose as the smell on his da's breath rejuvenated the taste clinging to the back of his throat. The big man took another shot before spinning the lid back on.

"So, Joe. What do you know?"

Joe looked at him blankly.

"What I mean to say is; how are you? You know? What with your mate...um?"

"Tommy."

"Yeah, Tommy. What with Tommy dying, are you going to be okay?"

"Aye. I'll be fine."

"Good. That's good."

They sat in silence for a moment. The cows had gotten used to them and were moving about, though still keeping their distance. Joe thought they were the most useless animals in the world. Slow and dumb. No redeeming physical features. Just waiting for that sledgehammer to the head and mutilation on the butcher's cutting block. Probably nice to have no worries though. Eat and shite and sleep. All day long. Lucky fuckers.

"So, me and my ma were in McVeigh's house earlier."

"Oh, aye?"

"Yeah. He's weird. Big poster of Bruce Lee, half naked, over the fireplace. Fuck all furniture. And everything looks too clean and tidy."

"Ah, a neat freak. All the better for us. It'll make things much easier to find. So when do you want to do it?"

"Well, I know he's got a Gaelic match on tomorrow night. He'll be running around in shorts on the Beechmount Leisure Centre pitch for seventy minutes. Kick-off's at seven."

"So I'll meet you at seven. Outside the video shop on Beechmount Avenue, okay?"

"Dead on." Joe drummed his fingers on the thick plastic tabletop. "Can I get another shot of that whiskey, then?"

Liam lay in his bed, wide awake, quilt kicked to the floor and shivering in his boxer shorts. He didn't want to sleep. He couldn't face the nightmare lying in wait. Every time he closed his eyes he could see Tommy Four-Eyes; his ashen face scrunched. His squinting eyes peering at him over the top of the thick-rimmed glasses on the end of his sweat-slicked nose. Liam's final image of his dead friend perfectly preserved in his mind. While he lay awake it was a silent image. But the dreams would come and give Tommy the power of speech, and Liam knew he couldn't handle the asthma-strained voice of accusation. Not yet.

He rolled onto his side and watched the passing glow of headlights on the closed vertical blinds. Outside, life moved on. According to his digital alarm clock it was still Wednesday night, but only just. Tommy had died almost seven hours ago. Another car rumbled down Liam's street, oblivious to the tragedy. He tried to imagine dying on a Wednesday evening in the middle of the summer and cringed. There'd be a remembrance mass in September at St Paul's chapel on Cavendish Street. The teachers and priests would pretend they'd suffered a loss to their school and parish. Tommy's memory would be dragged through roses and still come up smelling of shite. You didn't have to tell the truth about dead kids, but plenty of people would remember it in silence. He'd died running from a cop after kicking the shit out of a yuppie and stealing from him. It'd be left out of the service, but not the local paper.

And of course, there'd be questions. Who were the other kids? Why had they not given themselves up? What were the cops going to do? Where were the witnesses? When would the others be caught? How could they let a friend die?

Just after the accident he'd phoned Joe in a panicky blur and stupidly admitted his fault in Tommy's accident. He'd panicked and hung up while Joe stammered. Then he'd gotten a wave of missed calls and text messages from the other Rockets asking if he and Tommy had made it. Rather than tell the truth or attempt to come up with a story, he'd turned off the phone. Then he'd slinked around the City, blending in as best as he could, for two hours to avoid meeting the others on his way up the road. Apparently they hadn't been stupid enough to phone his ma's house and rouse suspicion. He found her on the armchair by the TV, drinking vodka and orange juice and watching Big Brother. His da had gone to the pigeon club.

"You want dinner, son?"

"No, ma. I had a fish supper in the park."

"And you wonder why you can't lose your puppy fat?"

Same old same old. He'd gone to his room and left his TV on for a few hours, mimicking normality. When he flicked it off he couldn't remember one show he'd watched.

Enough. He rolled off his bed and landed lightly on the floor. A well practiced movement from countless midnight excursions. He pulled on his jeans, muffling the rattle of his open belt buckle by closing a chunky fist over it. Then he unrolled and wiggled into the Ben Sherman T-shirt and navy NYC hoodie from the floor. He padded down the stairs, sticking to the side closest the wall to reduce the risk of creaking floorboards. Probably an unnecessary precaution as both his ma and da's snores cut through the night like a pair of stuttering chainsaws. He got to the bottom of the stairs and still hadn't decided what he intended to do. The general idea was to get fucked up and maybe steal a few hours of escape. But he was out of grass and the off-licences closed at eleven. Some of the taxi ranks still sold cider after hours, but not to kids his age and not without a phone order. His ma's vodka might do the trick, but only as a last resort. She marked the bottle and could tell when it had been watered down no matter how drunk she got.

Hoping the night air would bring inspiration, he slipped out the front door and took to the streets. He picked a maze-like path through the terraces of Beechmount, towards the Springfield Road. Most of the younger kids had been dragged off the streets for the night, but small groups of teenagers were dotted about the area, gathered at street corners, smoking, drinking, murmuring and laughing. Liam wasn't in the mood to listen to the inevitable verbal abuse. He avoided all the corner crews by backtracking and taking alternative routes. On the Springfield Road, he considered climbing the gate into the nearby Dunville Park to look for the rest of the gang. Maybe scrounge a bottle or two. But they'd want to hear about the accident. They were bound to know by now. It'd have worked its way out from Joe and from Tommy's family.

Instead he pulled up his hood and cut through Waterford Street putting the three-storey shop buildings between him and the park across the road, then surfaced onto the Falls Road at Clonnard. He trudged down the road's slight decline, towards the city, still not knowing where he wanted to go. A gust of wind swept up a blue plastic bag and rolled an empty Harp lager tin towards him. He sidestepped the low-flying bag and kicked the tin off the footpath and into the road. A passing private taxi ran over it. The dull crimp resonated in the still night and Liam shuddered as unwelcome thoughts of Tommy Four-Eyes squished flatter than the tin swamped him. His stomach churned and his mouth watered but he swallowed hard and moved on.

He stopped at the Falls Road Library. As usual, it featured the wino-of-the-week seeking shelter from Mother Nature in the enclave doorway of the red sandstone porch. The scraggly tramp sat in cross-legged meditation, his head bowed and drool strings clinging to his stubble-coated chin. His rolled sleeping bag lay beside him, forgotten in drunken blackout or awaiting more urgent need in the wee small hours of the night when the ancient and mystery-stained woollen coat's protection wouldn't be enough. Under the brown ceiling of his wrinkled and weather-beaten face, two bottles of Mundies fortified wine stood to attention. One had given up half of its contents, the other looked full. As Liam got closer he could see the seal hadn't been broken on the second bottle's tin screw-top.

Liam reckoned he'd be doing the dipso a favour by taking the unopened bottle. He eased himself up the concrete steps leading to the doorway, paying care not to scuff the soles of his trainers and wake Sleeping Brutal. Holding his breath, he bent at the waist and gently wrapped his hand around the neck of the full bottle. The wino stirred. Liam paused, heart thudding. He felt his chest tighten as his lungs craved air. The wino's shoulders slumped slightly and his hunched back rose and fell in a slow steady rhythm. Liam lifted the bottle and hugged it to his fluttering chest. A little braver, he took a deep breath and sighed it back out. The wino snorted.

"Whaffuck?" He sat bolt upright and squinted at Liam. "Fuckaya doon?"

"Sorry, mate. I was going to leave you some money for it." Liam shoved a hand in his pocket, making a show of hunting for the money he had no intention of parting with.

"That's my fucking bottle you hood bastard." The wino's gravelly voice gurgled through a mucus-filled throat. He hacked and spat a big green gob. It landed by Liam's trainer.

Liam glared at the gelatinous bubble of phlegm, framed by the hem of his drawn up hood, as the wino struggled to his feet. Blood roared in his ears. "You dirty fucker. Were you trying to spit at me?"

"My fucking bottle. I'm going to kick your hole."

"Did you just spit your manky, rotten slabber at my Nike Airs?"

The wino wobbled and tottered like a zombie Pinocchio, but managed to stay on his feet. He stumbled into his half-drank bottle of Mundies and it bounced forward. The thick green glass hit the concrete hard but didn't shatter. The wino recoiled at the sudden clunk and tripped over his drink-heavy feet. His head hit the sandstone behind him with a sledgehammer thump. He didn't seem to register any pain from the fall. With determination cut into his leathery brow, he jerked his legs back in an attempt to get them under him again.

Liam's internal temper thermometer threatened to spew boiling mercury. Kids like Tommy died every day, but guys like this lived on. He stepped over the wino's spittle and scooped up the second wine bottle. His fists clenched around the neck of each bottle, held at his hips like a gunslinger's revolvers.

The wino almost made it to his feet, but then flopped back onto his ass again. He looked up at Liam with hatred in his squinty eyes. "Give me my drink, dickhead."

"Oh you want it?" Liam raised the half-empty bottle in his right hand. "No problem, mate."

Liam swung the bottle from his shoulder to his waist and slammed it into the wino's forehead. The wino's eyes widened slightly and his lower jaw flapped loose. Liam went at him with a slow-motion Lambeg drum roll. Right, left, right, left, buppa-buppa-buppa-buppa-boom. Half aware he'd lost control, he stepped back and placed the full wine bottle on the ground. Then he twisted the cap off the half-empty one and sloshed the remains over the beaten and bloody tramp at his feet. He pulled a fake Zippo lighter from his pocket and snapped it lit. Against all of Hollywood's conventions, the wino didn't burst into a fiery mass when Liam dropped the naked flame on the drink-soaked woollen coat. The lighter puffed out on contact.

Liam turned his back on a passing car and saw the sleeping bag. The car disappeared up the road and he lit two cigarettes with his retrieved lighter in shaky hands. He stuffed them into either end of the roll and tucked it under the unconscious, dead or dying man. Liam's knees wobbled as the smell of burning synthetic wafted up. *What the fuck are you doing?* He thought. He stumbled backwards, and half-turned to run. The wino moaned and Liam froze. He looked at the bloody mess with a sleeping bag billowing black smoke tucked under his knees.

Blood dribbled over the wino's unshaven chin. "Drink."

Liam looked at the full bottle he'd set down before trying to douse and burn the tramp. Blood-matted hair clung to the side. He fought the urge to puke. "Oh, fuck, mister. I'm sorry."

"Drink."

Other cars passed, paying no attention to the scene. The shadows thrown by the deep-set doorway hid the beaten tramp's face. A hooded figure at midnight served as part of the furniture in Liam's part of the world. Don't bother what doesn't bother you. He kept his hood up and his back to the road.

"Please. Drink," the wino said.

Liam understood. "Okay. That's how sorry I am. I'll give you more drink."

Crying, Liam fell to his knees and lifted the gory bottle. He twisted off the lid and tilted the bottle's lip towards the wino's mashed mouth. Wine and blood mixed. The tramp swallowed. Liam sniffed back watery snot and rubbed his eyes. Pillars of black smoke thickened and rose into the night sky. Growing tongues of flame licked at the air. Liam poured the wine until the fumes from the burning sleeping bag spun his head. The wino sighed and Liam retreated, glassy weapons in hand and fat tears rolling off his face.

The battered drunk showed no pain as the sleeping bag puffed alight. His woollen coat caught seconds later. He closed his eyes; passed out from smoke inhalation or shock. The dipso was fucked. Then Liam couldn't see him. Blurred vision and acrid smoke mercifully combined to filter his revulsion at what he'd just done.

"What the fuck am I going to do?" he asked the night.

A gust of wind tumbled up the road. It gently ushered him. *Move on.*

166

Chapter 11

Louise grabbed Joe's bony shoulder and shook him awake. He groaned and gently pushed her arm away. She whipped his duvet off and dumped it on the sock-littered carpet, exposing her stripped-to-the-boxers son to the fresh air pouring through the open window.

"Joe, it's past one in the afternoon. Get up."

"I'm freezing." He turned his back on her and curled into the foetal position.

"Would you not take a minute to put on a pair of pyjamas before you go to bed?"

"They don't fit."

She took in his knobbly spine and how his skin stretched over his shoulder blades. He'd shot up too quickly for his puppy-fat to keep up. She'd have to cook steak for dinner more often.

"Come on, you big string of piss. I've got sausages and soda farls downstairs. Hop in the shower and I'll get the frying pan out."

Joe unrolled himself and looked at her through one half-open eye. "Sweet. I'll be down in a minute."

"Yeah, I thought that'd get you moving."

Downstairs, the oil had only started popping in the pan when Joe tramped in wearing his navy bathrobe and dripping water over the linoleum. Louise shook her head and smiled.

"Will it be long?" he asked.

"No. Stick the kettle on for me and go watch some TV. I'll bring it out to you."

Joe hummed as he filled the kettle and plugged it in. Louise watched him swagger the short distance to the living room, lost in his own internal soundtrack. She wondered if Dermot had actually done something useful for once and cheered Joe up. It'd take a lot longer to win her over, or even earn a smidgen of her respect, but she had to admit, Dermot had impressed her. She'd let the meetings continue but hoped he wouldn't lose interest in the fatherhood thing and disappear in a few weeks.

She piled eight sausages and two whole sodas on Joe's plate and buttered some toast for herself. In the living room she watched Joe smother his sausages in tomato ketchup and shove them between the halved sodas. With each bite, a dollop of sauce plopped onto the plate on his lap. He purred like a cat as he chewed.

"Enjoying that, son?"

He nodded and tore another chunk off his sandwich. A thin line of ketchup ran down his chin and he wiped it away with the heel of his palm.

She waited until he'd cleared his plate before making conversation. She didn't need to wait long.

"So, you had fun last night?"

Joe nodded. "Yeah, it was class."

"What'd you do?"

Joe sipped at his tea before answering. "Drove around a bit. Had a chat. Nothing much." He hid behind the red and blue Spider-Man mug again.

Louise guessed there was more to it than that, but she didn't press him. He deserved to blow off a little steam. "So, how do you feel about Tommy?"

Joe's face reddened and he put his cup on the arm of the chair. "I feel a bit guilty about it this morning."

"Why?"

"I sort of stopped hanging about with him and a few of my other mates and I keep thinking I should have been there to look out for him. Like maybe it wouldn't have happened if I'd been with him."

"Well, Joe, sweetheart, I think your time is up when it's up. Even if you were there it probably wouldn't have made a difference."

Joe bit his thumbnail and looked thoughtful for a few seconds. "Yeah, you're probably right."

"And anyway, I heard something earlier that's made me thank God you weren't with him."

Joe's eyebrows met above his nose and he tilted his head back a little. "What did you hear?"

"Stephen phoned me after listening to the morning news on Radio Ulster. Tommy was running away from a peeler when he got knocked down. He'd been with a gang of kids who'd just robbed some guy on Fountain Street and got spotted in the act. They're saying that The Wee Rocket gang is expanding, or at least working further from home."

"Who's saying?"

Louise shrugged. "The news people, I suppose. Did you know he was in that gang?"

"I don't want to talk about it anymore."

"Oh, right. I understand. But if you have anything on your mind or you have any questions about life and all that stuff, you know you can talk to me, don't you?"

"Aye."

"And Stephen says he'd be happy to talk to you too; if you want a man's opinion, like."

"I've got my da to talk to now. Why would I ask McVeigh for anything?"

"He just wants to let you know he's there for you."

"Dead on."

"No really, he seemed genuinely interested. He's taken a shine to you, I think. Maybe you remind him of himself when he was younger."

"Tell him thanks, but no thanks."

"There's no need to be like that, Joe."

"Whatever." He lifted the Sky TV remote, flipped on the digital listings and glared at the TV screen.

Louise reminded herself that he'd been through a lot in the last few days. "Okay, son. Sorry for pushing it."

Joe glanced away from the screen for a second and shot her a quick half-smile. "Thanks."

"So what are you going to do today?" she asked.

"Ach, not much. Meeting my da at seven."

"Oh, really? He's very keen."

"Yeah, I guess."

Although suspicious of Dermot's sudden interest she decided to let things lie. She was actually a bit relieved that Joe would be out by seven. It meant she could go see Stephen's match without bringing up the topic and upsetting him again.

Dermot shoved the old warped door shut behind him, muffling the jackhammer clatter from the roadworks outside. He slid the deadbolt in place automatically. Upstairs, he found Emily sitting on the bed base, flicking through a newspaper as she chewed on a red ballpoint pen. He hung his jacket over the corner of the door. The squat seemed a little tidier and the air smelt faintly of potpourri.

"When did you learn how to read?" he asked.

"Fuck off, darling." She pulled the pen out of her mouth and drew a circle on the page.

Dermot sat beside her and glanced at the paper. "The Property Finder?"

"I need to get out of here, Dermot. This place is depressing the shit out of me."

Dermot pointed to the ad she'd just circled. "I'm not going to live in East Belfast, love."

"Why not?"

"It's a cultural thing. A Brit chick like you wouldn't understand."

She rolled her eyes. "Well you take a look through the ones I've circled and cross out the dodgy areas. I'm just marking all the two bedroom apartments going for five to eight hundred a month."

"Fuck, rent's gone up here in the last few years."

"It's still dirt cheap compared to Hackney."

"Did you just defend Belfast, Emily? I thought you hated this place."

"I'm looking on the bright side." Her voice had a slight edge of reproach to it.

"Good for you."

"So are you going to help me or what?"

Dermot checked his watch. "I'm meeting Joe soon. He's going to cut his teeth on the footballer's house tonight. Remember?"

"Fine." The edge softened a little. "Did you go see the fence then?"

"Aye. Everything's okay there. He's still in the trade and happy to take a look at whatever I come across."

"Including motors?"

"No, but he gave me the number of another guy."

"Go and make some money then. We'll need a deposit and a month's rent. If we're not out of here by the end of the week, I'll cut your fucking balls off."

Dermot left her to her bad mood. The prospect of a good old-fashioned burglary lifted his spirits. He had a lot of talent for car theft, but he enjoyed house-breaking more. After all these years it still got his heart thudding in his chest when he opened another person's cupboards, drawers and wardrobes in search of valuables.

To save time and hassle, he flagged a private taxi and hopped out at The Beehive, the Beechmount residents' unfriendly local. He arrived five minutes early, but not before Joe. His gangly protégé loitered outside the video shop puffing on a fag. He spotted Dermot and raised his hand in a splay-fingered salute. Dermot nodded and crossed the street to meet him.

"What's the craic, Joe?"

"Same old. You not driving today?"

"A big strapping lad like McVeigh would hardly drive to the Boucher Road from here. I figured we'd just take his car if we needed to move fast."

"Seriously?" Joe hunched his shoulders and sniggered.

"What's so funny?"

"Wait until you see his motor."

"Is it one of those silly wee Fiats or something?"

"Not even. Come on, sure. I'll show you."

They took their time dandering up Locan Street, wary of attracting unwanted attention. As they approached McVeigh's house Joe sniggered again. He pointed up the street.

"It's the blue one. Well, it started off blue, I think."

Dermot glanced at the old Escort as they passed it. Then, without breaking stride, he checked out the front of McVeigh's house, scanning for an obvious weakness in security. No alarm, but he had a brand new PVC door and double-glazed windows. The brass door handle had a decent lock, unlike the weak night-latches he was used to. They'd have to check out the backdoor. After soaking up the details from his initial sweep he led Joe to the right and onto Ballymurphy Street. He pulled two fags from a fresh twenty-deck and handed one to Joe. Father and son stood facing each other and nattering through a cloud of smoke. Nothing suspicious about that.

"He drives that piece of shit?" Dermot asked. "Are you serious?"

"Yeah, I think he bought it off aul Mackers."

"Mackers! So that ancient bastard is still flogging clunkers to idiots. Thought he'd be dead by now. Must drop by and say hello to him."

"Well, he's still in the same house. Me and my mates tried to buy a runabout off him last year, just for a wee tear. He told us to fuck off."

"Well, I'll teach you how to get by without him. Next time we go driving I'll let you hotwire it." Dermot flicked his half-smoked fag onto the road. "Right, time to get down to business. We're going in the back."

Joe nodded and dragged back the unlocked security gate at the mouth of the alley separating the houses on Locan Street and Beechmount Street. A knackered pram and a couple of rusting bikes lay in a tangled jumble close to the gate, waiting for the council to come and dispose of them. Crisp packets and plastic Fruit Shoot bottles cluttered the uneven cement path. A dog squatted at the far end and left a steaming coil for some kid to run through.

McVeigh's numbered wheelie-bin stood sentry outside his backyard gate. Dermot smiled at the fact that the gate was one of the old wooden ones. It'd pop right off its hinges without too much fuss. After a quick check up and down the alley, and a cursory glance at the small number of windows they could be spotted from, he threw his shoulder into the gate. It juddered back on its creaking hinges and Dermot almost toppled over. The big eejit hadn't locked the deadbolt. He shook his head and slipped into the yard. Joe followed close behind him.

The yard was the cleanest Dermot had ever seen. No moss on the ground or bird shit on the windowsills. Two patio plants in terracotta pots sat in the middle of the yard to make the most of the sun's daily path. And with not one beer tin ring-pull or cigarette butt to be found, it looked like the sad bastard actually hoovered outside.

He tried the backdoor. Unlike the gate, McVeigh had locked it.

"So what now?" Joe asked.

"You any good at climbing?"

"Don't know."

"Well, with those long arms and legs you'll take to it like a duck to water."

Dermot visualised a path from the yard to an open window on the first floor. The bubbled glass marked it as the bathroom. The house had been a standard two-up-two-down, but like most of the houses in Beechmount, it had a backyard extension to accommodate a modern kitchen and an indoor toilet. This particular extension had a Legoland look to it. The bathroom sat on top of the longer ground floor extension. The staggered, flat roofs looked like a couple of steps. They'd be as easy to climb.

###

Stephen stood in front of the referee, palms to the sky and shoulders raised. His baggy green, white and yellow jersey flapped in the wind. Between them, lying at their feet, the St John's centre-forward lay curled up and moaning.

"I was going for the ball," Stephen said. "The wee man must be into amateur dramatics."

The ref looked to the umpire on the sideline who shrugged. He hadn't seen it.

"Told you, ref. I didn't do nothing to him."

"McVeigh, I know you're a dirty bastard. I'll catch you next time."

"Ah, ref. That's uncalled for." He winked at the balding, self-important prick.

St John's made their substitution and the fresh meat jogged onto the pitch with a look of terror on his face. A young player Stephen hadn't seen in the blue and white strip before. It was probably his first season on the senior team. Stephen checked the time. Five minutes left. He'd leave this one alone. There wasn't enough time for him to make a difference. St John's trailed by three goals and a point.

The huge score difference meant there'd been no real need to take out their starting forward, but Stephen couldn't pass up the opportunity to get in a sly dig. Sometimes personal vendettas took precedence over necessity. Marty McShane had made him look bad in a friendly match last season. Cheeky fucker had run rings around him for the whole seventy minutes and when Stephen went to shake his hand at the final whistle, Marty blanked him. Stephen hated that kind of bad sportsmanship. He'd given nothing away when they met again. Every time Marty took possession, Stephen came in hard and fast. In the final ten minutes the ref hadn't caught up with the ball on the break and it fell into Marty's hands. Stephen didn't waste his chance. Marty charged for the goal, mind set on salvaging a little pride. Stephen loomed just outside the box, about ten yards from the oncoming forward. He spat over his own shoulder for dramatic effect then sprinted head on at Marty and stuck a knee in his groin as they collided.

Sweet revenge.

They played a little extra injury time and Davitts conceded a few points, but St John's had done too little too late. Stephen shook hands with the fresh centre-forward and jogged towards the changing rooms. He caught sight of Louise on the sideline and gave her a little wave. She stuck her fag in her mouth and waved back, then pointed towards the car park. He nodded to signal he'd meet her there after his shower.

Nobody mentioned his dirty tackle in the changing room; communal showers being no place for easy innuendo. After drying off and dressing, he went to the car park with Wee Paul. Louise smiled at both of them as they approached. Stephen enjoyed the sight of her in her bright pink vest top and light blue jeans. There wasn't even a hint of flour on her summery ensemble.

"Hiya, boys."

Wee Paul clacked his tongue and winked at her. Louise giggled at his semi-fake leer.

"Paul says he'll give us a lift up the road, Louise."

"Ach sure, it's a nice night. Why don't we dander back to yours?"

"He just got a new motor. Let him show it off."

"Really? Where is it, Paul?"

"It's the red Clio over there." Paul pointed to his girly city-car, huddled in the corner of the car park.

"Oh. My. God! That's gorgeous."

Stephen nudged Wee Paul's ribs with his elbow. "Told you, mate."

"Told him what?" Louise asked.

"I gave him a lift down here. He told me that it's a woman's car."

Louise raised an eyebrow and pouted. Stephen wanted to plant a big sloppy one on that sexy mouth; ashtray breath be damned.

"What?" he said. "Don't tell me you think that's a pimp-wagon."

"And what do you drive, Captain Caveman?" she asked.

"That's a fair point. Paul, lead us to the fanny magnet."

Louise shook her head, but couldn't fight off the smile tugging at the corners of her mouth. On the way to the car, Stephen felt a teensy bit guilty about his remarks. Wee Paul wore a slight blush, though he hadn't sniped back. Not yet. Then the car's interior smothered Stephen's guilt again. He couldn't hold his tongue.

Before he buckled up, he turned to face Louise in the backseat. "Why do you think Paul decided to go with black seat covers with little red love-hearts instead of pink?"

Louise looked out her window. "Don't be ignorant, Stephen. The car is red. Red and pink clash."

Stephen sniggered then clapped Wee Paul's tense shoulder. "Only slagging, mate."

"I know." But he didn't turn to look at his passenger.

"Then smile."

Wee Paul drew his lips back from his clenched teeth.

"It's a lovely car, Paul," Louise said.

Stephen couldn't resist. He pointed at the rear view mirror. "The Betty Boop air freshener is a bit much though."

Wee Paul sank the toe and the Clio skittered forward with a tyre-spinning squeal. Stephen opened his mouth to comment on the reckless manoeuvre but Wee Paul cranked the stereo to drown him out. ABBA's upbeat *Mama Mia* bass line blasted from the speakers. Even Wee Paul couldn't help grinning.

"Fucking Sinead!" He ejected the CD and frisbeed it out the window. "We've had this car two days and she's already taken it over. May as well hang my balls on the mirror instead of those furry dice she's after." Although he laughed, he made it sound like a joke with a jag.

"Will she not be pissed that you threw out her CD?" Louise asked.

"Ach, she's got millions of them. And not one of them is in its box. She'll not even realise."

Stephen fiddled with the stereo. DAB digital. A bit flash, but fun to play with. He found a classic heavy metal station and nodded. *Welcome to the Jungle*. Wee Paul tapped his thumb on the steering wheel in time with the snare drum. Stephen heard Louise sigh softly in the back, but he didn't risk asking her if she wanted to pick the music.

They pulled up to his house halfway through an Iron Maiden track. The chorus was cut short as Wee Paul killed the engine.

"Mate," Wee Paul said. "Your front door's open. I could swear I saw you slam it shut."

Stephen leant forward to look past his teammate. "Fuck. Come in with me. The fuckers might still be in there." He twisted in his seat to face Louise. "Wait there until we check this out."

Worry creased her face as she nodded.

Stephen took a deep breath to steady his nerves. Before his brain could make a coward out of him he hopped out of the car and charged into his house. In the living room he stood statue still, straining his ears to detect the intruder's position. Nothing. Wee Paul came in and stood beside him.

"TV's still here, mate," Wee Paul said.

"Shush, will you?"

Wee Paul huffed air through his lips but held his tongue. Stephen listened for another few seconds.

"You check upstairs," Stephen said. "I'm going to the kitchen."

"What? Why don't we stick together?"

"Because I want to be down here if someone bolts down the stairs."

"Aye, after they've stabbed me? Dead on. You go upstairs and I'll follow you."

"Fine. You fucking pussy."

Stephen clumped up the stairs, deliberately trying to warn any would be attackers that he was on his way. He couldn't get rid of Wee Paul's idea that an armed lunatic waited for them in his bedroom. Getting stabbed by a dirty wee hood had to be one of the worst deaths he could imagine. He went to the main bedroom with an idea to start at the farthest room from the front door and work his way back. Wee Paul stuck to his heels like a shadow. He eased the door open and stepped in with his knees slightly bent, ready to duck or pounce.

"There's nobody in here," Wee Paul said.

"Aye, thanks for that, mate. Just you keep me up to date."

The room seemed untouched. Bedclothes unruffled, the wardrobe and chest of drawers neatly shut, clock radio, TV and Xbox all present and accounted for. He checked the other bedroom and the bathroom. Nothing out of place.

"This is weird, mate. Why would someone break into your house and take nothing?"

Stephen shrugged. "Maybe they were looking for cash."

"Do you keep any in the house?"

"Just a few quid in the kitchen to pay the window cleaner and get milk. I use my Switch card for most things."

"Well, we may check the kitchen then."

Downstairs, all was in order. Even his jar of change on top of the fridge had been left alone.

"Are you sure I closed that front door properly?" Stephen asked.

"One hundred percent. I thought you were going to pull it through the frame, in fact."

"This is fucking weird."

He unlocked the backdoor and stepped into the yard. His gate sat open and the guttering from his kitchen extension lay on the ground by the wall. It looked like it'd been used as a handhold by an amateur scumbag. Squinting against the setting sun, he traced an alternative route into his home and tightened his lips. Somebody really had broken in. He hadn't noticed at first glance, but his bathroom window was opened much wider than usual. But why hadn't they taken anything?

"Stephen," Wee Paul peeped his head around the doorframe. "Come on back in and look at this."

He followed Wee Paul to the living room. Now that his adrenaline blinkers had faded he noticed it before his friend pointed it out. His mystery visitor had drawn a crude pair of breasts on his Bruce Lee picture. And across his stomach they'd scrawled one word.

"FRUIT!"

Paul only allowed himself to smirk after he'd parked the Clio outside his own house. After all the shit McVeigh had given him, he didn't even feel one bit guilty about it. He'd left the big man trembling with rage in his living room, glare fixed on his defaced icon. After he explained the situation to Louise and advised her to give McVeigh some time to cool down, he took his own advice and sloped off.

Wee Owen waved out at him through the window. He gave his son the thumbs up and climbed out of the car. Sinead half-smiled up at him from the sofa as he dropped his kit bag at the bottom of the stairs.

"There's tea in the pot if you want one, babe," she said.

"Thanks. I quite fancy a coffee though."

"Suit yourself."

He hesitated for a second, but she made no indication that she intended to get up and make him one. He rolled his eyes and went to the kitchen. On the countertop he found a plastic bag from *Wheels R Us*, the car accessory shop. He poked inside and found a large Playgirl Bunny decal. It looked as if it would fill a large portion of the Clio's rear window. Paul forgot about his coffee.

"Sinead?"

"Yeah, babe?"

"What the fuck is this?"

"Paul! Watch your language. Owen's..."

"Get in here."

"Who the fuck do you think you...?"

"*Get in here, now!*"

The sofa springs creaked as Sinead dragged herself off the cushion. She trudged slowly into the kitchen, as if on her way to the gallows. Paul flexed the muscles in his jaw, all the more wound up that she seemed to possess no ability to rush. He wanted to charge and shake her until the teeth rattled in her head.

"What's wrong?" Her meek voice cracked and sprang up an octave.

"This." Paul held the plastic bag in front of him at arms length.

"What about it?"

"It's the last straw."

"But..."

"But nothing. You've hijacked that fucking car from me. Bad enough that I bought the model you were wetting yourself over, now you're going to tart it up to make it look like even more of a

181

girl's car? I can barely sit in it without taking a reddener as it is. But this bunny sticker? Fuck! Do you want to just stick a pair of tits on me now? Call me Paula?"

"Paul, you're acting like…"

"Shut up. Just shut up. Nothing you say right now is going to help."

Sinead's lower lip quivered. Her big brown eyes moistened and she sniffed, but she didn't speak. Paul took a deep breath.

"There are going to be some changes in this house, Sinead. Starting now." He dropped the plastic bag on the floor between them. "That's not going on the car. Get a refund, store credit or burn the fucking thing. But keep it away from *my* car."

Sinead nodded.

"I'm heading out for a few hours. You put Owen to bed, tidy the place up a bit and make me a sandwich to take to work tomorrow. It's time you started pulling your weight. And don't you dare yap about your sciatica. It never flares up in the club on Saturday night."

Sinead wiped her wrist across her wet cheeks. She nodded again, defeated before she realised they'd been fighting. Relief flushed through Paul's body. Too much had been left unsaid for too long. He knew what his family thought of his wife. It'd never been said out loud, but they picked their barbed questions with expertise. *Sinead looks tired this week. Have you her working too hard in that house? Does Wee Owen always ask you for his dinner before Sinead? Where's Sinead today? Cleaning the house? Oh, Sleeping? Well, I suppose Wee Owen is hard work, isn't he? I mean, look at you; you've lost more weight.* And it was all a polite way of saying, *Sinead's a lazy bitch.*

He checked his pockets for cash and keys then swept past his wife and straight out the front door. Wee Owen raked back the vertical blinds and waved at him through the window again. Paul gave him another thumbs up and gunned the engine. He'd get the child some sweets to make up for leaving without spending any time with him.

Without admitting to himself where he was headed, he took the Falls Road into the city. Belfast opened late on Thursday night. He could have gone to Castlecourt Shopping Centre for a browse and a bite to eat. He could have strolled up and down Royal Avenue and rated the window-shopping women on a scale of one to ten. He could have gone to an internet café and played online pool until closing time. But he didn't. Instead, he navigated the city's one-way traffic system and found himself trundling up Linenhall Street, evaluating the Lycra-skirted goods.

After his first pass he looped the loop down Ormeau Avenue, onto Bedford Street and back onto the meat market stretch via Clarence Street. On his second ogle he spotted a girl that stood out from her contemporaries. Long leather jacket. Wavy blonde hair. Arrogant chin tilt. She looked like Buffy the Vampire Slayer. Wee Danny sometimes watched it. The show was stupid, but the wee blonde had plenty going for her. He pulled up to Buffy-a-like's stretch of kerb before the big brain could overrule the little one. Cold sweat trickled from his armpits to his floating ribs as he wound down the window.

"Hiya… love."

"You looking for company, darling?" Her Cockney accent contradicted, yet highlighted, her American style.

"Um… what way…?"

"Do you want directions or a fuck?"

Paul blinked. "No… I'm looking for… um… you know?" He laughed at himself. She would hardly knock him back. "Look, I want a shag."

"That's the spirit. First time?"

"No. I mean, aye. Like…"

"Shall I just get into the car?"

"Yes, please."

"I'm not cheap."

"Okay. I have money."

"Good. So long as we both understand how this works, we'll both have a good night."

Paul held his breath as she slinked by the front of the car and slipped in the passenger side. The little car rocked slightly as she settled into her seat. She gave Paul a slow, sexy wink.

"Does your missus know you've got her car out?"

Chapter 12

Liam studied Tommy's dead face. It didn't freak him out. It didn't even look like Tommy. No glasses. Pale skin pulled taut across reconstructed cheekbones. Freckles disappeared by makeup. He stepped back from the white coffin after what seemed like a respectable viewing time. He didn't force tears. His poker face would be construed as a mask of shock by the people gathered at Tommy's wake. The hushed chatter in the lamp-lit living room continued through Liam's performance. Drug-numb from his replenished grass stash, he kept guilt and grief at bay.

By the sandwich-laden sideboard, the Fegan twins shook his hand in turn. Liam approved and offered each of them a half-smile and a sigh. It seemed grown up and suitably serious behaviour in the presence of the white coffin. Tommy's box glowed against the backdrop of drawn curtains. A dead kid in his parents' living room. What a fucked up tradition. Liam nodded towards the front door and the twins stepped out of the house with him and into the summer twilight. He'd had better Fridays.

"Did you hear about the dipso at the Falls Road Library?" Matt Fegan asked.

Liam shook his head. Maybe a little too quickly. Matt didn't seem to notice. He licked his lips and smiled.

"Burnt to a fucking crisp. Set himself on fire with a fag or something. Too drunk to wake up and put himself out."

Liam's skin burned in a hot wave of guilt and relief. *Just another dead dipso*, he told himself. If it was written off as an accident, then he could rest easy over the whole thing. The story kept him out of trouble at least. And maybe in time he'd forget the smell of the burning sleeping bag... He swallowed hard and grasped for a distraction.

"You shouldn't be talking about that." Liam said. "We're here to remember Tommy, not think about some aul wino. Who's got a fag?"

"I need something stronger to smoke," Eddie Fegan said. "Have you any grass on you?"

"Not here, mate. It'd be disrespectful."

"Oh, right. Matt, give Liam a fag."

The younger twin tilted a half-empty pack towards Liam.

"Cheers." Liam lit up and pulled smoke into his cottony mouth. "I'm dying of thirst. Could murder a tin of Fanta."

"Sure we'll dander to the shop," Matt said.

Liam knew the twins were more interested in questioning him than smoking his grass or joining him in a quest for Fanta. He also knew he'd have to tell his version of the Tommy Tragedy sooner or later. He decided to tackle it head on as they walked.

"Go ahead and ask me."

"About what?" Eddie asked.

"About the other day. About getting chased by that peeler. About Tommy getting splattered all over the road."

"I heard they found bits of him in the grounds of City Hall," Matt said. "That has to be about fifty yards from those traffic lights."

Liam tried not to laugh. "Don't be so fucking stupid. Where'd you hear that?"

The twin frowned. "Don't know. I just heard."

Liam imagined one of the Goth kids sitting about the green outside City Hall casually flicking Tommy's ear off his shoulder. Then he remembered the screaming girl at the traffic lights, the beads of Tommy's blood on her face, and it wasn't funny anymore.

"Well it's shite. Don't let me hear you say that again, all right?"

Matt gave Liam a hard stare but kept his mouth shut.

"So what did happen?" Eddie asked, shaking his head at his brother.

"Well, me and Tommy ran like fuck to keep the heat off you lot. I've never ran so fast in my life. And fair play to our Tommy, he matched me step for step. I thought we were going to make it. The cop was falling behind, the wee green man was lit up, we could have disappeared into the crowd and everything would have been sweet. But then Tommy had one of his asthma attacks."

"Did he tell you to leave him behind?"

"No, Eddie, but he was really fighting to breathe. He couldn't say shit."

"Poor wee bastard."

Liam nodded. "Aye. It was desperate. I did what I could for him. The lights had changed and the traffic was picking up speed, but going full tilt I'd have made it. No sweat. I couldn't leave Tommy to get scooped though. I grabbed his arm and tried to give him an extra boost across the road. Tommy nodded like he was telling me we could make it."

Their saunter up Beechmount Avenue slowed to a halt within spitting distance of the shop. Liam flicked his fag butt onto the bonnet of a parked car. He took a deep breath.

"Then what?" Matt asked. The sick fucker wanted all the gory details.

"We stumbled on the last lane. I might have tripped over Tommy's feet or he might have got caught up in mine. Either way, we only stayed upright by clinging on to each other. Then I was falling towards the footpath. Almost took out a bunch of Spanish tourists. I heard something skidding. Then a thick, wet thumping sound. That's when the screaming started."

Matt leaned forward, wide-eyed and barely breathing. Eddie fidgeted, pulling at the short sleeves of his striped T-shirt and shifting his weight from foot to foot. He chewed on the inside of his pale cheeks. Liam inwardly congratulated himself on a job well done. His carefully planned version came out sounding natural and weighed down by anguish. He just needed another joint to smother the pangs of guilt gathering strength in the pit of his stomach.

"But..." Eddie paused, scrunched up his face and tried again. "But if the two of you were clinging on to each other how come Tommy didn't land on the footpath with you?"

Liam dropped the corners of his mouth and pushed out his lower lip. He looked Eddie right in the eye. "Don't you see, mate? Tommy pushed me. The last thing our Tommy ever did was save my life. Now that's a fucking mate."

Matt whistled long and low in appreciation. Eddie shook his head slowly. They'd bought it. Every last bit of it. Liam looked away from them, like he needed a minute to collect himself.

"I'll be back in a minute. That Fanta's not going to walk out to me."

The cover of the shop allowed him to drop his morose expression for a moment. A smile spread across his face as he lifted a can from the back of the cooler to make sure he got one of the coldest. After paying, he cracked open the tin in the shop and gulped down the first half. Heaven. Back outside he offered a swig to the twins. They both declined. Liam noticed something different in their manner. He figured they were in awe. A kid they grew up with had died to save their best mate. They had to respect that.

###

Joe rapped Wee Danny's door and enjoyed the solid thunk of knuckle on wood. The PVC doors, all the rage a few years ago, just didn't produce the same sound. Mister Gibson had been right to pass on the Housing Executive's offer. He'd taken the double-glazed windows but bought himself a solid pine front door with money from a whiplash claim. A little spyhole had been fitted into it. Danny couldn't reach it.

"Who is it?" Danny's snare drum voice travelled through the wood loud and clear.

"It's me, Joe. Let me in, would you?"

"Not by the hair on my wrinkled ball bag."

"Just open the door, dickhead."

The security chain rattled and the lock slid open. Danny opened the door a couple of inches and peeked out.

"You on your own, Joe?"

Joe shoved the door open, jolting Danny back a few steps.

"Yes, I'm on my own. Why are you acting like such a fruit?"

Danny spoke over his shoulder as he led Joe through the living room and into the kitchen at the back of the house. "I just can't be arsed with people. Everyone's telling me what I should be doing. I've been keeping a low profile until I get my head around the Tommy thing."

"Any luck with that?"

"Fuck, no. I still don't even believe it."

"I was just about to call around to his wake. Come with me. You'll believe it when you see him."

"Are you fucking nuts? Why would I want to do that? I didn't go to my granny's wake. I'm fucked if I'm going to Tommy's."

"You should say goodbye."

Wee Danny's chuckle sounded like a cancerous cough. "He's already gone, mate. We don't get to say goodbye."

"The funeral's not until Sunday. He'll be at his ma's until the hearse picks him up."

"That's not what I mean."

Joe opened the fridge and found a load of crappy vegetables. "Have you any biscuits or crisps?"

"No, my ma does the shopping on Saturdays."

"I bet there's wee bowls of crisps and plates of chocolate biscuits at Tommy's house."

Wee Danny ignored the observation. "I mean, do you see the point of wakes?"

"I don't see the point of loads of things, but that's life."

"What do you think Heaven's like?"

"It's probably shit. Like a Christmas mass. All that singing and rejoicing."

"Maybe it smells like incense. That'd be okay."

"It'd be better if it smelled like weed."

Wee Danny laughed a real laugh. "And you lay about on huge clouds of toke-smoke."

"And Pringles grew on trees."

"Hah, yeah. That'd be fucking sweet." Wee Danny unlocked the backdoor, beckoned for Joe to follow him into the yard and lit two fags. He passed one to Joe.

"Cheers, mate. I'll buy a pack later."

"No sweat." Wee Danny puffed a line of smoke rings and they floated off into the still air. "Do you think we'll go to Heaven?"

"Aye."

"Do you?"

"Kids don't go to Hell. We're, like, immune until we're eighteen."

"How do you know that?"

"It just makes sense. Why would God want to send a kid to Hell when there's plenty of murderers and kiddie fiddlers out there to keep the fire going? We're not altar boys, but we're not evil or anything."

"So you'd say Tommy definitely went to Heaven?"

"Of course. Sure he was the one that talked the Fegan twins out of taking knives out on our hunts. He'll probably get one of the nicest clouds for that."

Wee Danny nodded. "Yeah, you're right. He was the best of the lot of us, wasn't he?"

"He was a fucking saint."

They flicked their butts and had an unofficial minute's silence in honour of Tommy Four-Eyes. It ended with the blare of a car horn from a neighbouring street and the laughter of kids messing about. Joe thought he should get Danny out of the house, even if only for a trip to the shop.

"Come on and we'll go get some fags, mate."

Wee Danny pulled a twenty-pound note out of his pocket and waved it at Joe. "My ma gave me this yesterday to cheer me up. Know what we should do?"

"Tell me."

"Buy cigarettes, cider, chips and chocolate. Then we should find a nice spot to sit and fill ourselves up while we remember some more shit about Tommy. That'd kick the balls out of any fucking wake."

Joe's stomach rumbled agreement and they were on their way within the minute. Wee Danny seemed to be back to his old self as he gabbed on about the shite he'd been watching on TV all day. It seemed he wanted to save the Tommy-speak until he had a wee drop in him. Joe half-listened while his mind wandered. He kept getting flashback images of his da sniggering as he defaced McVeigh's Bruce Lee poster. They'd done little else after going to all that trouble to get in. His da had rooted about in a few drawers and took photos of some bills and letters with a real cracker of a digital camera. Joe didn't ask why. He just wanted to get out before McVeigh got home. Distracting his da with questions would have held them back.

"It'd be a good idea, wouldn't it, Joe?"

Wee Danny's direct question snapped Joe back into their conversation. "Aye, yeah. Good idea." He hadn't a clue about what he was agreeing with.

"Right, well, you phone Liam and I'll call the twins and they can pass it on to everyone else."

Shite. "Um… you go first." There was a chance he'd catch what he'd missed if he heard what Wee Danny had to say to the twins.

"Why?"

"Because… they're probably together anyway. No point in making two calls if one will do the same job."

Wee Danny shrugged and conceded. "Hiya, Eddie? Yeah, it's Danny. Me and Joe are just heading to the off licence. We thought it might be good to all get together and have a wee memorial night for Tommy."

Joe inwardly cursed himself. He wasn't in the mood for a big gathering. He should have paid attention to Wee Danny's prattling. And Liam hadn't been in touch since he phoned Joe and told him about Tommy's accident. Joe wanted to talk to him about how Tommy had died and why he thought it was his fault. He would have to keep his questions to himself until he got Liam alone.

"Aye. Yeah. No, like just have a bit of a session and tell stories about the guy. Aye. The whole gang. Liam with you? Well, see what he thinks." Wee Danny crossed his eyes and pulled faces for Joe's entertainment while he waited for Eddie to get back to him. "Yeah? Right. Okay. I'll ask him."

Joe flicked his head back. "What is it?"

"They just want to know where to meet. You pick."

"How about Clarendon Dock? Down by the Seacat?"

"What for?"

"For a change. It's dead chilled out down there."

"There's plenty of places around here. We don't need to go that far."

Joe tutted. None of his mates ever wanted to go any further than the Lower Falls. "We'll just go to Dunville Park then."

Wee Danny nodded and passed it on. They agreed to meet in an hour to allow enough time to get a hold of the rest of the gang.

"So let's get that chip then," Joe said, "before I eat you."

They tucked into their takeaway food in the bus shelter at the park gates. It seemed as good a spot as any. Black taxis and busses trundled by as the rush hour congestion thinned. Considering the mild weather, Dunville Park was pretty vacant. A couple of families lurked around the play area, but they'd more than likely be on their way within the hour. They'd have the whole place to themselves. All the better for relaxing. It only ever took a snide remark or even a dirty look from some nosy prick to turn things nasty. Combine the usual malarkey with a fucked up week like the Rockets just had and it was a recipe for disaster.

"What about your da then?" Wee Danny asked.

"What about him?"

"Has he been cool to you or what?"

Joe stalled for a few seconds, amazed by how much had gone on in just a few days. He hadn't even had time to tell Wee Danny about stealing the Honda or breaking into McVeigh's. "Ah, mate, if Tommy hadn't died, this might have been the best week of my life."

"Seriously? How come?"

He started with an in-depth description of Emily, a serious indication of his da's success, and went on to tell his best mate about the joyride and the burglary.

"And you never asked him why he was so interested in McVeigh's paperwork?"

"No." Joe Shrugged. "I'm sure I'll find out sooner or later."

Wee Danny shook his head. "And the teachers are always going on about your potential too. You've not got two brain cells to rub together."

"I'm too busy rubbing your ma's..."

"Hey," Wee Danny said. "Let the man who lives in a glass whore house throw the first stone."

"What the fuck's that mean?"

"It's a famous quote, you goon."

Joe creased his brow. "You're full of shit, wee lad."

"No, I'm full of useful information. That's how I've already figured out what your da is going to do with McVeigh's details."

"And are you going to tell me?"

"Identity theft."

"You what?"

Wee Danny rolled up the greasy paper bag he'd eaten his chips from and dropped it at his feet. He rubbed his hands dry on his jeans and burped. "Our Paul told me about it. He had to do a course on something called Data Protection before he was allowed anywhere near a phone. If somebody else gets a hold of a customer's address and bank account numbers or internet banking passwords they can start applying for loans and credit cards and all sorts. Then it's party time."

"And the customer pays all the bills?"

"Now you're getting it."

"Fuck, imagine how much debt they'd be in."

"You're not really focussing on the bigger picture."

"What's that?"

"Your da can buy you shitloads of stuff when the money starts pouring in."

Joe didn't share Wee Danny's single-minded enthusiasm. Stealing someone's DVD player from their house was one thing. Taking their identity? Fucking hardcore. He almost felt sorry for McVeigh. Almost.

"Here they come, Joe." Danny nodded towards the pedestrian crossing at the bottom of the Springfield Road.

Liam and the twins had made it first. They waited at the lights for the traffic to stop. It seemed that Tommy's fate had sent a blunt reminder of their mortality. Any other day they'd have stepped off the kerb and expected the cars to stop. Joe shot them a quick wave. Matt Fegan returned it with a lightning-fast salute. Nobody yelled insults. Joe didn't like that. The hype and banter was missing. They hadn't even gotten within speaking distance and already the awkwardness glared.

Together, the five of them trudged down the gentle slope to the benches at the bottom of the park. They sat and rustled blue plastic bags. Bottles of cider hissed as the lids spun off and plastic cigarette lighters crackled alight.

"So, are the rest coming?" Wee Danny asked.

Liam nodded.

"And are they bringing the craic?"

"I fucking hope so. You'd think someone died."

A couple of sniggers sounded among them. Joe hoped they could fan those sparks of laughter into something warmer.

Matt wiped cider foam from the corners of his mouth. "Mickey, the two Franks and Kevin were already knocking about together when I called them. Said they'd come and meet us after they'd been to see Tommy. Have you two been already?"

"Aye," Joe said. "My ma phoned me as soon as she heard he was home. Me and Danny were part of the first bunch. We didn't stay long. Felt a bit in the way." Joe glanced at Wee Danny. The wee fellah barely nodded, but his eyes thanked Joe.

"I know what you mean, big lad," Eddie said. "That kind of shite's for grown ups."

"I thought he was a bit old for a white coffin," Matt said. "Are they not for wee tiny kids, like?"

Joe shrugged. "It's probably just a matter of taste these days. Nothing really means anything anymore."

Liam made a noise somewhere between a sigh and a whistle. "Nothing means anything. That's so fucking true, mate. Nothing means anything. Anything means nothing. That's just rolling about in my head now. Fuck."

Joe, Wee Danny and the twins shared a puzzled look. Liam studied his bottle of Buckfast tonic wine. Joe hated that syrupy, medicine-tasting shite. The thought of drinking something a bunch of crusty old monks had stepped in turned his stomach. Liam didn't seem to mind. He gulped a quarter of the bottle in one go.

"Jesus, Liam," Eddie said, "take it easy or you'll be on your hoop. That stuff sends you loopy."

"I'm already loopy. The whole nothing-means-anything world is loopy. We're not even strapped in. Just wandering around on this merry-go-round like we're not going to fall off it some day and go hurtling towards the sun. Or a black hole. Fuck. Imagine that. Looping the loop in a black hole."

Joe clicked on. "He's smoked a shitload of grass, hasn't he?"

Matt and Eddie nodded.

"When? Was he stoned at the wake?"

"Not that I know of," Eddie said. "We duked down an alley and shared a spliff not long after leaving Tommy's house. Liam hogged it though. He'll probably whitey."

"Ach, for fuck's sake," Wee Danny said. "We'll get fuck all craic out of him tonight."

"I think he's entitled to it," Matt said. "He saw Tommy die."

"Oh." Wee Danny pulled his fags from the pouch on the front of his hoodie. He tossed one towards Liam, landing it on his lap. "Sorry, Liam. I never thought…"

Liam moved in slow motion. He picked up the fag, held it at eye level and smiled. Then he tucked it behind his ear. His face went slack for a moment, then he slapped his own jaw. "You got a smoke, Danny?"

Wee Danny tilted his head back and looked down his nose. "Are you fucking with me?"

Liam blinked slowly and smiled. "Yeah." He turned to the twins. "I could smoke either one of you under the table. Whitey? Me? Fuck off."

The mood lifted after that and before long the other four Rockets arrived. They brought a new energy with them and kicked off the stories about Tommy. The more the gang laughed the quicker they drank and the bottles emptied fast.

"Let's get more," Joe said.

"We could do that," Liam said, "or we could have some of this shit." He waggled a small cellophane baggie of grass at Joe. "Let's have a few joints in honour of our fallen comrade."

Most of the boys cheered. Joe didn't.

"That doesn't seem right to me, mate."

Liam squinted at Joe. "Why not?"

"Tommy wasn't a toker, Liam. He didn't even smoke fags."

"Fuck off."

"No, that's right," Danny said. "It would have fucked with his asthma."

Liam threw an irritated glance at Wee Danny then turned his attention back on Joe. "I don't remember him not smoking."

Joe had been avoiding Liam's eyes all night. He'd thought it the best way to avoid an imagined accusation over Tommy's accident. Now Joe fastened on Liam's red-rimmed eyes and matched his cold stare. "He didn't make a big deal about it. I guess you never noticed."

"Never noticed? Me and Tommy Four-Eyes were best mates."

"Ach fuck off, would you? You used to torture the poor wee lad."

"It was only a bit of banter. He gave as good as he got."

"Whatever you say, Liam."

"Didn't he give up his own life to save me? If I was such a bully then why would he do that?"

"Is that why you phoned me crying your lamps out about how it was all your fault?"

Liam lifted his empty Buckfast bottle and threw it. Joe flopped to the side. The heavy glass bottle glanced off his upper arm. Wee Danny jumped up and went for Liam. The twins went to Liam's side, fists raised. Joe clambered to his feet and put a hand on Wee Danny's shoulder.

"It's all right, Danny. Leave it be."

"Fat fucking wanker. He needs another hiding. Teach him a bit of respect."

"Leave it, mate."

"That's right," Liam said. "You're not one of us anymore, you fucking dwarf. You neither, Joe. We've got on just fine without the pair of you. Better in fact."

"Just chill out, Liam. We're here to remember Tommy, not to fight."

"Really, Joe? Seems to me you forgot about us all pretty soon after you left the gang. One of us had to die before we got so much as a phone call."

The other four now stood behind Liam and the twins. Joe and Wee Danny were no longer one of them. They'd left the gang and lost their loyalty. Getting home in one piece became Joe's top priority. To do that he'd have to keep his simmering mate under control. He leant in to Wee Danny and asked him to be cool with a hurried whisper. Wee Danny nodded but maintained his aggressive stare.

"Okay, we've all had a bit to drink and a very fucked up day. I don't want this to get out of control. Me and Danny will just head on and leave you guys to it. Smoke your brains out. I shouldn't have said anything."

Liam, confident and cocky in his new position of command, smiled. "Aye, you should have kept your gob shut. We were happy to have a drink with you for old time's sake, but you had to fuck that up. Bounce. And take your wee boyfriend with you."

Joe wrapped his arms around Wee Danny and strained to hold him back. The wee pit bull was stronger than he looked.

"Come on, Danny, relax. We can't win this."

"Maybe not." Wee Danny spat the words through bared teeth. "But I can get a few digs into that fat cunt before I go down."

"Leave it, mate. We'll get our chance another day, okay?"

Wee Danny relaxed and Joe loosened his iron grip. "Fuck these wankers. We can drink at my place, Joe."

The long walk to the park gates was made longer by the jeers of the Rockets.

###

Danny felt his skin turn red every time he thought about Liam Greene. The fat fucker had turned on him and Joe faster than a starved dog. Humiliated them. It'd be a long time before he forgot about that. But if nothing else, his anger at Liam had taken his mind off Tommy Murray. Until his ma started yapping on about the funeral.

"You'll have to borrow a tie off our Paul, son."

"Sure I've got my school tie."

"Catch yourself on, wee lad. You're not showing me up at this funeral with your raggedy Corpus Christi tie. Get over to Paul's house now and find out if he has a spare one. And make sure it's black."

Danny was too familiar with that tetchy tone of voice and he wasn't stupid enough to protest any further. Muttering, he tugged his red Nike hoodie on and hit the street. Drizzly rain instantly coated his face. Typical Irish summer. Scorching sun for a couple of days then the clouds opened up for twice as long. It was a nuisance. Sheltered drinking haunts were far harder to come by. He lit a fag and cupped his hand around it to keep it dry.

Paul lived just two streets away but Danny slowed his pace, giving himself time to enjoy the entire fag. He flicked the butt before rapping on Paul's door. The bluish flicker of the TV danced on the living room blinds, drawn to cut out the glare on the screen. Nobody came to the door. Usually Wee Owen would be bouncing off it, half wetting himself to see who had come and what they'd brought for him. He tried the handle and the door swung open. The bass rumble of movie dialogue travelled into the hall.

"Paul?"

"I'm in here."

Danny realised he'd been holding his breath. He let out a lungful of air. In the living room, Paul sat in his pyjamas watching a black and white film on one of the free movie channels. Beer tins littered the floor around his feet. The room smelt of Chinese takeaway.

"You having a wee party in here or something?"

"Sort of." Paul glanced at the floor. "There might be a full tin amongst that lot if you want one."

"It's a bit early, Paul. Not even twelve. I only got out of bed half an hour ago."

"I thought you young ones were more hardcore than that."

"Have you not been to bed?"

"Nah, I had a wee doze here. I was getting caught up on some TV time now that I finally have the house to myself."

"Where's Sinead and the child?"

"Don't know, mate."

"What?"

"We had a fight on Thursday night. I stormed out. By the time I came back she'd packed a bag and gone."

"Fuck. Have you not tried calling her or anything?"

"Are you kidding me? I've been waiting for a break like this for ages. I'm not wasting the opportunity. I phoned in sick yesterday and I'm just going to take a wee holiday by myself until she decides to come home."

Danny couldn't believe Paul's attitude. The guy looked like he hadn't a care in the world. It was nice to see him that way. "Fair fucks to you, mate."

"Cheers. I have to admit though…"

"What?"

"I'm quite impressed with Sinead. I always thought she'd be too lazy to leave me."

Danny got a tie off Paul and promised not to tell their ma about Sinead. Before talking to his brother, he'd been wound up tighter than a spring. Joe talking him into giving up the gang, Tommy dying, Liam doing everything he could to push his buttons.

Everything had turned upside-down. But Paul had found a bright side to his wife and child leaving him. He could do the same.

At home, he held the tie over his head like an Indian warrior presenting a scalp to his chief. His ma nodded approval and went back to ruining lunch. He threw the tie over the banister for safekeeping and bounded up the stairs. His ma shouted after him, complaining about elephant herds and heavy feet, but Danny's buzzing mind had no room for hangover consideration. He'd gotten beyond anger and frustration and had found his silver lining. Now he needed to phone Joe.

"Yeah?"

"You sound like you're still in bed, you lanky string of piss."

"All right, Danny? What's the craic?"

"I've been thinking about last night."

"Ach, mate, just forget about it. Liam's a wanker, and if the rest of them want to lick his balls we're better off without them."

"Aye, I know."

"So why are you calling me at this time of the morning?"

"It's lunchtime, you lazy bastard. Get out of your scratcher."

"Just tell me what you want."

"I want to meet your da."

"What? Why?"

"Because he sounds like the kind of guy I'd like to work for."

Chapter 13

Nothing drew the crowds like a child's funeral. Even a scummy wee fourteen-year-old thug of a child.

Stephen didn't look out of place standing at the back of the chapel. The pews had been jam-packed when he'd arrived at St Paul's and now the aisles were filling up. His spot by the big wooden double-door gave him the best view of the mourners, both seated and arriving. He thought he'd be able to tell the Rockets from the nosy schoolmates. The palest, nerviest kids would top his list of suspects. Those with fascinated and darting eyes would be crossed off.

One of the first kids Stephen noticed sat close to the back. At every creak of the main door's hinges, his head swivelled on a thick neck spilling over a stiff white collar. Stephen remembered the cheeky fat fucker giving him lip the Saturday after poor wee Missus McKinney got mugged. Joe and Wee Danny Gibson had come along and saved the dickhead from a good punch in the head that day. He made a mental note to ask Joe about him.

According to Louise's text an hour ago, she'd be attending the funeral with Joe. He wasn't surprised that he couldn't spot her in the crowd. Running late came easy to her. She seemed to enjoy it. At this stage she'd be spending the service outside in the rain. She'd forget her umbrella too.

The people in front of him obscured his view of the white coffin at the top of the aisle and that was fine. He wasn't there to pay his respects. The little scumbag didn't deserve his sympathy, but Stephen couldn't help but feel bothered by the sight of a coffin that size. Whether or not the wee lad deserved it, he still found the scene depressing.

The organ accompanied the sullen choir and tears rolled. The priest's rumbling voice bounced around the chapel walls. Stephen fidgeted. He checked his watch at five minute intervals, bored now that he couldn't scope out prospective targets. He was eager for the service to end so he could get out into the air and get a good look at the guilty-faced kids. Especially any gravitating towards Joe's fat friend. He bowed his head respectfully and yawned into his hand. As soon as the queues to receive communion formed, he slipped out into the fresh air.

"Stephen!" Louise waved at him with more enthusiasm than the occasion called for. She didn't seem to notice the dirty look from the biddy beside her. Joe loomed to her right, dressed in new trousers that actually met his shoes. But even in the funeral-standard black tie and white shirt his hassled teenage face dashed his best chance at looking smart. He scratched at his head, obviously missing his baseball cap. Stephen plastered on a smile for Louise's benefit as he fantasised about shaking Joe until his teeth chattered.

"Hiya, Louise. Did you get held up?"

She smirked, "Yeah. What am I like? I'd be late for my own fu…" The sentence drifted off. She glanced at Joe then turned back to Stephen. "Anyway, it's a huge turnout, isn't it?"

"Aye. Must have been a popular kid."

Joe grunted.

Stephen ignored him. "What do you say we make our way up to the City Cemetery? It's hardly raining at all now and we'll be there before the hearse if we get a bit of a head start."

Louise scraped her fingers through her damp hair. "Aye, we might as well."

"Can I stop off at ours and get changed?" Joe asked. "This tie's choking me."

"No you can not. Catch a grip. Just wait until after Tommy's been buried."

The disapproving biddy cleared her throat. Stephen nodded to her but Louise focussed on Joe, waiting to shut down any argument he might make.

"Right, okay," Joe said.

On their way up the road, Stephen could feel Joe's eyes on the back of his head. The lanky teenager straggled behind to avoid conversation. Stephen reached out for Louise's hand just to wind the bastard up. She squeezed his fingers and smiled at him. His chest hitched a little. He gave her a wink and raised her knuckles to his lips and almost forgot about Joe.

Typically schizophrenic, the sun put on its happy face and chased away the rain. Stephen shrugged off his jacket and carried it over his shoulder but suppressed the urge to whistle. The three of them instinctively slowed their pace, making the most of the brief summery moment. The City Cemetery gate came into view, and much too soon they passed through it and found the freshly dug hole.

Louise nudged him. "Oh, there's Missus Morgan from the bakery. I'll have to go say hello or she'll take the hump with me. I'll be as quick as I can."

Stephen checked out her sway as she joined a bit of mutton in lamb's clothing for a chinwag. No time to waste, he turned to Joe.

"So this Tommy fellah was a mate of yours, then?"

Joe took a moment to compose a poker face. "Aye."

"He was a scumbag, though."

Joe's nostrils flared. His lips barely moved as he spoke. "I've met worse."

"I fucking bet you have."

Joe looked away. The muscles in his jaw flexed.

"In fact, I reckon you can help me, Joe. I'd like to meet a couple of these worse scumbags you know. Actually, I'd be interested in meeting a gang of them."

"Fuck off."

"You see, that's a normal answer in this situation, and I can respect that. But I don't have time to pussyfoot around you. So here's the deal. You give me the name of that fat kid I've seen you hanging about with right now, and I'll leave you alone. If you don't, I'm going to take you up here tonight and bury you beside the Murray kid. A grave this fresh will be a cinch to dig. Easy-fucking-peasy."

Stephen glanced over his shoulder to see Louise still deep in conversation with Missus Morgan. He felt happy with the way things were going. Then he saw Joe's face. The kid's smart mouth curved into a smirk.

"That's all you want? His name? Sure you could ask anybody on Beechmount that. Anybody that matters, like."

"I don't want it from *anybody*. I want it from you."

"And then we're quits?"

"For now."

"What about my ma?"

"She's a great shag."

Joe's smirk slipped for a second and Stephen relished it. But it returned, and seemed genuine. "Whatever. I've seen the way you look at her. You like her. As soon as I can, I'll make sure she dumps you."

"Like I give a fuck about that Millie cunt."

Joe glanced over Stephen's shoulder and raised his eyebrows. "Hiya, ma."

Stephen's stomach flip-flopped and he turned on his heel, already anticipating a slap from Louise. She still stood where he'd last seen her, smoking a fag with her workmate.

Joe chuckled.

By some miracle, Stephen reigned in a burst of white-hot rage and restrained himself from stomping Joe into the ground. He hissed through his teeth. "You little fucker. You'll regret that."

"Mate, quit talking like you're in a movie. Fucking relax, okay?" Joe patted his pockets and located his phone. "Have you got your mobile with you?"

"Why?"

"The sleeked fat fucker I used to chum about with is called Liam Greene. I'm going to give you his phone number."

Stephen could feel the onset of a migraine. "What for?"

"I'm sure it'll come in useful. And Wee Danny is going to love me when I tell him."

From behind, Stephen heard a hurried clip-clopping and took a deep breath. Blood pumped through his muscles, but he tried to relax them. Louise tapped his elbow.

"God, I thought she was never going to stop talking. Were you okay without...? Are you boys swapping numbers? Ach, that's brilliant."

Joe gave her a big, goofy grin. "Aye. Turns out we've more in common than we thought. Isn't that right, *Stevie?*"

A cold raindrop hit the back of Stephen's neck and he raised his eyes to the black clouds above. The heavens opened up and pelted down on them. Louise nodded towards the gate at the bottom of the cemetery's hill. The hearse crept up the path, window wipers swishing.

"Typical, eh?" Louise said. "The day was just starting to look up."

Dermot saw Joe and his friend before they saw him. As he approached the entrance to the Movie House cinema on the Dublin Road, the teenagers leant into each other, shielding a lighter's flame from the wind. It always amused him when kids befriended their physical polar opposites. The phenomenon tended to highlight the negative aesthetics, rather than the positive. Joe looked too tall and awkward and his little mate appeared malnourished and weak. They both looked like fish out of water.

"How's the lads?" Dermot bellowed his greeting to give them a start. It worked.

They turned as one, ready to face a threat. Joe blinked then laughed.

"Hiya, da."

"Fuck me, Mister Kelly. I near shit myself."

"Sorry, couldn't resist. Danny isn't it? Joe told me you wanted to meet me. Hope I haven't started off on the wrong foot."

"Ach, no. I can take a bit of banter."

"Good man yourself. How's you, Joe?"

"All right. Bit of a shitty day, like."

"Oh aye?"

"Yeah. It was Tommy's funeral today."

"Shite. You never said. I'd have come along."

"Sure you never knew the guy. No point you getting depressed about him. Anyway, I want to forget about it now. Figured if you hadn't been, we wouldn't have to bring it up."

"Say no more, Joe. So, Danny, what did you boys want to talk to me about? Joe was his usual cagey self on the phone earlier. Maybe you can enlighten me?"

Danny looked up and down the street. "There's an awful lot of people about here. Can we go somewhere?"

"There's a bowling alley not far from here. Not the most private place in the world, but the rumble and clatter makes it hard to listen in on someone's conversation."

"What do you think, Joe?" Danny asked.

"Sounds sweet. But I've never been bowling before."

"It's a piece of piss, son. Good enough craic too."

"Cool," Danny said. "Let's go."

Before Dermot had left for London, the Superbowl on Clarence Street had still been in its childhood. On entering it for the first time in over a decade he found that the years had not been kind to the entertainment complex. A pair of bouncers hovered by the door, their manner cold and no nonsense. Threadbare industrial carpet added little comfort to the hall. A wall of dated arcade machines flickered, flashed, wailed and blared. Kids cursed at them as they pumped pound coins into the hungry slots. A long-haired, bearded man propped himself up at the customer service desk with his back to the public. His interest had been hijacked by the rack of maroon and cream bowling shoes sorted by size. He dangled a small pair by the laces as he gave great thought as to which slot best suited them. The only notable change since Dermot's last visit was the lighting on the alleys. The uneven laminate-floored lanes glowed a hazy blue. The scoreboards proclaimed them modern glow-in-the-dark lanes. Dermot thought they looked like they'd been lit by bug zappers.

"This place is class," Danny said, without an ounce of sarcasm. "All futuristic and all."

"Yeah," Joe said. "Let's get started."

The bearded weirdo hooked them up with freshly deodorised, ill-fitting alley shoes and brought them to their lane. Dermot paid for Joe and Danny and offered to get them a drink from the bar.

"Just a Coke, please," Joe said.

"Want me to put a wee vodka in it?"

"Ah, yeah. That'd be cracking."

"Same for you, Danny?"

"Yes, please, Mister Kelly."

"Look, kid. If we're going to have a wee drink and a chat tonight, you'll have to stop calling me that. If you can't use my first name, call me mate or something. Mister Kelly makes me feel like your maths teacher."

"Okay... mate."

Dermot paid the extortionate price for a pint of beer in a plastic glass and two vodka and Cokes. He checked out the blue felt pool table on his way back to the lane. Two men in their twenties played for fun. He hoped he could find someone to challenge for drinks after the bowling. Either that or he was going home sober.

He sat the drinks on the little table beside the ball return. Joe gave him a fag.

"Thanks a million," Danny said.

"No worries." Dermot raised his plastic glass. "*Sláinte*, lads."

They slurped on their drinks and puffed on their fags.

Dermot tapped ash into a foil ashtray. "So, we're in relative privacy. What's the story?"

Danny did the talking. "Me and Joe had to abandon a profitable gig we had going when we got word of outside interest. We've been out of pocket since then. Joe tells me that you're the type of person who knows how to make a few quid. So we were wondering; do you have anything going at the minute that we could help you with?"

"You're asking me for a job?"

"Well, yeah. I'm too young to work in McDonalds and my ma doesn't give me fuck all. I need money for fags and cider."

Dermot admired the little squirt's ballsy attitude. He slipped into negotiation mode. "Well, if Joe's vouching for you, that's good enough for me. So consider this interview a success. Next we need to talk about terms and conditions."

"What do you mean?" Joe asked.

"He's talking money, mate," Danny said. "What do you think is fair, Dermot?"

"Well, most crews operate a profit sharing arrangement, usually based on individual experience and reputation. But you guys are still wet behind the ears, and a bit of a business risk. I think we'll need to go with a standard payment per job over a probationary period."

"How much and for how long?"

"You don't mess around, do you, Danny? Let's start with thirty quid a job for at least six weeks and see where we go after that."

"Thirty sounds a bit low, Dermot. How about fifty?"

"Thirty-five."

"Forty."

Dermot winked at the wee man. "You got it, mate. You drive a hard bargain." He paused for a few seconds to sip on his pint. "Of course, if I'm paying out eighty quid every time we do a job together, I'll have to make sure it's worth my while too. We can't afford to fanny about with stealing car radios or shoplifting, lads."

"We're up for anything," Danny said.

"I bet you are. Are you two free the night after tomorrow?"

They nodded in unison. Danny licked his lips, like a dog anticipating a juicy steak.

"Great stuff. I've just the thing to see what you two are made of. But for now, let's do some bowling, eh?"

Paul stretched out on the double bed, moaning with pleasure as his joints popped and cracked. You just couldn't beat a Monday morning lie in. He rolled over, determined to stay wrapped up warm and cosy until noon. He drifted towards unconsciousness then jolted when his mobile went off. Its factory preset ringtone chirped as it vibrated on the flatpack bedside cabinet. He snatched it up and pressed it to his ear.

"What is it?"

"Are you in bed?" Sinead's voice jabbed his eardrum.

"Aye. What do you want?"

"Well, isn't it well for you? Force your family out of the house so you can bunk work and sleep all day. And here's me minding our son all by myself."

"Aye, I'm sure your mother hasn't helped you one bit. I suppose you sat in the whole weekend, afraid to ask her to babysit her only grandchild. Dead on, babe. I feel for you. Now, what do you want?"

"God, you're so cold-hearted. I'm phoning to see if you want to sort things out. All of this can't be good for Wee Owen."

"You're talking as if I booted you out. You left of your own accord. So we'll talk when I get over the pain you caused me by walking out with my son." He yawned. "I reckon I'll be in the right emotional place to tackle this in about a week. Chat to you then, okay?" He disconnected the call and turned off the phone.

But the bitch was determined to keep him awake. His landline squawked for attention and burying his head under the pillow didn't help. He tramped down the stairs in T-shirt and boxers and whipped the phone's jack out of its socket. It was too little too late for now, but it'd be one less possible wake up call on Tuesday morning. He went to the living room and flopped onto the sofa. At least he could get back to his stack of unwatched DVDs.

After *Kung Fu Hustle* he zapped a microwave burger and chomped it down. He snacked on crisps during *Land of the Dead*. To lighten the mood he decided on an Adam Sandler flick. He vetoed *Big Daddy* and went for *Mister Deeds*. By the time those credits rolled it was almost dinnertime. He stood, stretched and purred like a fat tomcat. He'd lounged long enough. Time to groom.

He swayed gently in the shower as rivulets of steaming water encased his body. Nobody rapped the door, called for him to hurry up or ran the cold water tap in the kitchen. He practically slept on his feet. His mind flashed with images of his night with Buffy the Vampire Slayer. Classy ones. Black and white, like an artsy French soft-porn flick. Her white thighs and black leather coat. Black pouting lips and wavy white hair.

He needed to see her again.

Rather than throw some clothes on and speed down to Linenhall Street like every part of his being screamed at him to do, Paul forced himself to take his time and build the anticipation. In any case, he had no idea what time a prostitute started her workday at. It wasn't even a sure thing that she'd be working that night. But fuck it, he'd take the chance. He shaved, clipped his toenails, moisturised the bags under his eyes, doused himself in Calvin Klein aftershave and flossed his teeth. Dressed in his FCUK boxer shorts, Diesel jeans and Ben Sherman shirt, he felt smoother than a waxed James Bond. In fact, there was a good chance Buffy would fall in love with him and he'd sweep her off for an adventure, *True Romance* style. But at the very least, he'd have a cracking shag.

By seven o'clock, Paul sat in his reclaimed Renault Clio. He parked at the stretch of kerb he'd picked Buffy up from the previous Thursday. The engine idled and he listened to a biographical piece about Sinead O'Connor on BBC Radio Ulster. It lasted half an hour, and not much longer after it ended, the girl he'd waited to see strode around the corner. She moved with MTV attitude, energetic and placing each footstep to an internal rhythm. She snapped back her head to whip an errant blonde wave out of her face. Paul wondered how much it would cost for a striptease to Aerosmith's *Crazy*.

She spotted his car and went straight to the open driver side window.

"All right, darling?" She leant into the car and kissed his cheek. "You waiting on me?"

"Aye."

"Aw. Ain't you sweet?" Just like last time, Paul's heart went giddy-up as she crossed his path to get to the passenger door.

"Hiya," he said as she settled into her seat.

"There's something different in here."

"Oh, I changed the seat covers."

"Yes you did. And the plain black is a lot more masculine. I miss the Betty Boop air freshener though. I love that little slut."

Paul grinned at her. "I've had a bit of a clear out. Here and at home. It's been... refreshing."

"Good for you. What you going to do when she comes crawling back?"

"You don't miss much, do you?"

"I've seen it all, darling. I could write a book."

"They say everyone has a good book in them."

"Why haven't they written them then? I'll tell you why. Because they're full of shit. Wankers."

"I love your accent."

"Yeah, I get that a lot here. So what we going to do tonight?"

Paul cleared his throat and took a deep breath. "Do you want to go to the pictures?"

"You what?"

"You know… the cinema?"

"Yes, I know you meant the cinema. But I think you're a little confused. You don't have to take me out on a date. Did you forget how this works?"

"I've been watching movies on my own all day. I'd like to watch something new and then talk about it with somebody afterwards. I'll pay you your usual hourly rate. Then afterwards, maybe we can do what we did last time?"

Buffy studied his face, as if she expected him to burst into laughter. Her blue eyes stared right into his soul. He held her gaze, desperate for her to take him seriously. Finally she nodded.

"Sounds great to me, darling."

Paul rubbed his hands together before pulling out onto the road. "Fucking sweet."

He asked Buffy to pick the film and she went for a Wayans Brothers comedy. Something ridiculous about a midget posing as a baby. Chewing gum for the brain. They got a seat in the back row and snuggled into each other. Buffy threaded her arm into his and rested her head on his shoulder. Paul felt seventeen again. The opening credits rolled.

"This is probably going to be a piece of shit, you know?" Paul said, whispering into her ear.

"Yeah, I know. But I wasn't in the mood for anything too intellectual."

"Well, you struck gold with this one. I bet it's ninety minutes of fart and dick jokes."

"Do you want to leave?" It wasn't a snarky question. Her voice was sincere.

"Not at all. I'm here with a stunner like you. I'm happier than a pig in shite."

She sighed theatrically. "Shakespeare wouldn't be in it."

As predicted, the film pumped out vulgar jokes and an idiotic plot. Paul found himself enjoying it. Sitting with Buffy, he didn't feel the need to suppress the laughter that came naturally from time to time. He didn't fear her judgement. Occasionally, they glanced at each other and rolled their eyes. She didn't have a problem with the adolescent crudity the Wayans had built a franchise upon. No doubt, she'd encountered a lot worse.

The film reached its third act and Paul got a little fidgety. The jokes had been played out a little too long, and he knew exactly where the plot was going. He shifted in his seat for the millionth time. Buffy patted his thigh.

"All right, darling?"

"Aye. Just a wee bit bored."

She ran her hand up and down his thigh, inching closer to his crotch with every length. "Oh, yeah? Can't have you complaining of boredom on me customer survey. I'll have to do something to enhance your experience."

Paul pushed his hips forward as Buffy's hand brushed against his erection.

She bit his earlobe. "I think I know what you need."

Paul whimpered a little as she inched down his zip, popped his button and sank her hand into his jeans. She hooked her fingers into the waistband of his boxers and pulled it down. He sprang out of confinement. With a panicked side-to-side glance he determined that they were the only ones in the back row, reducing the odds of him being done for indecent exposure.

Buffy wrapped her hand around his shaft and worked her wrist with brain-swelling slowness. Paul tuned out the movie soundtrack, melted into his seat and closed his eyes; a Cheshire Cat grin spread from ear to ear.

Chapter 14

Liam ran his fingers along the rack of football tops. They swung back and forth on their hangers like a lazy wave. The feel of the shiny material sent a shiver down his spine. Celtic, Man United, Liverpool, Arsenal, Chelsea… all the top teams in every size. And only a few footsteps from the shop door.

"Can I help you, son?"

Liam shook his head, dismissing the man behind the till. "I'm just looking."

"Well, give me a shout if you can't find what you're after," the man said – though he meant, *I've got my eye on you.*

Liam shuffled about the shop for another minute, checking price tags and humming along to the radio, then left Lifestyle Sports empty-handed. The Fegan twins and the rest of the gang loitered about the car park of the Park Centre shopping complex. Situated on the Donegal Road, near the St James area of West Belfast, the complex was within walking distance of Beechmount. Or running distance, depending on your intentions. Liam had a new plan.

"What about you, lads?"

Eddie Fegan spoke for the rest of the gang. "Dead on, Liam. What's the craic here then?"

"I've another move planned. Did you bring me down that hoodie?"

Matt pulled a green and white striped sweater from a Tesco carrier bag and tossed it to Liam. He shrugged out of his Adidas tracksuit top and pulled the borrowed hoodie on over his T-shirt.

"Your cousin doesn't do subtle, does he?"

"He's a buck-mad Hoops fan," Matt said. "But sure, it's a disguise."

"So, what's the plan?" Ginger Mickey asked.

"Did you ever see that show, *Supermarket Sweep*?"

"Aye, our ma loves that shite," Eddie said. "You run around the shop throwing beans and biscuits and all that craic into your trolley until the time runs out. I could chin thon poof of a presenter. He does my head in."

"Well, I reckon we could have our own wee *Supermarket Sweep*. Except we'll call ours *Sports Shop Sweep*. Just follow my lead."

They fell in behind Liam and moved as one. He led them to the side door. Earlier, he'd scoped it out and noticed the pretty-boy security guard looked a bit softer than the skinhead Rottweiler-man they had on the front. They breezed past the useless bastard with their hoods drawn up and the guy acted like he hadn't even noticed them. Probably afraid he might get his hands dirty or his hair messed up. The gang stormed through the centre and the shoppers parted in front of them like scuttling pigeons on a city footpath. Liam savoured the feeling of power coursing through him. The general leading his army of bad bastards through a defeated country. They were fucking untouchable.

Within sight of the sports shop he turned to face them, walking backwards to maintain momentum. "Okay, I'll distract the man behind the till and the twins will keep an eye out for the security guards. The rest of you grab as much shit as you can carry. Stay the fuck away from the sale racks. We're lifting the in-season stuff only."

They flooded the shop, whooping and howling like lunatics as they spread out. Liam lifted a snooker cue from a display stand and charged at the wide-eyed shop assistant. He swung the cue like a baseball bat and clunked the prick with the fat end. The guy folded up and disappeared behind the counter. Liam laughed and rounded the counter. He came down hard with a couple of sledgehammer swings and made sure the fucker laid still.

The till looked pretty simple. A number pad and a bunch of symbols. Liam mashed a few random buttons and the till drawer popped open. Stuffing two handfuls of cash into his pockets, he looked across the shop. The boys were doing great. "Twenty seconds left. Hurry the fuck up."

He laid a few more wallops into the man at his feet and cheered himself on. The shaft of the cue cracked. Blood coated the cellophane on the business end. Two more whacks and the cue snapped in half. He waved the thin end in the air. "Five, four, three, two, one. Right, get out to fuck."

They flocked together and piled out of the shop. Security tags set off the alarm system as they passed through the sensors. Heads turned, but nobody moved to stop them. Too much sense. Liam led the charge with the broken cue held out in front of him. He glanced over his shoulder and saw they'd lost some of the clothes, leaving a multicoloured trail in their wake. It didn't matter, what he'd lifted from the till and what clothes they held onto would add up to their largest score to date.

"Out the front door. Anybody tries to grab you, hit them and keep running. Then scatter!"

All that stood between the gang and the automatic doors was the Rottweiler security guard. The mad bastard hunkered down a little and spread out his tree trunk arms as if he would catch all seven of them at once. Liam didn't give doubt time to flourish. He sped up.

"Get out of the way, dickhead!"

The guard shook his head.

Within kicking distance, Liam lashed out with the cue. The jagged wood cut across the security guard's cheek. Skin parted like a straining zipper. The guard didn't seem to notice. He grabbed Liam's head and hugged it to his chest like a goalkeeper with a football. Half suffocated and fearing that his brain would pop out the top of his skull, Liam tried to hit the guard with the broken cue and grapple the python-thick arms with his free hand. A couple of hour-long seconds later Liam felt his new claustrophobic world tilt. The pressure on his head and neck disappeared. Unseen hands pulled at his striped hoodie and dragged him backwards. He blinked away tears and cleared his vision. Matt, Eddie and Ginger Mickey fought with the guard. The big man tried to restrain them with armlocks and bad language. His opponents worked together, unrestricted by laws of reasonable force and professional ethics. They scratched, bit, spat and attempted to gouge.

Liam charged into the fray. "Come on, lads!"

The two Franks and Kev might have been right behind him. He didn't know. Tunnel vision cut out all distractions. He shoved Matt Fegan out of his path, aimed the shaft and lunged forward.

The security guard doubled over and gasped a huge breath. Liam stumbled backwards. He looked down at his hand. Empty. The big fellah straightened and patted the area around the shaft jutting from his stomach. A patch of crimson on his white shirt blossomed out from the wound. He held his bloody palms out to Liam and paled. The circling Rockets drifted back. Eyes bulged. Nobody made a sound.

Then a passing group of Millies let rip with a chorus of ear-piercing shrieks. They scattered in all directions, some charging deeper into the centre, some sprinting back out to the car park. All of them screaming for help.

Liam pushed his panic way down deep. Crammed it on top of his guilt and fear. "We're fucked if we don't split. Wake up, lads."

"*He's* fucked, Liam," Ginger Mickey said.

"It's just a wee gash. He'll be fine."

The guard toppled backwards, bashing his head on the tiled floor. Some of the boys hissed in empathy.

"He's definitely fucked, Liam."

"Stop using my name, Mickey. Come on. The peelers will be here soon."

Kev Watson pointed a shaking skeletal finger at the unconscious man. "There'll be prints on that cue, man."

"See you and that *CSI* bullshit?" Liam hesitated for a second. "Ah, fuck. Fine."

Liam stood above the guard, placed a foot on his barrel chest and gripped the smooth wood. "Remember that movie, *King Arthur*? No?" He waited for someone to laugh or smile. Nothing. "Jesus, you cunts are a barrel of laughs."

"Come on, Liam." Kev said. "I think I can hear sirens."

"Right, right. Fuck's sake." He gritted his teeth and wrenched the shaft from the wound. It came far easier than he'd expected and he almost lost his balance. He raised a hand to his hood to keep it in place. CCTV cameras in the West were usually out of focus or out of film, but there was no point tempting fate. "Okay, let's get the fuck out of here."

###

Stephen's thumb hovered over the green button on his mobile. He'd scrolled to a contact labelled 'scumbag'; the number Joe had given him for Liam Greene. He shook his head and pushed the red button instead. *Wise up,* he thought. *Are you going to just call him and invite him to meet you for a kneecapping?* He set the mobile down on the arm of his sofa and gazed up at his framed poster of Tony Jaa, Bruce Lee's modern day replacement.

In truth, now that he had his target lined up, he had no idea what to do. It had all been about the chase. About hunting down the wee fuckers responsible for so much hurt. About making a difference to his community. It became something else as he thought about the reality of street justice.

An anonymous call to the PSNI would be least messy. But what would come of it? Would the wee bastard tout on the rest of his gang under interrogation? Would it end in a satisfying conviction? Would they learn anything from a few years in a young offenders centre? No. None of that balanced up with the weight of the gang's crimes.

They needed to be dealt with in the only language they understood. And Stephen needed to know he could mete out the punishment in cold blood. Revenge on the football pitch when temper, adrenaline and testosterone whooshed through the veins was easy. But to drag a fourteen-year-old into an alley… and there was more at stake than a two match ban.

And that kind of penalty sent out the wrong signals. Journalists and politicians would have a field day. It had paramilitary punishment beating written all over it. That wouldn't help his community. And if the wrong people got wind of the maverick vigilante's identity, it wouldn't help him.

For once in his life, he had to keep a cool head on and find a subtle way to deal with his problems.

And Liam Greene wasn't the only problem.

He phoned Louise.

"What about you, big lad?"

Louise's boisterous greeting tugged at the corners of his mouth. "Hiya, love. You up to anything exciting?"

"Nah, I came off the early shift a couple of hours ago and had nothing more exciting planned than tidying Joe's room."

"Can he not tidy it himself?"

"Are you joking? He can barely keep his arse clean."

"That's a thought I could live without."

"Sorry. So what's on your mind?"

"Why do you ask?"

"Usually you just text me to tell me your coming over." She paused for a second. "Wait a minute. Is this a break up call? Fuck me, that's the kind of thing you do face-to-face after you hit your twenties."

"Um."

"It is, isn't it?"

It should have been, but now that the time had come it seemed like the last thing he wanted to do. "No, this isn't a break up call." And having said it, it felt right.

"So why the pause? Are you just losing your bottle? I don't need you hanging around me just because you're afraid I might shout at you."

"No, it's not that." So what was it? She'd led him to the Rockets. What else did he need from her?

"Well?"

"I just wanted to tell you... I... I... really like you, Louise."

Silence swelled for an agonising five seconds, and then a genuine giggle broke the tension.

"And I... I... think you're a fucking weirdo," Louise said. "But I like you too. Hang tight. I'm coming around to yours. Have you condoms or will I pick some up on the way?"

###

Joe curled his fists to stop himself biting his nails. The heater in the stolen five-door Fiesta pumped out cooked air.

"Can you turn off the heat?"

His da twiddled a couple of knobs on the dashboard. It seemed to make little difference. Joe thought about opening the window but didn't want to risk getting snapped at. Since he'd picked him and Wee Danny up, his da had been quiet and unsmiling. Wee Danny had asked for some music from the backseat and gotten no response. Now they were parked on a road near Queen's University, though Joe had no idea where. He'd never been in this part of the city. Hadn't thought he ever would.

His da stared out the window at a little supermarket. A squat man with thinning white hair wearing a checked shirt manned the shop floor. A student-type wandered up the aisle counting coins in the palm of his hand. It looked like he was the only customer. He left without buying anything.

"Okay, boys. Time to see what you've got. Joe, you're the wheels man tonight. Daniel, you're coming with me."

"It's Danny."

"It's nothing at all until this is over."

Joe thought about making a *Reservoir Dogs* reference, but chickened out. "I don't know about driving. I've no idea where I'm going."

His da pointed out the front windscreen. "That way until I tell you different."

"What am I going to do?" Wee Danny asked.

"Wave this about." Joe's da handed Wee Danny a rusty hatchet. "I'll do the talking."

"Okay, Dermot." Wee Danny didn't ask any questions, though if he was anything like Joe, a million of them must have been whizzing through his head. His da wasn't exactly dishing out the details.

"Right, let's go."

As they jumped out of the car, Joe shifted himself over the handbrake to sit behind the wheel. He pulled the seat forward slightly and fastened his seatbelt. Then he unfastened it. He wondered if he should be ready to hop out of the car if his help was needed or if he should stay with the car no matter what. He fastened the seatbelt again. His da and Wee Danny crossed the road and headed directly for the shop. They covered their faces at the front door, his da slipping on sunglasses and pulling a Liverpool FC scarf up over his nose and mouth, Wee Danny drawing his hood up.

Joe watched as the shopkeeper almost leapt out of his skin. Wee Danny waved his axe and Joe's da whipped a pistol out from his jacket. Joe felt his mouth dry up. *A gun.* His da was waving a gun in some poor fucker's face. He'd expected a knife or a baton or something a little less hardcore, but he'd underestimated the situation.

The shopkeeper nodded and held both hands up, begging for calm. Wee Danny really got into his role. He swiped the chewing gum stand off the counter with his hatchet and the white-haired man bounced back into the cigarette display. Joe's da pulled a bin liner from his pocket and slapped it down on the counter. He jabbed his pistol at the cigarettes and the till. The shopkeeper swiped the bag off the counter and shook it open. He tried to straight-arm the cigarettes on the top shelf into the bag but they scattered in all directions, most of them landing on the floor. Wee Danny hacked a lump out of the counter top and the shopkeeper dropped to his knees to scoop up the errant fags.

Wee Danny looked up at Joe's da, probably seeking approval. The big man clapped Wee Danny's shoulder with his free hand.

And then the shopkeeper sprang to his feet with a luminous-green baseball bat in his hands.

Joe's heart skipped a beat at the thought of seeing his da shoot someone. The smaller man drew back and put his whole body into a murderous swing. Joe's da skipped back and shoved Wee Danny forward. Into the arc of the bat.

It connected with Wee Danny's skull. Joe's best mate flopped sideways. He hit the big shop window and slid down it, like a boneless corpse. The shopkeeper dropped his bat and wiped his hands down the front of his checked shirt. Joe's da stepped over Wee Danny and clocked the stunned man with the butt of his gun. Blood sprayed and the guy went down cupping his broken nose in his hands. Joe's da tapped a button on the till and the drawer popped open. He grabbed a handful of cash and bolted.

Leaving Wee Danny in a heap on the floor.

Joe's da yanked open the car door and clambered into the passenger seat.

"Fuck. I think he's hit his silent alarm, Joe. Go, go, go!"

"We can't leave Wee Danny behind."

"Didn't you hear me? There'll be peelers all over the place in minutes. Drive!"

"What about Wee Danny?"

"He'll be okay."

"He might be dead. Was he still breathing?"

"Forget about him, Joe! We have to get the fuck out of here! NOW!"

"But he's a mate."

"He's expendable. You're all expendable."

Joe shook his head. "So you would have left me behind, too? Fuck you!"

226

His da pulled back a fist and Joe flinched. "Okay, okay." He peeled out into the road, missing a private taxi by inches. Their car lit up like a dance floor as the angered taxi driver flashed his high beams and laid on his horn.

"Fuck me, Joe. Open your eyes. I taught you better than this."

"Fuck yourself, you bastard!" Joe's voice cracked and spittle flew. Rage burned red hot in his cheeks. He gripped the steering wheel and wished for the strength to rip it off its column and wrap it around his da's neck.

"Just keep her between the lines, will you?"

"Why didn't you shoot the fucking shopkeeper? What did you have to throw Wee Danny at him for?"

"The gun's not loaded."

"What?"

"I wasn't going to shoot someone over a few packs of fags and a day's takings. What do you think I am?"

"A yellow cunt."

"Watch your mouth, son."

"Don't you dare call me son, you spineless bastard! You're not supposed to ditch your mates. I shouldn't have left him behind."

"Look, I know you're upset, but Wee Danny will be fine. Young fellahs like him have concrete skulls. He'll maybe get three years in a borstal and his record will be scrubbed clean when he turns eighteen. It's too late for us to do anything for him now."

"I can still do *something* for him, *Dermot*."

Joe yanked the steering wheel to the left and mounted the kerb. Dermot shrieked as he slammed into the passenger door window. Joe homed in on a huge, red postbox cemented into the footpath.

Dermot scrambled for his seatbelt when he realised Joe's intention. "Fuck. Stop."

Joe screamed like a madman. The car hit the postbox. Its bonnet crimped. Joe's seatbelt locked and catapulted him back into his seat. Dermot collided with the dashboard and the windshield. The car pivoted around the sturdy postbox and skittered out onto the road. It came to a rest across both lanes. Joe fought to pull air into his winded lungs. Dermot groaned; alive, but barely conscious. Joe unbuckled his seatbelt and shouldered his door open. He wobbled away from the wreckage on Bambi legs.

"Were you driving that car?"

Joe squinted at the source of the question. A young woman, struggling with a Cairn Terrier trying to choke itself on its own lead, studied him in the orange haze from an overhead streetlight.

"No, Missus. I was in the back. I'm lucky to be alive."

"What about the driver?"

"He's still in there. I'm going to find a phone box."

The dog lady instantly lost interest in Joe and crept towards the car. She probably wanted a good story to bring home. Why stop and chat to a dazed teen when there might be a maimed victim impaled on his steering column and bleeding to death? Joe did his best to steady his gait. He could do without any unwanted attention and the inevitable joyrider accusations. He glanced over his shoulder and saw that some cars had stopped on either side of the buckled Fiesta and the occupants were out to investigate. He'd slipped away in the nick of time. Dermot was probably good and fucked though. The thought of it spurred him on. He made his way back towards the shop. Back towards Wee Danny.

Minutes later he could see the twirling blue lights from a cop car. Rather than stand at a distance looking guilty, he closed in on the scene and melded in with the growing crowd of onlookers. If anybody noticed his shaking legs and chattering teeth they made no indication of it. He could see Wee Danny still in the same spot Dermot had left him. A young peeler stood at the door, barring access and throwing the occasional glance at the downed teenager.

The shopkeeper wasn't in sight. They'd probably taken him out the back to make a statement.

An ambulance wailed and wove through the scant traffic and Joe felt relief flood his body. They wouldn't bother with the siren if they were picking up a corpse. Joe stood around to watch the paramedics bundle his mate onto a gurney. Wee Danny pawed at the air once and then lay still, but it was enough to satisfy Joe.

Chapter 15

Paul wound a strand of Emily's blonde hair around his index finger. They sat in the back of the red Clio, pink-skinned, and breathless. He noticed that she furrowed her brow a little and glanced at his hand.

"Sorry," Paul said. "Is that annoying you?"

"Not at all, darling. But you shouldn't care if it is. You're paying me, remember?"

Paul kissed her nectarine-smooth cheek. "That's no reason to take you for granted. I feel happier now than I have in years. I'd say this has been the healthiest relationship I've ever had. No mind games, no second guessing, no stress. Just sex with a stunningly beautiful woman."

He thought that her eyes might have softened for a second, but she blinked and the business look returned. "You Irish and your silver tongues. You'd give a girl silly ideas."

"Do you want to go for a bite to eat? My treat?"

Emily sighed. "Paul, have you been watching *Pretty Woman* or something? Let me help you distinguish Hollywood from real life. I'm not a whore with a heart of gold. I'm not looking for a knight in shining armour to rescue me. I'm not praying for a way off the street. I'm a prostitute and I make good money. More than you, probably. I have no intention of complicating a good life by hooking up with a client. No matter how charming he is."

"But we're agreed that I am indeed charming? That's a good firm basis to start the negotiations from."

"This isn't a negotiation, Paul. I don't want to date you."

"What if I let you pay your own way? You couldn't really call that a date. More like a business meeting."

"Pay my own way? Now you're really dreaming."

"Okay, why don't we go to McDonalds? That's as far from romance as you could get."

"Full marks for persistence, but the answer is still no."

Paul pecked her on the lips. The smell of her leather jacket danced in his nostrils. He kissed her again, and she responded, slow and tender. Their front teeth scraped together and their tongues slid over each other. Paul ran a hand from Emily's cheek, to her neck, to her shoulder, to her breast.

She broke the kiss and whispered into his ear. "No freebies, darling."

Paul nodded. "Will you give me a special rate for an all-nighter?"

"There's you getting all Richard Gere again."

"Seriously. Will you stay with me tonight?"

"Why?"

"I'd like to fall asleep after a long, slow shag, wrapped up with a sweaty sex machine."

"Sweaty?"

"Glistening, then."

"And what if you wake up in the morning and your house has been ransacked? You don't know me from Adam."

"I've nothing much worth stealing, to be honest. A budget brand widescreen TV and some integrated kitchen appliances. Unless there's big money in Fisher Price toys, it wouldn't be worth your while."

"It'll be expensive."

"I can afford half your hourly rate for eight hours."

"Most of which you intend to sleep through, yeah?"

"Yeah."

"All right, then, you silly bugger. You have a deal."

"Great, we'll pick up a big pizza on the way home. That'll be dinner and breakfast sorted."

"What's with you and food? Are you trying to fatten me up?"

"Nope, just making sure you don't run out of energy."

They zipped and buckled their way back to respectability and climbed into the front of the car. Paul's chest thudded and his groin tingled at the prospect of a whole night with Emily. They pulled out of the empty dockside car park and made their way to the city.

"Do you need to stop anywhere for an overnight bag?" Paul asked.

She patted the black leather handbag on her lap. "I travel light."

They drove on in comfortable silence until Emily's handbag began playing a generic dance beat. She apologised, probably more so for the crappy ringtone than the interruption itself, and fished her phone out of the bag.

"Hello? Yeah, I'm with a client... You what? Fuck... What about Joe?" Her mouth dropped open. "The little shit! What for...? Right, right, sorry. I'll see what I can do... Just off the Stranmillis Road... Okay... Calm down, all right? I'll phone you back in a bit."

"That didn't sound like good news."

"No, it wasn't, darling. My friend got himself into a bit of a mess. I'm going to have to help him out."

His heart sank.

"So our appointment is cancelled."

"Postponed, yeah?"

"Aye, okay."

"Thing is…" She laid a hand on his arm. "I'm going to need a lift to the Stranmillis Road. Maybe we could help each other out."

"I'm listening."

"If you play chauffer tonight, I'll give you a better price for an all-nighter tomorrow night."

"Give me two nights for the price of one and we have a deal."

She smiled at him. "Well good for you, you little haggler. You went in for the kill there." She shook her head. "Yeah, I can do that."

"Fucking sweet."

Paul altered his course and they were on the Stranmillis Road in ten minutes. Emily phoned her friend.

"We're on the road. Where are you? Okay. No, I don't see any cops about. Hold on." She turned to Paul. "Do you know where the Lyric Theatre is?"

"Aye. We're about a minute away."

"Great. Dermot? Yeah, we'll be there soon."

Paul wedged the Clio into a tight space at the kerb outside the theatre. Emily slipped out of the car and a tall man emerged from the shadowy alley leading to the back of the building. Emily had called him Dermot. Though bruised and bloodied, Paul recognised the face but couldn't quite place it. Outside, they exchanged a few words before she led him to the car. Paul guessed he was her pimp. The thought registered itself in a matter-of-fact manner. No jealousy. Not even when she reached out and gingerly stroked his face. Paul sighed and switched his mind to a simpler puzzle. Where did he know Dermot the pimp from?

Emily opened the passenger door and cranked the seat forward to climb into the back. "Hope you don't mind. His cribbage pegs will never fit in here."

"His what?"

"My legs." Dermot contorted his way into the seat. "She turns that Cockney shite on and off at random intervals. I keep telling her it makes her sound like a cheap *Only Fools and Horses* extra, but she insists that some of the punters lap it up."

"Where do I know you from, mate?"

Dermot rubbed his mouth then hissed in pain. He studied Paul's face. "Couldn't tell you."

"I thought I recognised you when I first saw you, but as soon as you opened your broad Belfast beak…" Paul tilted his head. "You're from Beechmount, aren't you?"

"I haven't lived there for a while now." His tone slipped from Jack-the-Lad to Jack Frost. "I've been away for a few years. Should have stayed away."

"That's right. I have you pegged now. You're Dermot Kelly. I used to buy E off you, before you were sent packing." He didn't know why, but he enjoyed watching Dermot squirm. "And do you know what? My wee brother, Danny, is your son's best mate. Fucking small world, eh?"

Liam curled up into the foetal position. He lay on the footpath by the traffic lights at the Beechmount Avenue and Falls Road junction. The Fegan twins loomed over him. A car screeched to a halt and Liam took one hand from his face to peek at it. The car's headlights silhouetted Matt Fegan, who stood with one leg raised over Liam's head. The car door opened and the driver started shouting.

"Hey, you. What the fuck are you doing? Get away from him you dirty wee knacker."

Matt lowered his leg and turned to face the hero. "Fuck off. This is none of your business."

"Maybe not, but two on one isn't right. And kicking him when he's down? You're scum. Why don't you try it with me?"

Matt hopped back over Liam and stood with his brother. They retreated a little every time the hero stepped forward. Liam covered his face with his arms, leaving just enough space between his forearms to see through. The hero knelt down next to Liam. A strong waft of aftershave emanated from his every movement. This was a man who spent a lot of time in front of the mirror. He placed a hand, heavy with white gold jewellery, on Liam's shoulder.

"You all right, big lad?"

Liam looked at his saviour's face. The guy watched the twins carefully, a hard expression on his face. Liam drew back his fist and punched the hero square in his balls. Eyes bulged, brilliant white against the heavily tanned skin. With a little squeak, he bent at the waist and cupped his assaulted nuts with both hands. Liam and the twins went to work. They left him lying in Liam's spot and jumped into the hero's sexy red sports car.

Liam whooped as he took control of the Mazda RX8 and punished the engine with his lead foot. The Falls Road became his midnight runway. Eddie shouldered open one of the rear suicide-doors and hung the top half of his body out into the night. Matt bounced up and down on the passenger seat like a kid about to piss in his knickers.

"Change gears, Liam," Matt said. "You're raking the fuck out of her."

"So?"

Liam jinked the car from side to side and Eddie scrambled back into a sitting position.

"The fuck are you at, Liam? I near fell out."

"Dry your eyes. What were you trying to do, anyway?"

"I wanted to see if your man was going to get up."

"You what?"

Eddie said nothing.

"Want me to go back and check?"

Before Eddie could protest, Liam attempted a 180 turn. He'd seen them do it in the movies. Heard the joyriders boast about their handbraking skills on street corners. Done it himself a million times on his Playstation. How hard could it be?

The car made a quarter turn then conked out.

"You're supposed to use the clutch," Matt said.

"You can drive the next one. Shut the fuck up and let me practice."

Liam turned the key and the car jumped. The twins sniggered, but knew better than to offer any tips. He pulled the gearstick into neutral and tried again. The Mazda purred. He jammed his right foot to the floor and the chrome-ringed tachometer's needle sprang right up into the red. The engine screamed and the car mounted the kerb as it completed the turn. Liam guided it out onto the oncoming lane, the coast clear for the time being. He eased off the gas, dropped the clutch and wrestled with second gear. It caught and they juddered forward.

He turned in his seat to smirk at Eddie. "See? Piece of piss."

"It wasn't me acting the driving instructor. Talk to Matt."

"Are we really going to see if this fellah's all right?" Matt asked.

"Well, if your Eddie is so concerned, I think we should."

"I wasn't concerned. I just wanted to know."

"Curious then. Let's find out."

Liam accelerated in second and the car jumped to fifty miles per hour. He inched towards the footpath. Towards the RX8's owner, lying still where they'd left him, on the lip of the kerb. One of his designer jean-clad legs had flopped onto the road. Matt fumbled with his seatbelt. Eddie hissed air through his teeth.

"Liam, don't." Matt raised his voice to be heard over the high-pitched revs. "You'll lose control if you hit the kerb."

"The sooner you learn how much control I have the better."

Mere feet away, Liam blasted the horn. The hero raised his head and peeped over his chest. The headlights picked out the tears in his brilliant white eyes. Then the shock. Then they were gone. Matt screamed and Eddie pounded on the back of Liam's seat, irritating rather than hurting him.

"Would you two buck-eejits calm the fuck down?"

Eddie popped his head through the gap between the front seats. He shushed his twin brother then turned to Liam. "Oh, fuck, Liam. That's fucked up. Your boy's at least lost his leg. It's a cert. The cops aren't going to write this off. Especially not so soon after you stabbed the security guard. They'll know they're linked."

Liam slammed on the brakes. Eddie saved himself from going through the windscreen by hugging the headrests on either side of him. Matt's seatbelt kept him right.

"First of all, look." Liam twisted in his seat and jabbed his finger at the back window.

The man knelt on the footpath, hands on his knees and his head hanging.

"Fuck me," Eddie said. "He must have rolled out of the way. Guess he was all right."

"Second of all…" Liam caught Eddie with a right cross as he turned to face him. The twin rocked back onto the tiny backseat. He wiped blood from his split lip. Matt grabbed Liam's arm.

"Out of order, Liam."

Liam headbutted Matt, catching his chin. It caused more shock than damage. "Keep your hands off me!" Liam peeled back his lips and glared.

Matt looked away. His chest hitched.

Liam turned back to Eddie. "What did we agree about the security guard?"

"Not to talk about him."

"Ever?"

"Never."

"So why did you?"

"I was freaking out. Liam. I wasn't thinking. Sorry, okay?"

"No, it's not fucking okay! Are you going to freak out if a peeler comes sniffing around your door? Are you going to freak out if one of us is scooped? Are you going to freak out if you have a nightmare? You wee shite-bag!"

Eddie's eyes burned into Liam. "After what happened to Tommy Four-Eyes? I better not."

"Shut up, Eddie," Matt said.

Liam said nothing. He settled back into his driving position and adjusted the rear view mirror. The kneeling man was now the standing man. Probably gearing up to becoming the running man. He threw the RX8 into reverse.

"Matt, I think I'll show your brother what I saw happen to Tommy. Though it won't be quite the same, because the wanker we just car-jacked is a stranger. But maybe he'll get a small taste of one of the things keeping me awake every night."

"Liam, please." Matt leant towards Liam, hands outstretched.

"I told you. No touching."

Matt snatched back his hands. "Okay, but we all need to chill. Your man's probably called the cops on his mobile already. If they arrive to find him splattered all over the road this place will be crawling with white land rovers. We'll get caught and hole-fucked.

238

If we go now, one cop car will do the West Belfast Tour. That gives us more time to get the fuck away. You don't want to be caught, do you?"

Liam filled his lungs through his nose and emptied them through his mouth. Maybe he did want to be caught, but he refused to even nudge that can of worms. He kept his head in the situation.

"I better not get caught with a car full of loose-lipped bitches, I suppose. I'll end up getting three hundred years."

Liam clunked into first gear. They drove up the Falls Road and through Andersonstown, suffering bone-jarring gear changes until they got to the Poleglass Roundabout.

Liam broke the silence. "Twinbrook or Poleglass?"

"Poleglass is mad as fuck," Matt said. "We'll be lucky to get out alive."

"Sounds perfect."

"Seriously, Liam. They're all psychos around there."

"They probably say the same thing about Beechmount, Matt."

Matt shook his head and smiled.

"What?"

"In our case, they'd be right, wouldn't they?"

Eddie piped in. "Apparently one in every three of us has killed someone."

Liam grinned. "All right, all right. We've work to do. Poleglass it is. If we stick together we'll be okay."

He enjoyed concentrating on the driving. By the time they were deep into the unknown he'd perfected his gear changes. He'd have to work on the parking another day.

It seemed like all of the houses were lit up from the inside. Liam wondered if any of the residents slept at all. As he looked at the clusters of teenagers on the streets he thought maybe Beechmount *was* a safer place. Or maybe he'd just gotten so used to the same faces in his own area that they barely registered as threats anymore. Either way, he didn't want to stop too close to anyone. He didn't like the way they all stared at his car.

"There's a chapel ahead, Liam. We could use the car park."

"Aye, that'll do all right, Matt."

They pulled into a space and got to work. Liam emptied a can of lighter fluid onto the seats and floor mats. Matt and Eddie stood behind him and twisted pages of the Andersonstown News into tapers. They lit a bunch of them, dropped them onto the seats and stood well back, waiting for the fire to catch. Black smoke belched from the open doors, swiftly followed by slender fingers of flame.

"Seems a real waste, that."

Liam spun on his heel as the first melting tyre popped. The comment had come from an older kid on a BMX. His white Carbrini hoodie glowed orange. Four others stood behind him. They cheered as another tyre exploded.

"We could have had a go before you wrecked it," BMX Boy said.

"All right, mate?" Liam said.

"Who you calling mate?"

Liam sighed. "Is there going to be a problem here? Because I couldn't be fucked breaking your legs."

BMX Boy turned to the four youths behind him. "You hear that? Couldn't be fucked breaking my legs." He turned back to Liam. "You've some balls on you."

He stepped off his bike and it clattered to the ground. Liam glanced at the four hoods behind him. They watched with hungry eyes, anticipating a satisfying show.

"Where you from, Legbreaker?"

Your ma, he thought. But even with the twins behind him, he'd have no chance of getting away without a serious kicking. He did his best to keep his smart mouth in check.

"Down the road a bit. We came up because we heard you can buy the best drugs in Poleglass."

"And do you have enough money for the best?"

Liam nodded. "Aye, but I'm not stupid enough to carry it on me. Awful lot of people getting mugged these days. I thought I could place an order first."

"Well… I might be able to help you. But I don't do shitty wee ten-deals. You're not going to waste my time over a bit of hash, are you?"

Liam had to swallow the insults on the tip of his tongue. BMX Boy wanted a good kick in the scones, but Liam knew they'd be safe if they had something to offer the prick. Different street, same rules.

"No, I'm not talking about a ten-deal, or even about hash. We're after some class A shit for a major party. It'll be well worth your while."

"How much you got to spend?"

"Three hundred."

BMX Boy had a shit poker face. His eyes almost rolled out of his head. Liam and the twins would live to fight another day.

"Right, give me your mobile number. I'll have anything you need in two days."

"Great. What's your name then, big lad?"

"Eamon, but most of the headers around here call me E Man."

"Dead on, E Man. Listen, would you and your mates walk us to the taxi depot? We don't want to get into any trouble on our way home."

"No sweat, mate. You'll be safe with us."

The rear tyres on the RX8 popped in unison. E Man offered his hand to Liam.

###

Stephen stretched out on the sofa. He set his beer bottle on the cork coaster on the wooden floor and aimed the remote control at the DVD player, skipping forward to the next fight scene. On screen, Jet Li opened a can of whup-ass on a gang of Chinese-American triads. One man against an entire crime organisation. If only life were so simple.

His doorbell chimed and he rolled off the sofa, sleek as a kung fu master. He hadn't been expecting company, so he readied himself to open his door to kids looking for a party to crash. The wee bastards tried it on every so often, thinking they'd get in by sending the prettiest girl first, then crowding in after her. He geared himself up to unleash a mouthful of abuse, and opened the door to Joe. The teenaged beanpole stood on the doorstep, shaking like a junkie. He cupped a cigarette in his hand. You can take the kid off the schoolyard...

"What the fuck, Joe? It's almost one in the morning. Why are you not at home?"

"Everything's fucked and I've nobody else to talk to. My ma keeps saying you want to get to know me. I'm desperate enough to test that."

"You're a real charmer, Joe. Come in. But lose the fag. This is a no smoking zone."

Joe flicked the butt into the street and stepped past Stephen. He stood in the middle of the living room until Stephen waved a hand at the armchair. Joe sat on the edge of the seat and Stephen sat on the sofa, placing one foot on either side of his beer. He wrapped a fist around the bottle neck and lifted it to his mouth. After a slow, satisfying swallow, he set his beer directly on top of the little wet circle in the centre of the coaster. Then he leant forward, resting his elbows on his knees and looked at Joe.

"So what is it?"

Joe licked his lips and glanced at Stephen's bottle. "Any chance of a beer?"

"When you're eighteen, maybe."

Joe sighed, but didn't complain. He took a plastic lighter from his pocket and fiddled with the flint. Little bursts of spark jumped.

"Joe, did you just come here for somewhere soft to sit or did you want to ask me something?" Then a thought occurred. "Or have you more info on them Wee Rockets for me?"

"What? No, I told you everything you need to know. Fat Liam Greene is in charge. The other six just follow his lead."

"What then? Spit it out for fuck's sake."

"You're mates with Paul Gibson, aren't you?"

"Aye, I suppose. We both play for Davitts, like."

"Will you get in touch with him and let him know his wee brother's in the hospital. Not sure which one, but last time I saw him he was bundled into an ambulance."

"Shit. What happened to him?"

"He got clunked on the head with a baseball bat."

Stephen scrunched his face up. "Nasty. What did he do to deserve that?"

Joe took off his hat and rubbed the crown of his head. Scalp flakes hopped like fleas. "We did something well fucking stupid tonight."

Stephen sat with his jaw hanging as Joe told him about the quality time he'd been spending with his father. He'd figured Dermot for a complete scumbag, but Joe's story put him into a whole new league.

"Jesus Christ. I can't believe your da took you and your fourteen-year-old mate on an armed robbery. And I thought your ma letting you smoke was bad. Fuck me. What chance did you ever have in life?"

"Look, I didn't come here so you could take the piss out of me."

"What did you come here for?"

"I thought we could help each other."

"Oh, I see. You want me to deal with daddy Dermot." Stephen snorted. "Why the fuck would I want to do that?"

"Don't you want to clean up the streets? Isn't that what your hard-on for the Rockets was all about? Playing vigilante? I thought you'd have jumped at the chance to take out someone like my da."

"I wanted to help out my community in a time of crisis. If Dermot is doing over shops in student land, why should I care? It doesn't impact on me or mine."

"Does it not? Armed robbery is only the tip of the iceberg, mate. He's been working more than one angle since he got back. You've plenty of reason to care."

"What are you talking about?"

"He's been in your house, McVeigh. Poking through your personal shit. He even photographed some of your bank statements. Ever hear of identity theft?"

Stephen launched himself out off the sofa and grabbed the front of Joe's hoodie. He hoisted him off the armchair and shook him.

"How do you know that? Were you with him, you wee fucker?"

Joe smirked. "It was me who wrote on Bruce."

Stephen dumped Joe to the floor. "You sneaky wee bastard. I should dance on your face."

"I'll tell my ma!"

"Not if I do a good enough job."

Joe rolled away, but Stephen made no move to follow him. He couldn't risk his relationship with Louise over Joe.

"Get off the floor, dickhead."

Joe stood and held his palms up to Stephen. "Look, I'm sorry for breaking in, okay? But now that you know about it, you can do something to stop your personal info being used, can't you?"

"Like kicking the shite out of your da? How convenient."

"I'm not asking you to give him a punishment beating."

"What then?"

"I need your protection. Do you think he'll just forget about the fact I left him for the cops? If he hasn't been arrested, I'm fucked." Joe blinked back tears as he waited for Stephen to react.

"You want *me* to protect you?"

"Well, I can't do it. He'd pick me up and break me in half. But you're built like a shithouse. So long as you don't turn your back on him, it'll be a piece of piss for you."

"Wait there."

Stephen went to the kitchen to fetch a fresh beer. He stood at the fridge thinking about Dermot Kelly. The bastard had violated his home. And that wasn't his first offence. Stephen's kidney still throbbed a little from their first meeting. And he'd stooped low enough to use kids, one of them his own flesh and blood, in an armed robbery. But even knowing all of this, Stephen couldn't see himself becoming a teenaged hood's bodyguard. But Joe didn't need to know that.

He popped the lid off his beer bottle and returned to the living room. Joe stood in the spot he'd left him.

"Joe, if your da is determined enough, the only way to stop him from hurting you will probably be to hurt him worse. Maybe even kill him."

Joe nodded. His face hardened. "I know. I've thought about that."

"If I were to do something to your da you'd be able to hold it over my head for the rest of my life. Let's face it; you'll never be a doctor or a barrister. What's to say you won't blackmail me when you're struggling to make ends meet on the dole?"

"I swear to fuck, McVeigh. I wouldn't do that. Getting rid of the bastard who fucked my best mate over would be enough for me. I'd be in your debt."

"But I've only got your word on that. I need something else. Some insurance."

Joe shook his head. Lost.

"Before I agree to something so serious, I need you on the same boat. I need you to deal with someone for me. Then you'll be in no position to blackmail me. We'll be evens."

Joe frowned. "Who?"

"Liam Greene."

Chapter 16

Dermot grabbed Emily's upper arm and spun her to face him. Her blonde waves billowed like a flamenco skirt. She caught his bruised face with a slap on her way around, the force multiplied by his own aggression.

"Don't you put a finger on me, Dermot Kelly. I'll bite your Niagaras off."

He rubbed his hot cheek. "I asked you a question."

"And I told you. It's business."

"You've never needed to stay out all night before. And it's only gone past six. Why do you need to leave so early in the evening? What's really going on?"

"Exactly what I told you. *Business. My business.* That's all you've ever needed to know before now. So sort yourself out, darling. You're losing grip."

"I think you have a boyfriend. Or someone who wants you to believe he's your boyfriend to get a few freebies."

"Sounds a bit like you."

"What's your point?"

"Are you jealous, Dermot?"

He curled his lip and instantly regretted it as it began to bleed again. "Aye, yeah. That must be it. I just don't want to share my common-law whore."

Emily gave him a sweet smile. "You know, we can fix that situation quite quickly. I'm beginning to think I'd be better off without you. I'm certainly making more money than you."

"Sure didn't I know it'd come back to cash? Never mind that I've been lifting and laying you. Making sure some sick fuck hasn't dumped you in the Lagan. Thought beyond making a quick score to try and build something we could both enjoy. Aye, go ahead. Fuck away off to your new boy and let him look after you like I have. I can do without the stress."

"Goodbye, Dermot. Come find me when you've gotten over your personal crisis, won't you?"

She shouldered her overnight bag, blew him a kiss and gave her ass a deliberate wiggle as she left the squat. A growl rumbled in the back of his throat and he punched the wall, cracking plaster and cheap chipboard.

He screamed at the closed door. "Fuck you then, you dirty wee scrubber!"

The bottle of Smirnoff whispered to him from the kitchen cupboard. He submitted to the silent seduction and poured himself a glass. It scorched a path to his belly and kicked the shit out of his stomach lining. He coughed and lit a cigarette to smooth out his riled throat. Then he poured another glass. This one went down a little easier.

After his third glass he decided to get up and out. The heartbroken drunk thing got boring when you'd no TV or tunes. He needed to find something to do. Or someone.

He gave himself a quick crotch and armpit wash before he threw on a fresh shirt. Feeling like a handsome bastard, he flagged a private taxi on Botanic Avenue and told the driver to take him to

Beechmount. He figured Joe wouldn't have been stupid enough to tell Louise about the previous night's disaster. Aside from that he'd been a model father to the boy, and his ma was bound to have thawed out a little as a result. With a bit of charm he might be able to snake his way into the house for a bit of adult company. If McVeigh happened to be there, Dermot could act innocent and ask for Joe. But if Louise was on her own… Well, he'd just have to play it by ear.

He rapped the letterbox. Louise answered the door in button up, cotton pyjamas. She frowned at him and he remembered the bruised face his vodka had numbed.

"Joe's not here. I don't think he was expecting you."

"It's not even seven yet. What are you doing in pyjamas?"

"I worked hard today. I fancied a wee bit of comfort. But more to the point; why do you reek of vodka? And what's up with your face? Have you been fighting?"

"Long story. Can I come in?"

"I don't know when Joe's coming home. He'd left before I came home from work."

"So how about me and you catch up? It's been a while."

"I'm well aware of how long it's been, Dermot. It's part of the reason I can't stand the sight of you. Remember?"

"And yet, you haven't slammed the door in my face."

Louise bit her lip and looked up and down her street. "Okay, you can come in for a cuppa, but only because you've really put in an effort to get to know Joe. I've noticed a real change in him since you started doing what you should have done all his life."

"Jesus! That was nearly a compliment."

"No it wasn't. But if you're going to continue seeing as much of Joe, we should be able to spend a little time in the same room together. Now's as good a time as any to start."

"And what about the big ginger fellah you've been seeing? Do you think he'd approve?"

"I don't need any man's permission to do anything. I'm not the stupid wee bitch you left holding the baby any more."

"But if he's due around here tonight he might get upset to find you entertaining."

"He's training, and more than likely heading for a pint after. You can stop wetting yourself. Though, I wouldn't relax too much. I'm sure he won't forget that sucker punch in a hurry."

"That was self defence!"

"Aye. Dead on. Look, just come in, will you? The neighbours' curtains are starting to twitch."

She brought a pot of tea into the living room on a plastic Carlsberg tray he'd stolen from The Beehive the night they first moved in together. He took it as a subtle signal that she still thought about him. Of course, that night had also been the cause of a massive row. He'd decided to stay on and drink the bar dry after last orders; even though he knew she wanted him to go with her and spend the first night in their new home together. The tray had been a peace offering. One that had nearly taken his head off, Oddjob style.

"This is weird," he said.

"What?"

"Sitting here as a guest. I used to live here, like."

Louise shrugged. "Things change."

"You haven't. You still look as good as you did back then."

"Well, you've gotten a bit fatter. You're still a good liar though."

"And you're still brutally honest." He rubbed his stomach self-consciously.

She sighed. "You do look better without the moustache though. Less sneaky. Wish I could talk Joe into getting rid of his."

"Ach, any kid who can grow one will. It impresses the other kids."

"I suppose. So where's what's-her-name tonight?"

"Emily? I think we've broke up. Pretty sure she's seeing other men."

"Really? And she seemed so prim when I met her. Goes to show — you can never judge a slut by her miniskirt."

"Hey! That was uncalled for."

"I owe you more than a few bitchy comments. Dry your eyes." And she smiled a little.

"Fair enough." He returned her smile. "I suppose you're wondering why I left you, eh? I could fill you in. Kill your curiosity."

"Don't bother. I used to wonder, but after twelve years I'm not interested in your excuses. You did what you did. I'm sure it could have been avoided, and I'm sure you'd deny that. But I don't care any more. So why relive it?"

He sensed the light mood shifting to a darker place. He needed to rein in the bad vibes. "Yeah, you're right. That's what everyone seems to be doing here these days. Moving on. I can't believe how much the city has changed."

Louise shrugged. "It's not something you think about on a day to day basis, but aye, I suppose it'd be weird for you. Last time you were here it was all security gates, bombscares and Brits patrolling the streets."

"Long may it continue."

"Fuck." Louise sighed. "This is all getting very deep. Maybe we need to have something stronger than tea. Lighten things up a bit."

"Now you're talking, sweetheart."

And when she didn't scowl at the old familiar pet name, he cheered himself on inside.

Joe took a deep breath of chemical-scented hospital air and then strode down the ward before he could chicken out. Wee Danny lay under a white sheet, drawn up to his chin. He wore a turban-like bandage around his head. His small face looked young and innocent.

"You awake, mate?"

Wee Danny opened one eye and looked Joe up and down. The other eye popped open and his devilish grin banished all innocence. "All right, Joe?"

Joe hesitated, a little relieved, but still expecting accusations of betrayal. "Aren't you pissed off at me?"

Danny's grin faltered. "Why, what happened? Nobody's really told me yet."

"What do you remember?"

"I got out of the car with your da, ready to do that job."

"And?"

"Well, that's it. I feel a bit like I've been drinking like a bastard. My head's banging and I've no idea how I got here."

"Fucking hell."

"Will you pass me a glass of water? I've been dropping some serious pain killers and feel a bit lazy."

"Yeah, yeah, of course."

Joe rushed to the bedside cabinet, almost tripping over a small wooden visitors' bench, and sloshed a measure of iced water into a plastic glass. He held it to Wee Danny's lips and tilted it, pouring a little into his mouth. Most of the water spilled onto his chin and ran down onto his neck.

Wee Danny spluttered. "Fuck's sake, Joe. You're soaking me, you eejit. Use that button to raise the bed and just hand me the water. I've a sore head, not a broken neck."

Joe stepped back and squinted at the button pad. "What if I hit the wrong one and fold you in half?"

"You're a stupid bastard sometimes. What kind of hospital would buy a bed like that? It's the top button."

Joe hit the button and Wee Danny screamed.

Joe whipped his hand away from the button pad. "Fuck, fuck, fuck. I'm sorry, mate."

Danny winked at him. "Just messing with you. Why are you making it so easy?"

"I'm a bit distracted, like. My best mate's got a broken skull."

"Fuck off! Have I?"

"Well, fractured. That's what they said when I phoned. I pretended to be your Paul when I was tracking you down. Do you really not remember what happened?"

"No."

Joe sighed and took off his cap. He sat on the wee bench and told the story for the second time.

"And you wrecked the getaway car for me? Fucking hell. Did your da get scooped?"

"Probably not, knowing my luck."

"You're in some deep shit, then."

"You're a real comfort."

"What are you going to do?"

"I went to see McVeigh last night. Asked him to protect me."

"Jesus, you must be desperate. What did he say?"

"That I have to get Liam Greene off the scene. Stop the Rockets from terrorising the streets. Then he'll look out for me."

"He might be asking a lot there. How are you supposed to do that?"

"I'm pretty sure I'd have to kill him."

The idea hung in the air between them.

Danny broke the silence. "Well, if it's a choice between you or him, you have to get rid of the fat fucker."

"I know, but how the fuck am I meant to do it?"

"I don't know. Offer him a Slim Fast milkshake or something? He might have a heart attack."

"Try and be serious, mate."

"Right, sorry. Must be the drugs."

"No worries. Maybe I shouldn't be putting this on you. You've enough to worry about."

"Ach, it's only a wee bump on the head."

"Not just that. Has the cop been in to see you?"

"What cop?"

"There's a uniform sitting outside the ward. Not exactly a genius though. I snuck in when he was trying it on with one of the nurses. I think they're going to take you in when you're well enough."

"Fuck."

"Sorry, mate."

"Your da's a real prick, you know?"

"Aye."

"I wonder what'll happen to me now?"

"Don't know, mate. But you're too young to go to the young offenders. Maybe the Juvenile Justice Centre in Bangor? Probably won't be as bad as a real jail."

"Ach, fuck it. Nothing I can do about it now. Tell you what though, if that fucker from the shop presses charges, I'm going to counter sue him for assault. How's using a baseball bat on a kid reasonable force?"

"You're a genius, mate. I'd never have thought of that."

"Of course I am. I guess the bastard didn't cause too much damage, then."

Joe stood up suddenly and reached into the pocket on the front of his hoodie. "Almost forgot. I have something for you."

He handed Wee Danny a Sony PSP. His friend's hands shook as he turned the portable games console this way and that in examination.

"Sweet. Where'd you nick this?"

"I bought it. I still had some savings from the Rocket days."

Wee Danny looked at Joe with huge round eyes. "Seriously? Wow."

"It was the least I could do."

"Look, Joe, I don't blame you for any of this. You'd already done enough when you abandoned the fucker on the road. We're cool, okay?"

Joe nodded.

"And when I'm not playing with this, I'll be using my superior brain to help you out, you slow fucker. I'll think of a way to handle Liam. Come and see me again, right?"

Joe had an insane urge to bend down and kiss Wee Danny's forehead. But he didn't fancy a punch in the eye. "No worries, mate. I'll be here tomorrow."

Paul raised his goblet of white zinfandel and clinked glass with Emily. At his request, she'd changed into a midnight blue satin nightdress he'd bought in Debenhams that day. The hem fell an inch below the perfect curve of her ass. As she crossed her legs and shifted position on the leather sofa, he caught a glimpse of black lace underwear. He'd flipped on the heating earlier, to keep her comfortable in her scant outfit, but after a sip of the ice-cold wine her nipples pushed against the low cut bodice. In the dimmed light her hair was burnished gold.

"I've got to say, Paul, this is a lot cosier than the back of your Clio."

"It's exactly how I imagined it."

"You get what you pay for."

Paul felt very comfortable too. He'd splashed out on some silk pyjama bottoms for himself, and matched them with a vest top that did justice to his toned arms. He'd considered going bare-chested, but figured that undressing added to the effect of a good shag. He glanced at his watch.

"Pizza should be here soon. I'm going to stick on a movie to watch while we eat. Any preferences?"

"You're the boss, darling."

He loved the sound of that. And it wasn't just Emily's accent that tickled him. It was the content. *The boss.*

"*Scarface*, it is, then."

He'd just popped open the DVD case when the doorbell chimed.

"Must be the pizza," he said.

Lifting a twenty-pound note from the mantelpiece on the way, he went to the door and answered it to Stephen McVeigh.

"Hiya, Paul."

"I thought you were the pizza guy."

"Nice to see you too. Can I come in?"

Paul leant one shoulder against the doorframe. He inched the door closed a little, restricting McVeigh's view of the living room. "I'm a bit busy at the minute, mate. Can I phone you later?"

"This is important."

"Here, why are you not at training?"

"I told you, this is important. I knew you'd given it a miss when you didn't call me to offer a lift to the pitch. Figured this would be a good time to catch you. Or am I interrupting a special occasion?"

Paul jumped on the opportunity. "Yeah, special occasion. It's our, um… anniversary."

"Paul?" Emily's cockney accent rang out from the living room. "Can I stick the kettle on?"

He poked his head back inside. "Yeah, go ahead." Then he turned back to McVeigh. "So, can I call you later?"

"I thought Sinead grew up in Twinbrook."

"She did."

"Then why does she sound like one of the birds off *EastEnders*? Whose anniversary are you celebrating?"

Paul shrugged to buy time. "She's just messing about."

McVeigh peeled back his lips in a shark-like grin. "You're full of shit. Who is she?"

"Nobody." Paul glanced over his shoulder. Emily still tinkered in the kitchen. "I'll fill you in later."

McVeigh looked him right in the eye. His lecherous expression melted into a serious frown. "I really need to talk to you about this. It's about your wee brother."

Paul rolled his eyes and widened the door. He directed McVeigh to the armchair and left him there to speak to Emily in the kitchen.

"Where's the pizza?"

"It's not here yet. That was a mate."

"Oh."

"I had to let him in."

"Oh?"

"Do you mind?"

"Mind what…? Oh, no, darling. You never said anything about a threesome. That'd have to be factored into our price."

Paul threw his hands up. "Whoa there, babe! I am *not* angling for that. Jesus, I've seen enough of that ginger beast in the showers at the club. No fucking way is he getting into my bed."

"Okay, okay. So what are you asking me?"

"Just wondering if you can wait about for a minute. He says he won't be long."

"What, out here?"

"Wouldn't you be embarrassed to meet him wearing that?"

"Um…" She stepped forward and offered her hand. "Hi, I'm Emily and I'm a prostitute. Have we met?"

"Sorry. I keep forgetting about that. Doesn't seem so important in the moment."

Emily tilted her head and the corners of her mouth twitched a little. "Ah, that's kind of sweet, I guess. Just don't forget when it's time to pay, all right?"

"Aye. Of course."

"Well, then. Introduce me to your friend."

McVeigh's tongue could have rolled out of his mouth and slapped down on the floor and he still wouldn't have looked any more gobsmacked. Paul got a little embarrassed by his staring teammate. He cleared his throat dramatically. McVeigh blinked and closed his mouth.

"Stephen, this is Emily. Emily, Stephen."

"Pleased to meet you, darling."

McVeigh shuffled his feet like a lust-struck teenager meeting a mate's hot older sister. "Hi."

They settled into their seats, McVeigh on the armchair and Paul beside Emily on the sofa, and stared at each other for a moment. Paul broke the silence.

"So, what's the mad panic?"

McVeigh glanced at Emily then to Paul.

"It's okay, mate. You can say what you want in front of Emily."

The big man shrugged. "Okay, then. I'm here to pass on some information you'll appreciate."

"Okay. Spit it out then."

"I know who's to blame for your Danny's… condition?"

"Condition? What are you talking about?"

"Well, you can't really call it an accident, can you?"

Paul's heart raced. He swallowed the sudden surplus of saliva filling his mouth. "What happened to Danny?"

"Haven't you heard?"

"Would I be fucking asking…?"

"Shit, calm down. I assumed your parents would have been on the blower to you by now."

Paul glanced at his house phone. The jack hadn't been replaced since Sinead's early morning wake up call. And he hadn't turned on his mobile for days to avoid her. Nobody could have reached him at his house. He'd been in the city since early morning, buying crap for his fantasy night and chilling out in coffee shops.

"Hold on a minute."

He bolted up the stairs and scooped his jeans off the bedroom floor. He fished his mobile out of the pocket and switched it on. Almost immediately, a series of text messages came through. The phone vibrated in his hand like a short-circuiting dildo. The messages all centred around one subject – *Wee Danny in the hospital. Fractured skull. Get your arse to the Royal to visit your brother.*

Almost breaking his neck in the process, he thundered back down the stairs and skidded to a halt at the bottom. McVeigh stood up, big hands open and palms out, face calm.

"Take it easy, Paul. You need to concentrate on my info."

"A fucking fractured skull!"

"Yes, I know. And there's a culprit. Just try to relax and I'll fill you in."

Paul sat down and held Emily's hand as McVeigh told Joe Philips's version of a fucked up night. At the mention of Joe's da, Paul shot Emily a glance and she looked back, ashen-faced. He held his tongue, not wanting to give away too much in front of McVeigh.

When the big man finished his recount, he stood up, eager to leave. "I'll not keep you from visiting Wee Danny. But give what I've told you some thought, okay? And come and see me when you decide what you want to do about it. I'll help you out if I can."

Paul nodded and brought him to the door. Then he wheeled on Emily. He said nothing. Just stared.

Emily nodded. "I can help you with this, darling. Go see your brother. I'll wait here for you, and we'll talk when you get back."

"Can I trust you? Will you not just fly out of here and warn your *friend* he's in trouble?"

She bent over the sofa's armrest, and even in a state of agitation, the sight of her ass, as the hem of her nightdress raised, formed a tent in his new pyjamas. She sat back down with her handbag in her hands and pulled out a wad of notes.

"This is all my money. I always take it with me because I wouldn't trust that shifty Irish cunt with a jam donut. But you can take it with you as security. I'll go nowhere without it."

Paul felt his resolve soften. She was on his side. Truly a friend in a time of need.

But he took the money. Just in case.

Chapter 17

Liam pumped up the volume on his stolen iPod. Hip hop beats and rhymes about dealing crack and pimping in the ghetto filled his ears. He bobbed his head while he cut open the large plastic baggy of cocaine with a penknife. The white powder puffed up as the cellophane split and dusted a small circle of desktop around the bag. Liam sat in his swivel chair and scooped some more powder out with the flat of his blade. He chopped the coke with the penknife, not sure if he needed to or not, then shaped it into lines. With a straw from McDonalds cut down to size and jammed up his left nostril, he hoovered up one of the white rails, gasping as it assaulted his sinuses. His eyes snapped wide open. He smiled.

"Not bad."

He snorted another line up his right nostril.

After a couple of songs he noticed his knees jittering. He needed to get out into the world. See people, do stuff, enjoy life. He'd come to terms with the Tommy thing. And the homeless guy thing. And the security guard thing. Sort of. The nightmares faded from his memory before the post-shower chill raised goose flesh as he towelled himself dry. The key was to spend less time in the shower; his thought tank. He'd become the king of speed showering. One minute flat, he got in, got washed and got the fuck out.

And now he had snow.

More than he could shove up his own nose. E Man had come through big style. The Poleglass dealer had phoned him that morning and they'd done an exchange in the Westwood Shopping Centre car park. Neutral territory. Liam figured that he could sell small baggies to the kids around his age. They wouldn't know if the deals were a little light or a tad overcharged. He'd probably make back double what he'd paid, so long as he was patient and careful. A couple of traits he now knew he needed to work on.

He left the house with the big bag of coke and a shitload of ecstasy in his schoolbag. If his ma broke a habit of a lifetime and decided to tidy his room, he could kiss the stash goodbye. It was safest on his person at all times. Before he could begin distributing he needed to do some shopping. Small cellophane bags, scales, baking powder and a calculator. Everything he needed to know could be found in his CD and DVD collection.

In keeping with his new decision to be careful, he decided to buy each item from a different shop. There were plenty to choose from on the Falls Road, all within walking distance. With the iPod still spewing super-bass beats and bad language direct to his brain, he added a swagger to his stride.

And almost jumped out of his skin when he felt a hand on his shoulder.

He turned with his fists raised. Joe Philips stared down at him. The lanky bastard took one step back, out of Liam's punching range. Liam tugged the earphones out of his ears and let them hang from the neck of his hoodie. Though he regretted freezing him out the week before, he couldn't show it.

"What the fuck are you at? Don't sneak up on me."

"I called your name, but you couldn't hear me."

Liam forced his shoulders to relax and took a deep breath. Joe stared.

"So, what the fuck do you want?"

"To give you a fair chance."

"At what?"

"Staying alive."

Liam's lips flapped as he blew out an exasperated breath. "Aye, dead on, Joe. Wee bit dramatic, maybe?"

"I'm serious, Liam. Someone wants to take you off the street. If that means hospitalising or killing you, they'll make it happen."

"How do you know this?"

"They came to me asking where they could find you."

"Did you tout?"

"No! Course not! But it'll only be a matter of time before they start threatening me. And let's be honest, the way you disrespected me after Tommy's wake, you could hardly expect me to go through too much to keep you safe."

Liam stared at Joe, waiting for more information. Joe was in no rush to give it up. He needed things to speed up. Slow Joe. Never in a rush.

"So, who's after me?"

"Stephen McVeigh."

Liam sniggered. "That prick? Sure he's nobody. I bet he doesn't even own a gun."

"He could pick you up and squish you like a grape."

"We'll see about that." He looked Joe up and down. "Thanks for the warning though."

"Aye, whatever."

Liam shifted his schoolbag from one shoulder to the other. Its weight reminded him of his new business venture. "Here. Do you want to buy some good shit?"

"What have you got?"

"E and Charlie."

"Charlie?"

Liam rolled his eyes. "*Cocaine.* I'll do you a cracker deal. For old time's sake."

"You're dealing now? What about the gang?"

"I'm an entrepreneur."

"A what?"

Liam sighed. "A business man, Joe. Jesus, you'd need some of this coke to shock your brain back into action. I'm expanding my horizons. I'll run the gang and sell a bit of chemical joy. No point standing still, you know?"

"You're going to get yourself killed, mate. That's some serious shite to be getting mixed up in."

"That was always your problem, Joe. You never wanted to take a chance. Since you and Wee Danny fucked off, we've been coining it in."

"Nobody ever got killed when I was the leader, though."

Liam bared his teeth. "Fuck you."

"Fuck yourself, fatso. I hope McVeigh takes you home with him and sticks his dick up your hole."

"Well, you may stop worrying about my back, you string of piss. Better start watching your own instead. Soon as I can get away with it..." Liam drew his thumb across his throat.

"Yeah, I'm real scared, Liam. You couldn't beat an egg."

Liam drew his fist back. But Joe moved like lightning. He shoved Liam with both hands. Liam just about kept his footing. Then Joe was right in his face. His breath warmed Liam's skin.

"Don't embarrass yourself, fatso."

Liam stepped back. "You don't know what I'm capable of."

"Why don't you show me, then? Right now."

"Suck my dick."

He turned on his heel and stormed away from Joe.

"You brought this on yourself, Liam. Don't say I didn't warn you."

Liam jammed the earphones back in, cutting Joe's tough guy act out. He added a knife to his shopping list. A big, sharp, dangerous fucker of a knife.

Stephen waved at the waiter and then shook a fist when the bastard walked in the opposite direction. Louise chuckled.

"Take it easy, Stephen. There's no rush."

"Sorry, I just like to order and then sit back and wait."

"But it's so lovely in here. The longer it takes them to serve us, the longer we get to sit here and people-watch."

"People-watch?"

"Yeah! God, have you never done that? Try watching people as they move, talk and don't talk. It's really interesting."

"I see. You might call that people-watching. I call it nosiness."

"Ach, you're no fun. It is gorgeous in here though, isn't it? I love all these beautiful Chinese statues and all the red curtains, carpet, tablecloth. It's just so rich and vibrant."

"Aye, red's a very powerful colour in Chinese culture. And the guys that own this place? They're some of the most rich and powerful restaurant owners in the industry. It's the best restaurant in the city. The original, before they expanded into a chain. I've always loved it here."

"I've never been anywhere as nice as this. Thanks so much for taking me."

Stephen beamed at Louise. He loved that she was so taken with The Red Panda, the busiest and most expensive Chinese restaurant in Belfast. A lot of its trade came before and after the shows playing at The Grand Opera House across the street, so the clientele was mostly dressed to the nines, even on a Thursday night. Stephen was of the mindset that if you were going to go out, you should make the effort and go out in style. And Louise had certainly made the effort.

She wore a classy black and white print dress. Cut high and long to leave it all to the imagination, but hugging her hips to guide it along just a little. It looked new, or unworn. She'd been to the hairdressers and her black roots had been taken care of. The hair itself was scooped and twirled into a stylish shape. Almost formal, but not quite. But the makeup had been self-applied, and the only thing that let the image down a jot. She'd been a mite stingy with the red lipstick and it made her lips look thinner than they really were. Stephen had a thing for good, full lips. She had them, but didn't know how to make the most of them. Maybe he'd pay to get her a makeup lesson for her birthday or Christmas. He still didn't know which would come first.

Finally, a stunning Chinese girl in a black skirt and red blouse, sporting a little red streak in her jet black hair, arrived at their table with a notepad.

"Are you ready to order?"

Louise looked at Stephen and nodded, signalling he should order for both of them. He loved those little old fashioned values that she allowed to surface from time to time.

"The first thing I'd like you to get for us is a couple more drinks. I'm on the Tiger beer and she'll have another glass of Chardonnay. You not going to write that down?"

"I have a good memory, sir."

"Okay, good. We'll have a mixed platter for starters and a chicken curry for my... um... date. And I'll have Peking duck."

"Very good. Rice or chips?"

"One of each, please."

Stephen thought he might have caught a little sneer at that, but he gave the pretty face the benefit of the doubt.

"I'll be back shortly with your drinks."

"Thank you."

Louise sighed. "Wasn't she just so beautiful?"

"Never really noticed."

"Aye, dead on. God, so elegant and pretty and doll-like. Fucking bitch." She laughed at that, but not very sincerely.

"Well, tonight I've all I want to look at in you. You look fantastic, babe."

"Ach, thanks love. You're not so bad yourself, in that shirt and tie. Don't be drinking too much. I want to take my time undressing you tonight."

He reached under the table and stroked her calf. "That's an invitation I won't pass up."

"Yeah, you'd be wise not to. I'm going to make your toes curl."

His pulse sped up and he got a little hot under the collar. She always knew exactly what to say and when to say it.

The waitress plonked their drinks on the table and interrupted his hungry stare. Stephen raised his beer bottle and Louise tapped it with her wine glass.

"Cheers, beautiful."

"Same to you, big lad."

Taking her at her word, he sipped slowly on the imported beer. She winked at him over her glass. He decided it was the best time to break his news to her.

"Louise, I have to talk to you about something. Well, someone. Joe told me a very fucked up story about Dermot."

The cheer faded from Louise's face. Her too thin lips disappeared. "*Joe* told you? When did you two get so close?"

"We swapped numbers at the funeral. Remember?"

"And what? Now you guys spend your time talking about me?"

"What? I'm talking about Dermot. What are you talking about?"

Louise blinked and her face softened. A dimple creased on cheek as she half-grimaced. "Sorry, ignore me. I got the wrong end of the stick."

Stephen raised an eyebrow. "So do you want to hear about Dermot's behaviour or what?"

"Aye, sorry. Go ahead."

Stephen talked about Joe and Dermot breaking into his house first. Louise sat and listened in stunned silence. As he relayed the tale of the armed robbery disaster she visibly fumed. One of her hands latched onto a lump of linen tablecloth with a white-knuckle grip. The other hand never strayed far from her glass of wine. Stephen stopped there and waited for her to vent some anger. Then he would offer to sort things out for her.

"I can't believe that anyone, not even Dermot, could be so stupid," Louise said. "Either you've been fed the wrong information or you're making it up. If you want to have a go at Dermot for embarrassing you with a sly dig, then be a man and admit it. I could respect that."

"Could you lower your voice? People are staring."

"So?"

"So your Beechmount is showing. This is a classy place, you know."

"Ach, fuck them." She stood up. "And fuck you too, you fucking snob."

Stephen sat back, bowled over, and watched Louise leave. She zigzagged between the tables of curious diners. As her tense form disappeared out the door, Stephen reached across the table and picked up her glass of wine. *Thank fuck the crazy bitch didn't completely let herself down and throw her drink at me,* he thought as he gulped down her leftovers. He was about to get up and leave when the starter arrived. He looked up at his waitress.

"Is it too late to cancel the main course?"

Poker-faced, she shook her head.

"Great. Bring me a couple of beers to go with this platter and then come back in twenty minute with the bill, please."

The waitress scurried off and Stephen drew his mobile from his inside jacket pocket.

"Hiya, Paul. You ready to do something about this Kelly cunt? Good. I'll see you later."

Danny opened his eyes. Joe sat on the wee bench at the side of his bed. He looked bored.

"All right, mate?" Danny said. His voice sounded croaky to his own ears. He cleared his throat and immediately regretted it. Pain flared in his head and black dots swam across his vision.

"Aye. I was just waiting for you to wake up. You snore."

He blinked away the dots. "Everybody snores. How long have you been here?"

"About an hour. They told me not to wake you. Even though it's visiting time, like."

"Well, this isn't the zoo, mate. I'm not lying in this scratcher to entertain people, you know?"

Joe chuckled. "Fuck me. Same old Danny. Nothing would get you down, would it?"

"Not for long mate, no." He shook his head to emphasise the point then stopped when it felt like he'd bounced his brain off the inside of his skull. "Fuck, is this headache ever going to shift?"

"Have you tried to get morphine off them yet?"

"Aye, but they're having none of it."

"Want me to ask?"

"Nah. I'll charm them around. There's one wee nurse who keeps saying she wants to bring me home. I'd go too. She's fit as fuck."

"Could be worse then, eh?"

"Fucking right. So what's the craic?"

"Got something on Liam."

"Oh, aye?"

"Yeah. I found out he's trying to break into dealing. And not just blow. He offered me coke and E tabs yesterday. That's serious shit."

Danny smiled wryly. "Fat fucker just wants to be 50 Cent or something. It's all good in the hood, what?"

"True. Anyway, we should be able to use this against him. Tell some fucking dissident dickhead about him and see if he gets snatched up and trailed off to the forest."

"Do you know any dissidents?"

Joe sagged. "No. I was hoping you or your Paul would."

"No, mate. My family's Provo all the way. What big Gerry says goes. Anyway, so far as I can tell, all the dissident shit is happening in Newry and South Armagh. Probably amounts to just a couple of farmers with a spud gun making threatening phone calls at this stage."

"Well, can you see an angle?"

Danny fought to keep his eyes open as a fuzzy wave of exhaustion washed over him. He yawned then winced as the effort intensified his headache. Then an idea sparked.

"There's a wee nurse in here who wants to take me home with her."

Joe gave him a sidelong look. "Aye, you told me."

"Did I?"

"Just there now. You okay?"

"I'm fine. Anyway, this nurse; she's as fit as fuck."

Joe nodded.

"And she lives in Poleglass. That place sounds mad. Every week she sees kids from her area coming in here to get treatment for overdoses or bad pills." He yawned again. "Said that one weekend there were three teenagers who'd all bought ecstasy off the same dealer. One of them died and the other two only just pulled through. They'd all gotten bad shit from the same batch. It's like Russian Roulette."

"What's that?"

"Jesus, Joe. Read a book or something, will you? It's like, you never know with some drugs when you're going to get something that fucks you up in the wrong way."

Danny closed his eyes for a second while Joe got his head around the concept. It felt a little like the room was swaying. How he imagined it would feel like to lie down on the deck of a boat. He opened one eye and focussed on Joe.

"I think I see what you mean, mate." Joe said.

"Yeah, Joe. Something to think about, eh?"

Danny closed his eye and let the waves gently rock him. He could hear Joe's voice, but not what he was saying. He realised that the pain in his head had faded to nothing more than a bit of pressure behind his eyes. Bliss.

Then he opened his eyes.

Joe had turned into his brother, Paul.

"How the fuck did you do that, mate?"

"What?"

"Holy shit. You even sound like him."

"Danny, are you okay?"

"Is it still Friday?"

"Aye, Friday evening."

"Oh." His brain caught up with the new situation then gave him a jolt of pain to wake him up. "Oh, right. Is Joe away on?"

"He wasn't about when we got here." Paul flicked his head towards the foot of the bed.

Danny's sleep-heavy eyes widened. "Holy Jesus. Are you here with our Paul?"

Buffy the Vampire Slayer's sexier sister nodded. "Yeah, darling."

"Wow."

"Emily, would you get him a Mars from the shop?"

"Yeah, sure."

Danny watched her until she disappeared around the corner. Then he turned to Paul. "Who the fuck is she?"

"A friend."

"Does Sinead know her?"

"Never you mind. How are you today?"

"Tired."

"You've done nothing but sleep since you got here."

"Because I'm tired."

"Well, I know what happened. I just want you to know I'm going to put it right."

"What do you know?"

"That Dermot Kelly used you as a shield and left you to take the heat for him." Paul sighed and the corners of his mouth drooped. He looked older.

"I was thinking about touting to the cops. Get him lifted." Danny waited for the standard republican lecture. It didn't come.

"I don't think they'd find him. But I know how to track him down."

"Joe told me McVeigh was going to sort it out."

"McVeigh came to me because he knew I'd want the satisfaction. And it just so happens I'm shagging Kelly's bird, so I'll be more help than he could have known."

"Fuck off!"

"Shush. You keep that to yourself."

"Can I tell Joe?"

Paul paused then scrunched up his nose. "Ach, why not?"

"Class."

"So anyway, she's agreed to help me and McVeigh get our hands on Kelly. We're going to tear the fucker apart. And if he's still alive after we're done, we're telling him he's got one day to leave the country."

"You'd do that for me?"

"You're my wee brother."

"Cheers, Paul." Danny rubbed his eyes with the heel of his hand. It came back wet. "I'm in a shitload of trouble, aren't I?"

Paul nodded and put a hand on Danny's chest. "Afraid so."

"What's going to happen?"

"Don't think about it right now. I want you to get better. Then you can worry about what comes next."

"Okay."

"Because as soon as you're out of that hospital bed, I'm going to slap you so hard you'll be right back in it for a week."

Danny smiled and closed his eyes.

Chapter 18

Stephen's multi-coloured Escort shuddered to a halt on Stranmillis. Light from the Mace corner shop bathed the kerbside parking space. He winked at Emily in the rear view mirror.

"All set?"

"Ready as I'll ever be, darling."

Wee Paul fidgeted in the passenger seat. He twisted his spine to look in on the blonde honey and give her an encouraging smile. Stephen experienced a pang of jealousy. Absurd, because Wee Paul had been completely open about his business arrangement with Emily, but he could see subtle signs of friendship between them. And with things the way they were between him and Louise, the adulterer and the prostitute looked like Romeo and Juliet.

Emily fished a phone out of her handbag and called Dermot.

"It's me, Dermot. Yeah, I want you to come see me for a chat. I've missed you, but you won't get me back without some serious grovelling. Meet me in the little coffee shop above the bakery. The one run by that miserable cunt and his mother. Yeah, we'll get some privacy there. Don't keep me waiting."

She disconnected and dropped the phone back into her bag.

"Is he coming?" Stephen asked.

"Yeah."

"How can you be sure?"

"We've had tiffs before, darling. He knows what side his bread is buttered on. And he *always* comes."

"We better get this heap of shite out of sight," Wee Paul said. "Reverse it up into this street. We'll still have a view of the coffee place."

Tucked in behind a 3 Series BMW on St Ives Gardens, they watched the café for Dermot's arrival. The narrow one way street accommodated two rows of parked yuppie and student cars. Even Stephen's rusty heap would be hard to spot in the line up. Emily hummed softly in the back. Not an unpleasant sound, but a little upbeat in the circumstances.

"There he is," Wee Paul said. "Who's he with though?"

"I don't fucking believe it," Emily said.

Stephen squinted. His grip tightened on the steering wheel.

"Oh, shit," Wee Paul said. "That's Louise isn't it?"

Stephen grunted. *What the fuck is she playing at?* His chest swelled, pushing against his seatbelt, as hot blood pumped through his veins. He wanted Dermot's head on a plate.

Emily sighed. "Oh, Dermot. You are a berk."

"You don't sound that bothered," Paul said.

"I'm not. I feel sorry for the idiot. Obviously he thinks he can make me jealous by bringing his ex-wife along. But I don't give a fuck about him. No more than I could care for a pimp. He's always been my errand boy and that's it. I threw him the odd fuck as a little treat, but now he's gotten all puppy love on me. He must have damaged his brain in that car crash."

"Well, let's finish the job then," Stephen said. "Come on, Paul."

"I'll come with you, boys."

"No," Paul said. "You stay out of the way. We don't want you getting hurt when it all kicks off. That's what we agreed, remember?"

"And we agreed that when we thought we were coming to see Dermot on his own. Which one of you two is going to punch that girl's lights out if she decides to go Amazonian warrior on you?"

"Nobody is going to punch her lights out," Stephen said.

"She might have a point, Stephen. You said yourself she was pissed at you. And I've seen her fight. She's fucking vicious."

"Right, fine. Let's just get in there and fix this wanker."

Emily led the way. A little bell above the door tinkled as they entered the bakery. A sour-faced woman with Brillo Pad hair and tiny eyes swimming behind large round glasses stalked out from the back.

"Can I help you?"

"Room upstairs for three?" Emily asked.

"Plenty. I'll be up to take your order in a few minutes."

"Take your time, love," Wee Paul said.

The aul doll pursed her lips and nodded curtly. "See you up there."

They tramped up the narrow staircase. Dermot and Louise's voices drifted down to Stephen's ears, but with the roar of blood in his head he couldn't make out the words. Something light, judging by Louise's giggles. Emily rounded the balustrade and the conversation came to a dead halt.

"Don't stop on my account, Dermot."

"Emily, you've met Louise."

"Hello, darling."

Stephen topped the stairs as Louise raised a timid hand to wave at Emily. She blinked furiously, as if trying to wash away an illusion. "Stephen? What are you doing here?"

"I'm going to have that chat with your *ex*, babe. You might want to take a walk with Emily."

"Why, what are you going to do? I never took you for a petty thug. Don't let me down."

"Sorry, darling," Emily said, "but you are coming for a walk with me. Whether you want to or not. These boys have a lot to talk about."

"Fuck off, slut."

"Now don't be a bitch, darling. There's no reason why we can't be nice to each other."

The two women, neither of which Stephen would want to fuck with, gave each other the hairy eyeball.

Dermot broke the silence with a gravelly forced cough. "Emily, did you bring these two here to harm me?"

"Why yes I did, Dermot. It's been a long time coming. And when I got all the facts about your disaster last Tuesday night, how could I not? That little boy could have died."

"We're meant to stick by each other. Watch each other's backs."

"Stick by each other? Is that why you brought Louise with you?"

"I was pissed off. I just wanted to fuck with your head. But it's not as if I called Rent-a-Goon to sort you out over a disagreement. Call them off, love. We can do this sensibly."

"I don't think they could be called off, even if I wanted to. You've given them both a vendetta now, darling."

"When I'm finished with them, I'm going to cut your pretty face up."

"You're a hard man, aren't you?" Stephen said. "Using kids to do your dirty work and threatening women. Well, let's see you get through me then. But it might be a bit more of a challenge this time. You'll not get to sneak up behind me."

Dermot stood up, tipping his chair back, and turned his palms out by his hips. "Come on then, big lad."

Louise jumped to her feet and intercepted Stephen as he strode forward to knock lumps out of the scummy bastard. She put her hands on his chest and made eye contact. "Stephen, don't do this. Please."

"How could you go back to this cunt?" Stephen asked. "Did you forget all the shit you went through when he ditched you and Joe?"

"I'm having coffee with him, not sucking his dick. I came to see him to talk about our son. And I wanted to ask him about this armed robbery you were…"

Louise disappeared from his view and a white light flashed. He went down, landing on his side. The sneaky bastard had blindsided him. And whatever he'd hit him with had been heavy. Stephen's hand came away from his temple slick with blood. He'd been split open. Grabbing at a chair and a table, he fought to get to his feet. Knives, forks and a wine bottle with a candle stuffed into the neck clattered to the floor as he pulled at the tablecloth. Most likely he'd been clobbered with a matching candleholder.

When he got back on his feet he could see Wee Paul and the scumbag trading punches. The wee man moved like lightning, placing four or five digs for every glancing blow his opponent dealt. A Tasmanian Devil on speed couldn't have kept up. Dermot was empty-handed and fucked.

"Stop that! Stop that! What are you doing?" The clipped squawk whip-cracked from the top of the stairs.

The po-faced biddy had come up to take their order and stumbled upon chaos. Her shrieking distracted Wee Paul. He glanced over his shoulder in her direction, taking his focus off Dermot for a split second. Dermot pushed himself out of the corner and took the advantage. His hand shot out and Wee Paul screamed. The smaller man stumbled backward, both hands jammed against his left eye. Blood dribbled down his cheek. Dermot rubbed his thumb on the hem of his T-shirt.

"My eye! My eye! Fuck, fuck, fuck!"

Dermot grinned as Wee Paul rolled about in agony. Stephen screamed. No words. Just a guttural roar. Dermot snapped his attention back to Stephen. They eyeballed each other like duelling gunslingers. Stephen scooped the tumbled wine bottle from the floor and launched it across the room. It glanced off Dermot's shoulder and smashed against the wall. Stephen lifted a chair and tossed it. Bull's-eye. Dermot toppled like a skittle.

"Get out of my café! I'm calling the PSNI! And my son!" The aul doll scampered down the stairs. Her squealed threats faded away.

Stephen paid her little attention. He knew they'd have enough time to finish the job before the first Land Rover arrived. The beaten and bleeding scumbag clambered to his feet. But Stephen had the rat cornered. He stalked across the dull patterned carpet. Then Louise crossed his path to join Emily by Wee Paul's side. Dermot reached out and grabbed a handful of bleached hair. She shrieked as he pulled her into a rough chokehold. Then he held the jagged bottleneck an inch from her face. The half-melted candle still protruded from the bottle's mouth.

"Stay back, dickhead." Dermot's battered lips parted as he sneered.

"You fucking scummy fucking bastard. I'll fucking kill you."

"No. You'll stay the fuck back. Isn't that right, Louise?"

Louise spat her words through clenched teeth. "You get one chance to let me go, Dermot. I'd advise you to take it."

Dermot chuckled, a humourless and painful effort. "I'll take my chances."

Stephen couldn't help but cringe as Louise reached behind her and grabbed hold of Dermot's balls. She threw her head back, smashing it into an already punished face. Wiry muscles bunched in her forearm as she squeezed. Dermot emitted a thin yelp and folded over. He dropped the bottleneck and clutched his sac with both hands. Louise push-kicked his floating ribs and he flipped onto his back. Stephen watched her take him apart in awe. She drew back her foot to crash it into his skull. But Dermot reached out and snatched her weight-bearing leg from under her. Stephen was shocked into action. He darted forward and tried to catch her. Too late. Her head cracked off the edge of a table as she went down. Stephen dropped to his knees by her side.

Dermot groaned as he struggled to his feet. Stephen ignored him. Louise was his only concern. He put a finger under her nose. The warmth of her breath flooded him with relief. He stroked her cheek.

"Louise. Louise. Come on, love. Wake up. Are you all right, babe?"

She groaned a little, and he knew she would come to.

Fucking Dermot Kelly!

Stephen looked up, ready to leap into action and dance all over Dermot's head. But the scummy bastard was moving again. He lashed a roundhouse kick into the already damaged side of Stephen's head. Stephen flopped to his side. He threw his own leg out, clipping Dermot's heel and toppling him forward as the fucker tried to escape. Then Stephen tried to push himself off the floor. Time to finish the job. But black snow floated in his vision and he almost puked. His strength abandoned him. He lay on his side and breathed deep.

Dermot crawled to the top of the stairs. He used the balustrade to haul himself to his feet. Clutching the banister, he staggered down the stairs. Stephen watched the bastard from the floor.

"Go on then, you sleeked cunt." Stephen's hoarse yell caused fresh agony in his skull, but his anger wouldn't allow silence. "I'll get you another time. And it won't be just a beating. I'm going to cut your throat and dump you in the Lagan."

Dermot nodded and waved his middle finger at Stephen as he sank from view. Stephen tried to force himself to chase him down and break him in half, but it was a losing battle. He couldn't even sit up.

"Stephen." Emily whispered for his attention.

"What?"

"I'm a great believer in contingency plans."

She sat by Wee Paul and stroked his hair. The one-eyed GAA hero had gone pale and eerily quiet. Emily's mascara had run to give her panda eyes, but she curved her lips in a grotesque grin.

"What are you talking about?"

"I've some insurance organised. Everything's going to work out, darling."

Drum and bass pumped through the walls and poured out onto the street. Joe sucked down a deep breath of summer-drizzly air. The familiar metallic scent zinged on his sinuses. He shouldered open the front door of the Greene family home. Liam's parents had gone for their monthly jaunt to Donegal and the Rockets were making use of the free house. In each hand, Joe held carrier bags stuffed with party food. If you're going to gatecrash, you better bring some goods. The musty tang of hash hung in the cloudy open-plan hallway and living room. He could feel the music in the floorboards, passing through his rubber soles and raising the hair on his calves.

Ginger Mickey Rooney was the first one to spot him. He scurried to the kitchen and came back with Liam and the Fegan twins. The jungle track died and all eyes turned to Joe. He felt as welcome as a preacher in a whorehouse.

Liam broke the silence. "You've a brass neck on you, son."

"I'm not here to start anything. Just wanted to say sorry for what I said the other day. You weren't to blame for Tommy."

"I don't need you to tell me that."

"I know, but I needed to say it. I've been a dick. Let's just get over this. It's gone too far for no reason."

Liam looked around the room to gauge his gang's reaction. They offered him very little. A few shrugs, but nothing decisive. His call.

"It's probably the drugs, Joe, but I'm with you. There's no need to keep this stupid feud going." Liam pointed at Joe's carrier bags. "What's in the bags?"

Joe liked what he heard, but he didn't relax. He needed his wits about him in case Liam was leading him on. "I brought a peace offering. Food and drink so we can eat and be merry. I'd have taken some drugs with me, but I knew you'd have that covered yourself."

"Fucking right we have it covered. We've been toking dope all night. But I've a bag of Es there to wake us up later on. I'm well up for some food too. I've a fuck off case of the munchies here."

A general murmur of agreement seconded Liam's desire to eat. Joe grinned and swaggered to the centre of the living room. He plonked the plastic bags on the pine coffee table.

"It's mostly shit I asked my ma to bring home from the bakery. Cakes and buns. I've a few bottles of Fanta there and all. You can't beat that with a big stick after a night on the weed."

"What the fuck are we waiting for, then?"

The Wee Rockets homed in on the sugary treats as one unit and decimated them. Icing sugar dusted the coffee table and white paper bags lay crumpled on the floor. Just as Joe thought he would,

Liam had scooped up all the apple sponge and made a pig of himself. A whole cake, right down the hatch. The greedy shite licked his fingers with a big smile on his face. Joe suppressed a stomach-punishing wave of nausea.

"Liam, I found a bottle of Dr Pepper in our house as well. You're the only fucker I know who likes that shit." Joe tossed the three quarter-full bottle to Liam. "Enjoy."

Liam smiled and twisted the cap off. He glugged the brown liquid down from the bottle.

"Tastes a wee bit weird. Kind of chemically."

"Ach, that's just the weed fucking with your taste buds, mate."

"Aye, probably. Cheers, Joe. Here, did you not get any cake?"

"My ma works in a bakery. Missing out on a donut or two will do me no harm."

"You sure?"

"Aye, no sweat."

"Well, take a seat at least. Matt, pass him a joint."

Joe sank into the sofa between the two Franks. Fra Collins half slept on his left, and Frankie Devlin fidgeted in his usual weasel-like way. Even stoned, Frankie's eyes never got a break from zipping around the room. A real ADHD kid. Joe sucked on the joint, but inhaled as little as he could. He'd have time to get fucked up later, in the safety of his own home. Right now, he was in the company of some true blue lunatics who were doing a piss-poor job of hiding their contempt for him. Joe was under no illusions. Liam was fucking with him. Acting the tomcat. But Joe had never been a mouse. And he was playing his own game.

The night rolled on and the mood remained light, then Liam passed around the baggie of E.

"Take it easy on these Doves, lads. One each. They're strong as fuck. E Man says they haven't been cut."

Joe fished four out of the bag as it passed under his nose. He palmed three and tucked one under his tongue then faked a swallow. "These are Doves, then? Me and Wee Danny dropped some Mitsubishis the other day. Do you reckon there'll be much difference?"

Liam shrugged. "These are better. For the big boys."

Joe gave him an unimpressed lip curl.

Liam swallowed his tab with a big gulp of water. "I heard about Wee Danny."

This is the start of it, Joe thought. "That right?"

"Aye. He got his head cracked open with a baseball bat."

Joe nodded.

"Were you not there to look after him, then?"

"No."

Liam sucked air through his teeth. "Stupid wee fucker. Still, maybe it'll knock a bit of sense into him. A wee sparrow fart like that trying to do an armed robbery? He must have been out of his tree."

Joe chewed on his lip, refusing to rise to the bait.

"I suppose he'll end up in the Juvenile Justice Centre. And the way he smokes, he may get his wanking hand greased up; for that's the only way he'll be able to keep himself in fags."

Even Fra Collins laughed at that. Joe felt his face light up, but he said nothing.

"You not going to stick up for your boyfriend, Joe?" Eddie Fegan asked. He licked his lips wolfishly.

Joe stubbed his joint out in the ashtray between his feet. He shook his head.

"Ach, Joe," Liam said. "Crack a fucking smile, will you? I'm only slagging."

Joe raised his eyebrows. The pill under his tongue had started to dissolve. He didn't want to give Liam an excuse to unleash the boys, but he couldn't encourage him to disrespect Wee Danny either. He stood suddenly. Liam flinched a little.

"I feel sick, Liam. Be back in a minute."

He ran up the stairs to a chorus of dry heaves from the Rockets. Inside the bathroom, he leaned back against the locked door. Encased in a greasy sweat, he took deep breaths in an effort to ease the ball of sickly panic in his stomach. Seconds ticked into minutes, but he didn't rush himself. He'd done it. He'd come in to the lion's den and was still alive to tell the tale. All he had to do now was slip out the window and let time do the rest.

But he couldn't leave it like that. Not after the way they laughed at Wee Danny. And really they may as well have been laughing at him. *Fuck you, Joe. What are you going to do about it?* They'd soon find out what he could do. There was no way he'd sneak away without enjoying the power of his moment. He needed to be in their presence again and relish knowing. Risky, but worth it. He spat the soggy E tab into the toilet and flushed it. Then he splashed some water on his face and went back to his spot on the sofa.

"You finish puking, you big Jenny-Anne?" Liam asked.

"Aye."

"You were gone long enough. We thought you'd fell down the toilet."

"Nah. I stopped by your ma's room and had a sniff around her knicker drawer."

The whole gang fell silent. Liam had them all climbing right up his hole. They were afraid to laugh at him.

"I'm only slagging, Liam."

Liam didn't drop the hard man glare.

"Seriously," Joe said. "I wouldn't touch your ma with yours."

Liam stared for another few seconds, then chuckled. "All right, mate. Fair's fair."

The music returned to cover up the iffy atmosphere. Joe just had to sit tight until the E worked its magic. Then he could have a quiet word with Liam and be done with the whole business. He lit a fag for something to do, then another off the butt, then another. Then Frankie Devlin leapt off the sofa and stepped up onto the coffee table. He waved his arms about and shrugged his shoulders in what was technically a dance. Most of the others laughed and cheered him on. Fra Collins simply gave him a thumbs up and closed his eyes again. It'd take a stick of dynamite in the arsehole to get that one going.

Then they were all up, jigging and jerking, except Fra and Joe. But Joe didn't have Fra's excuse. He forced himself to get off the sofa and act like the other lunatics. Trying to play the loved up clubber was not easy. He felt like he had lead in his shoes and his joints seemed to be stiffening, making movement awkward and laborious. And he didn't think his eyes were wide enough. Fuck all he could do about it though. So he threw his limbs about and hoped the others were too involved in their own bliss to notice his discomfort.

From the corner of his eye, he saw Liam slip off into the kitchen. Nobody else seemed to notice. Joe left the jittering loons to it and followed the fat bastard. He found him bent over the kitchen worktop with a piece of stripy plastic straw jammed up his nose. His eyes rolled about in his head. He snorted a line of fine white powder before acknowledging Joe.

"Why did you come here, Joe?"

"I want us to be mates again."

"I don't believe that for one second."

"Okay, then. I wanted to make sure I wouldn't come to harm."

"You think I would do something to you?"

"You're not the only one hearing things on the grapevine. The twins are loyal, but they've got big mouths. Half the hoods in

Beechmount know about the Park Centre thing. That's some body count you're racking up."

Liam rubbed his nose and sniffed. "I told them all to keep it quiet. What can you do? But there's no proof I did it, so why worry?"

"Yeah, you're right. Unless the security guard's family find out who you are and arrange a wee meeting."

"Are you threatening me?"

"Not at all. Just looking out for you. Remember I tried to warn you about McVeigh? Same thing."

"Except he hasn't done fuck all, has he?"

"Not directly, no."

Liam shook his head and got to work chopping and lining the coke with a video rental card. "You're just trying to melt my head. But it's not working."

"I heard that there's a lot of bad ecstasy coming out of Poleglass these days. Lot of kids in comas or dead. Now, if someone wanted rid of you, they could arrange for you to pick up a bag of that bad E. Am I right?"

Liam snorted another line. His smile stretched like a clown's. "Whatever."

"Some of that shit is cut with rat poison and bleach. If the dealer gets the mix wrong…" Joe wrapped his hands around his own throat. He let his tongue hang over his lip and made choking noises.

"Stop that."

"What's wrong, Liam? Worried you got a bad batch?"

"You took one too."

"Take a good look at me, mate. Do I look like I'm coming up? I flushed the pill."

"Doesn't prove they're bad. You can't know they're bad."

Joe nodded slowly. "That's true. I can't know. Those tabs are probably perfectly fine."

Liam's shoulders dropped in visible relief.

"But if the rat poison and bleach got into your system another way, the autopsy guy would match it with the ecstasy in your blood and come up with a cause of death. How did you enjoy that cake, by the way? And the Dr Pepper? Wash it all down for you all right?"

Liam dropped his plastic straw and card on the countertop and squared up to Joe. "What the fuck did you do?"

"Ach, maybe I'm just fucking with you." He laid a palm on Liam's shoulder. "Or maybe I'm looking out for number one."

Joe moved his hand from Liam's shoulder to grab his ear. He punched him in the stomach then rammed the side of his head against the countertop. Liam's eyelids fluttered. Still gripping the ear, Joe jerked him back and bashed his head off the black glossy surface. Liam's legs buckled. He shoved the fat fucker's head against the cupboard door. As Liam slid to the floor, Joe kicked the other side of his head for good measure.

The music in the living room kept the commotion from reaching the other Rockets' ears. Joe knelt by Liam's side. He popped the three E tabs he'd palmed earlier into his fat mouth then pinched his nose shut and pressed a palm to his lips. But the old trick didn't work. The subject probably had to be conscious.

"Fuck it, I've done enough."

Dissolving slowly in his mouth, the tabs might not be enough to cause an overdose, but the sweet rat poison from the cake and powdered bleach mixed into the Dr Pepper would work its magic. If Liam didn't die, he'd certainly be off the street for a long time. Joe decided to leave it at that. Give the wanker a chance for old time's sake. He rejoined the chaos in the living room. A minute later he slipped out the front door. The Rockets would find their fearless leader passed out or dead from a drug OD. Maybe it'd make them think about changing their ways.

But probably not.

Dermot staggered along the footpath. The pain from his beating lit up his nerve endings as the last of his adrenaline drained away. He smiled.

"You're a survivor, mate." His own voice sounded alien, but he drew comfort from the words.

Ahead, a group of students on their way to some pub or club parted before him. He lurched through the ragged guard of honour. One of the girls gasped, but none of them offered to help. They had their own problems. Dermot didn't give a fuck. He'd been battered half to death, and he'd never felt so alive.

But he'd come to the end of his affair with Belfast. The ginger prick and his wee mate had more reason than ever to kill him. And with that treacherous bitch Emily on their side, the squat wasn't safe anymore. But before he could go anywhere, he needed to pick up his cash stash. Then he'd be on the first bus to Dublin. And after that… he'd have to wait and see.

His conscience nagged at him a little over knocking Louise out. Such a rotten way to end things. He'd actually enjoyed catching up with her. But at the end of the day, he had to look out for number one. No chance of her forgiving him for waving a broken bottle in her face and then whacking her skull off a table.

He spat a huge crimson glob onto the pavement outside his squat. His appearance would draw a lot of nervous looks on the bus but it'd be unwise to waste time getting cleaned up. He needed to keep moving.

Climbing the stairs to the bedroom generated a fresh surge of pain. It crackled through his body like an electric shock. He fought through it but had to stand still at the top for half a minute until a wave of dizziness passed. As he stood there, he thought about Joe.

The bastard had too much of his ma's temper in him. He'd felt more than physical pain after they'd crashed into the postbox. His own son had betrayed him over a street runt. Left him to be scooped by the peelers. Dermot would never forget that. You should be able to rely on flesh and blood. Family should stick together. After all, he'd tried to include Joe in his budding empire. Mutually beneficial though it may have been, at least he'd been willing to pass on his wisdom while using him to get what he wanted. But he wouldn't make a mistake like that again. One less tie to the stinking city of Belfast.

He collected his cash and bundled some clothes into a holdall. After a quick root through Emily's stuff he found some painkillers. He popped four in his mouth and crunched them to dust, hoping they'd kick in quicker. The chemical taste turned his stomach, but he soldiered on. He half-stumbled down the stairs and opened the front door.

A silver Ford Ka idled at the kerb. Behind the wheel of the little city car sat an expensively suited ogre with slicked back hair. His left arm was trussed up in a sling. The driver's window slid open with an electric whir. Essex Boy, Tony Walsh extended his good arm through the opening. A sawn-off shotgun glared at Dermot.

"A little birdie told me I could find you here, sunshine. Thought I'd call by to see you."

"Ach, shite."

The muzzle flashed and thunder boomed. Dermot was blown back into the squat. Gut shot. He writhed on the uncarpeted hallway floor. Then Tony stood over him. He had the urge to plead, but the fire in his belly burned away the words on his tongue. He stared into the twin black circles of the shotgun. Tony bent at the waist and pushed the muzzle into Dermot's mouth.

"You shouldn't have played with the big boys, you sneaky Irish cunt."

Thunder rolled. And then it was over.

Epilogue

Joe woke up to the rattle, clatter and hiss of his ma cooking breakfast. The smell of frying sausages wafted up the stairs. His mouth watered. He rolled out of bed and pulled on his trackies and a Celtic top. After a long, spine-tingling piss, he shambled down the stairs.

"Morning, Joe."

McVeigh sat in the armchair, drinking from Joe's Manchester United mug.

"Did you stay the night *again*?" Joe asked.

McVeigh nodded. The right side of his face sported a fading scar. Joe could almost admit to himself that it suited the bastard.

"Where's my ma?"

"She's in the kitchen, son."

He didn't like McVeigh calling him son. Not one bit. But he bit back a nasty response.

His ma bustled in carrying a plate stacked with sausages and bacon. No bread. Not even soda.

"Oh! Morning, Joe. Didn't know you'd surfaced. You looking a wee fry too?"

"I got up when I smelt the food." He looked pointedly at McVeigh's plate. "Is there any left?"

"Of course. I'd not let you go without. Stephen doesn't eat bread, so there's extra soda and taty bread as well."

She disappeared back into the kitchen and got to work with the frying pan. McVeigh forked a sausage and ate half in one bite. Joe thought the ginger bastard looked far too comfortable. He spoke through a mouthful of semi-chewed sausage.

"So it looks like I'll be moving in with your ma."

"What?"

"Aye, I'm going to take her out for dinner tonight and ask her. What we went through the other month with your scumbag da made me realise how much I like her. Well, love her, really."

McVeigh unleashed a big dopey chortle.

"Are you winding me up?" Joe asked.

"Not at all. I'm deadly serious. Going to ask her to move into mine. But I'll move in here if she'd prefer."

Joe sat on the sofa before his legs could betray him. "Why are you telling me this?"

"Because, when she comes home to tell you about the idea, I don't want you giving her that hard-done-by face you always use. I want you to tell her you think it's a great idea."

"Why would I do that?"

"Because you owe me. Your da's gone. Liam Greene isn't, though, is he? He's still knocking about Beechmount."

"But he's not dealing or nothing. I've checked up on him."

"Aye, right." McVeigh sneered. "But even if he's not, it won't be long before he's back at it. I should've known you wouldn't deliver. Too much Dermot Kelly in you."

Joe sprang off the sofa. "Shut your mouth, you ginger cunt." Aware his ma wasn't far away, he hissed the words. And by some act of God, he stopped himself from swinging a dig at the big prick.

McVeigh reddened. "And that'll be one of the first rules I'll lay down when you're living under my roof. No cursing. And then, no smoking, no drinking, no drugs, no mates around after ten and *no lip*."

"I can't believe this shit."

"You'll thank me in the long run, kid. You might even have a chance in life if you've someone like me as a role model. Let's face it, you're doing a pretty good job of pissing it all away right now." He jabbed his fork in the air, struck by inspiration. "Here, if we get you off them fucking fags I could get you a trial for the Davitts under-sixteen's. You've the height to be a decent centre-back."

"Football?"

"Aye. Doors will start opening for you then. Believe me."

Joe felt as if the room was spinning.

His ma returned with his fry. She told him to sit and plopped down beside him on the sofa. While Joe and McVeigh worked through their laptop breakfasts, she had a cuppa and a fag. She smiled at each of them in turn. *We're her boys,* Joe thought. *Fuck.*

"Stephen, is it just the two of us tonight or will we ask Paul and Emily along?" Joe's ma asked.

McVeigh wiped grease from his lips with the heel of his hand. "Well, her and Dead-Eye Gibson are away for the weekend." He paused. "I wonder how much *that's* costing him."

"Shush, you. Emily's lovely. And, call him Paul, will you? You know that name winds him up something shocking. Not to mention how cruel it is. He lost his eye helping you out, you know."

McVeigh smirked. "Cruel? And what was it when he blew Sinead out for an English whore? When he left her to take care of that mental kid of theirs?"

Joe's ma shrugged and sucked on her fag. Her lips pinched down on the filter.

"Anyway," McVeigh said "He's not here to hear me, so what's the harm?"

She shook her head, fanning puffed smoke in a swirling arc. The smell of it tightened Joe's nicotine-deprived lungs. Before long, his plate was empty. He barely remembered one bite.

"I'm going to stick the kettle on," he said as he stood. "Anyone want more tea?"

"Aye, love."

"Please, son."

The wanker had fucking called him son again and his ma hadn't even batted an eyelid.

He plastered on a fake smile. "Coming right up."

In the kitchen, he lit a fag, leant against the worktop and watched the kettle boil. He couldn't live in the same place as McVeigh. It would drive him mental. Apart from McVeigh being a complete arse in general, he threw the Liam Greene thing in Joe's face every five minutes; a memory he could live without.

The Liam Greene thing.

If he'd put more thought into what he'd been doing the night he crashed the party, things could have been different. After a spell in hospital, Liam was back on the street. Joe would have to be on guard every time he went out. And Wee Danny wouldn't be around to back him up for at least a couple of years.

Joe thought about the big box of rat poison in his bedroom and the powdered bleach in the cupboard under the sink. He thought about how McVeigh took sugar in his tea; one of his rare dietary vices. He thought about how easy it would be to score a few tabs of ecstasy on the street. And how they were small enough to plant on even the most unlikely person. The original mix hadn't been right for that fat bastard, Greene, but with enough time to experiment, who knew?

He heaped two teaspoons of sugar into one of the cups then spat in it. A drop or two of poison would be as easy. And McVeigh, like all joiners, drank shitloads of tea…

Something worth considering, at least.

###

Acknowledgements

Gerard would like to thank the Arts Council of Northern Ireland for their support in writing this novel.

WEE DANNY

Incarcerated in a home for young offenders, Wee Danny Gibson has learned how to act in front of his teachers, his educational psychologist and the institute's supervisors. And if he continues to keep his nose clean, he could be rewarded with a day-trip to Castle Ward. But good behaviour is no easy task when his fellow inmates are determined to get in his face. Then there's Conan 'The Barbarian' Quinlan, a gentle giant who Danny feels compelled to look out for.

Friend or liability? Danny can't be sure, but he knows he needs to stay focussed on that little taste of freedom.

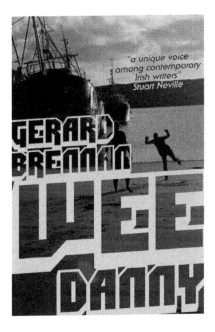